PENGUIN BOOKS

MISSIONARY STEW

Ross Thomas has been a reporter, editor, and public relations
director for numerous publications, radio stations, national
organizations, and political candidates in the United States,
Europe, and Asia. He is the author of eighteen previous
novels, some of which were written under the pseudonym
Oliver Bleeck. Mr. Thomas and his wife live in Malibu,
California.

Novels by Ross Thomas

(Under the pseudonym Oliver Bleeck)

MISSIONARY STEW

Ross Thomas

PENGUIN BOOKS

PENGUIN BOOKS
Viking Penguin Inc., 40 West 23rd Street,
New York, New York 10010, U.S.A.
Penguin Books Ltd, Harmondsworth,
Middlesex, England
Penguin Books Australia Ltd, Ringwood,
Victoria, Australia
Penguin Books Canada Limited, 2801 John Street,
Markham, Ontario, Canada L3R 1B4
Penguin Books (N.Z.) Ltd, 182–190 Wairau Road,
Auckland 10, New Zealand

First published in the United States of America by
Simon & Schuster, Inc., 1983
Published by Viking Penguin Inc. 1984
Reprinted 1985

LIBRARY OF CONGRESS CATALOGING IN PUBLICATION DATA
Thomas, Ross, 1926–
    Missionary stew.
    Reprint. Originally published: New York: Simon
and Schuster, c 1983.
    I. Title.
[PS3570.H58M57   1984]   813'.54   84-16678
ISBN 0 14 00.7413 9

Printed in the United States of America by
Offset Paperback Mfrs., Inc., Dallas, Pennsylvania
Set in Electra

MISSIONARY
STEW

1

HE FLEW INTO PARIS, the city of his birth, on a cold wet November afternoon. He flew in from Equatorial Africa wearing green polyester pants, a white T-shirt that posed the suspect question "Have You Eaten Your Honey Today?" and a machine-knitted cardigan whose color, he had finally decided, was mauve.

The articles of clothing, possibly Oxfam castoffs, had been handed to him out of a green plastic ragbag by Miss Cecily Tettah of Amnesty International, who had apologized neither for their quality nor their fit. The mauve sweater must have belonged to a fat man once—an extremely tall fat man. Morgan Citron was a little over six-one, but the sweater almost reached mid-thigh and fitted his emaciated 142-pound frame like a reversed hospital gown. Still, it was wool and it was warm and Citron no longer cared greatly about his appearance.

It was in a cheap hotel room near the Gare du Nord that Citron had been born forty-one years ago, the son of a dead-broke twenty-year-old American student from Holyoke and a twenty-nine-year-old French army lieutenant who had been killed in May during the fighting at Sedan. Citron's mother, obsessed with her poverty, had named her son Morgan after a distant cousin who was vaguely connected to the banking family. Citron was born June 14, 1940. It was the same day the Germans rolled into Paris.

Now on that wet, cold November afternoon in 1981, Citron went through customs and immigration at Charles de Gaulle Airport, found a taxi, and settled into its rear seat. When the driver said, "Where to?" Citron replied in French: "Let's say you have a cousin who lives in the country."

"Ah. My country cousin. A Breton, of course."

"He's coming to Paris."

"But my cousin is poor."

"Unfortunately."

"Yet he would like a nice cheap place to stay."

"He would insist upon it."

"Then I would direct him to the Seventh Arrondissement, in the Rue Vaneau, number 42—Le Bon Hotel."

"I accept your suggestion."

"You've made a wise choice," the driver said.

When they reached the Périphérique, Citron confided further in the driver. "I have a diamond," he said.

"A diamond. Well."

"I wish to sell it."

"It is yours to sell, of course."

"Of course."

"You know anything of diamonds?"

"Almost nothing," Citron said.

"Still, you have no wish to be cheated."

"None."

"Then we shall try Bassou and you will tell him that I sent you. He will give me a commission. A small one. He will also give you a fair price. Low, but fair."

"Good," Citron said. "Let's try Bassou."

* * *

Three days before, Citron had watched in the early-morning African hours, already steaming, as Gaston Bama, the sergeant-warder, brought in and ladled out the famous meal that eventually was to help drive the Emperor-President from his ivory throne.

Bama was then an old man of fifty-three, corpulent, corrupt, and slow-moving, with three chevrons on his sleeve that testified to his rank, the same rank he had held for seventeen years. For nearly all of the past decade he had been chief warder in the *section d'étranger* of the old prison the French had built back in 1923, long before the country was an empire, or even a republic, and still then only a territory of French Equatorial Africa.

The foreigners' section was in the small, walled-off east wing of the prison. That November it held not only Morgan Citron, but also four failed smugglers from Cameroon; a handful of self-proclaimed political refugees from Zaire; six Sudanese reputed to be slavers; one mysterious Czech who seldom spoke; and an American of twenty-two from Provo, Utah, who insisted he was a Mormon missionary, although nobody believed him. There were also three rich young Germans from Düsseldorf who had tried to cross Africa on their BMW motorcycles only to break down and run out of money a few miles outside the capital. Because no one had quite known what to do with them, they were clapped into prison and forgotten. The rich young Germans wrote home every week begging for money and UN intervention. Their letters were never mailed.

It was largely because he was bilingual in French and English that Morgan Citron had been elected or perhaps thrust into the position of spokesman for the foreign prisoners. His only other qualification was his gold wrist watch, a costly Rolex, that he had bought in Zurich in 1975 on the advice of a knowledgeable barkeep who felt that gold might be looking up as an investment. Just before the Emperor-President's secret police had come for him in his room at the Inter-Continental, Citron had slipped the watch from his left wrist and onto his right ankle beneath his sock.

That had been nearly thirteen months ago. Since then he had traded the gold links in the expansion band one by one to Sergeant Bama for supplementary rations of millet and cassava and fish. Infrequently, no more than once a month, there might also be some red meat. Goat, usually. Elderly goat. Citron shared everything with the other prisoners and consequently was not murdered in his bed.

There had been thirty-six links in the watch's gold expansion band originally. In thirteen months, Citron had parted with thirty-four of them. He knew that soon he would have to part with the watch itself. With his gold all gone, Citron was confident that his term as spokesman would also end. If not drummed out of office, he would abdicate. Citron was one of those for whom political office had never held any attraction.

Sergeant Bama watched as the skinny young private soldier put the immense black ironstone pot down near the bench on which Citron sat in the shade just outside his cell.

"There," Sergeant Bama said. "As I promised. Meat."

Citron sniffed and peered into the pot. "Meat," he agreed. "As I promised."

"What kind of meat?"

"Goat. No, not goat. Four young kids, tender and sweet. Taste, if you like."

Citron yawned hugely, both to express his indifference and to commence the bargaining. "Last night," he said, " I could not sleep."

"I am desolate."

"The screams."

"What screams?"

"The ones that prevented me from sleeping."

"I heard no screams," Sergeant Bama said and turned to the

private soldier. "Did you hear screams in the night? You are young and have sharp ears."

The private soldier looked away and down. "I heard nothing," he said and drew a line in the red dirt with a bare toe.

"Then who screamed?" Citron said.

Sergeant Bama smiled. "Perhaps some pederasts with unwilling partners?" He shrugged. "A lovers' quarrel? Who can say?"

"They went on for half an hour," Citron said. "The screams."

"I heard no screams," Sergeant Bama said indifferently and then frowned. "Do you want the meat? Four kilos."

"And the price?"

"The watch."

"You grow not only deaf in your old age, but senile."

"The watch," Sergeant Bama said. "I must have it."

Citron swallowed most of the saliva that had been created by the smell of the meat. "I will give you two links—the last two —provided there're two kilos of rice to go with the meat."

"Rice! Rice is very dear. Only the rich eat rice."

"Two kilos."

Sergeant Bama scowled. It was an excellent bargain, far better than he had expected. He changed his scowl into a smile of sweet reasonableness. "The watch."

"No."

Sergeant Bama turned to the private soldier. "Fetch the rice. Two kilos."

After the private soldier left, Sergeant Bama squatted down beside the ironstone pot. He dipped his right hand into its lukewarm contents and removed a small piece of meat. He offered the piece to Citron. For a moment, Citron hesitated, then accepted the meat and popped it into his mouth. He chewed slowly, carefully, and then swallowed.

"It is not goat," Citron said.

"Did I say it was goat? I said kid—young and tender. Does it not dissolve in your mouth?"

11

"It is not kid either."

Sergeant Bama peered suspiciously into the pot, fished out another small piece of meat that swam in the brownish liquid, and sniffed it. "Pork perhaps?" He offered the piece to Citron. "Taste and determine. If it is pork, you will not have to share with the Sudanese, who are Muslim."

Citron took the meat and chewed it. "It is not pork. I remember pork."

"And this?"

"This is sweet and tough and stringy."

Sergeant Bama giggled. "Of course. How stupid of me." He clapped a hand to his forehead—a stage gesture. "It could only be monkey. A rare delicacy. Sweet, you said. Monkey tastes sweet. There is nothing sweeter to the tongue than fresh young monkey."

"I've never tasted monkey."

"Well, now you have." The sergeant smiled complacently and looked around. The other prisoners were seated or squatting in the shade, none of them nearer than six meters, awaiting the outcome of the negotiations. When the sergeant turned back to Citron, the scowl was again in place and a harsh new urgency was in his tone. "I must have the watch," he said.

"No," Citron said. "Not for this."

Sergeant Bama nodded indifferently and looked off into the hot distance. "There will be a visitor this afternoon at fifteen hundred," he said. "A black woman from England who is a high functionary in a prisoners' organization with a rare name."

"You lie, of course," Citron said, wiping a thin film of grease from his mouth with the back of his hand.

Sergeant Bama looked at him and shrugged. "Believe what you wish, but she will be here at fifteen hundred to interview the other foreign scum. It is all arranged. You, of course, will be transferred to the isolation block and thus will miss the black Englishwoman. A pity. I am told she is a marvelous sight. Of course . . ." The sergeant's unspoken offer trailed off into an elaborate Afro-Gallic shrug.

"The watch," Citron said, understanding now.

"The watch."

Citron studied Sergeant Bama for several seconds. Over the sergeant's left shoulder he could see the private soldier approaching with a big pot of rice. "All right," Citron said. "You get the watch—but only after I see the black Englishwoman."

He was surprised when the sergeant agreed with a single word: "Good." Sergeant Bama rose then and turned toward the other prisoners. "Come and eat," he called in near English, adding in rapid French, which not all of them could follow: "We want you fat and sleek for when the black Englishwoman arrives."

The prisoners rose and started filing past the pots of meat and rice. The sergeant presided over the meat, the private soldier over the rice. The sergeant used a gourd ladle to dish meat into the prisoners' plastic bowls.

"What's this shit?" the young Mormon missionary asked.

"Monkey," Citron said.

"Oh," the Mormon said, hurried away with his food, sat down in some shade, and ate it quickly with his fingers.

Miss Cecily Tettah, who worked out of the London headquarters of Amnesty International, had been born on a large plantation in Ghana just outside Accra forty-two years before, when Ghana was still called the Gold Coast. After the war she had been sent by her cocoa-rich father to London to be educated. She had never returned to Ghana, never married, and, when asked, usually described herself in her splendid British accent as either a maiden lady or a spinster. Many thought her to be hopelessly old-fashioned. The few men lucky enough to find their way into her bed over the years discovered not only a magnificent body, but also an acerbic wit and an excellent mind.

13

Still a handsome woman, quite tall with graying hair, Miss Tettah, as she rather primly introduced herself to almost everyone, had been granted the use of Sergeant Bama's tiny office to interview the foreign prisoners. She sat behind the plain wooden table, a thick file open before her. Citron sat in the chair opposite. Cecily Tettah tapped the open file with a pencil and looked up at Citron with wide-spaced, bitter-chocolate eyes. She made no effort to keep the suspicion out of either her tone or gaze.

"There is no record of you," she said, giving the papers in the file a final tap with her pencil. "There're records of all the others, but none of you."

"No," Citron said. "I'm not surprised."

"They claim you're a spy, either French or American. They're not sure which."

"I'm a traveler," Citron said.

"I had an audience with the Emperor-President this morning." She sniffed. "I suppose that's what one should call it—an audience. He has agreed to release all of the foreign nationals —all except you."

"Why not me?"

"Because he thinks you're a spy, as I said. He wants to see you. Privately. Will you agree?"

Citron thought about it and shrugged. "All right."

"Not to worry," Cecily Tettah said. "We'll get it sorted out. Now then. How've they been treating you?"

"Not bad. Considering."

"What about food? You look thin."

"There was enough—just barely."

"Today, for instance. What did they feed you today?"

"Meat and rice."

"What kind of meat?"

"Monkey."

Cecily Tettah pursed her lips in approval, nodded, and made

a note. "Monkey's not bad," she said. "Quite nutritious. Almost no fat. Did they feed you monkey often?"

"No," Citron said. "Only once."

The Emperor-President's anteroom was an immense hall with no chairs or benches and a once magnificent parquet floor now ruined by cigarette burns and boot scars. The room was crowded with those who wanted to petition the Emperor-President, and with those whose job it was to prevent his assassination.

There were at least two dozen uniformed armed guards, plus another dozen secret police. The secret police all wore wide gaudy ties and peered suspiciously out at the world over tinted Ben Franklin glasses. The guards and the secret police stood. The threadbare petitioners sat on the floor along with a host of preening sycophants, a squad of sleepy-looking young messengers, and a pair of Slav businessmen in boxy suits who spoke Bulgarian to each other and tried to look forbidding, but whose wet friendly eyes betrayed their optimistic salesmen souls.

Citron also sat on the floor, his back to the wall, guarded by Sergeant Bama, who amused himself by shooting out his left wrist to admire his new gold Rolex. The sergeant smiled at his watch, then scowled at Citron.

"You will be alone with him."

"Yes."

"Do not lie about me."

"No."

"If you lie, then I might have to reveal what was in the morning pot. There are those who would pay well to learn its contents."

"Monkey," Citron said, knowing it wasn't.

The sergeant smiled a quite terrible smile that Citron felt he might remember for years. "It was not monkey," Sergeant Bama said.

"Last night," Citron said. "The screams. They sounded like children's screams."

Sergeant Bama shrugged and gave his new watch another admiring glance. "Some got carried away."

"Who?"

"I will not say." He glanced around quickly, then leaned closer to Citron. The smile reappeared, even more awful than before. "But you helped destroy the evidence," he whispered and then giggled. "You ate up all the evidence."

Citron stood throughout his audience with the Emperor-President, who sat slumped on the throne that had been cleverly crafted in Paris out of ebony and ivory. Citron thought it looked uncomfortable. He also thought the Emperor-President looked hung over.

"So," the Emperor-President said. "You are leaving us."

"I hope so."

"Some say you are French; some say American. What do you say?"

"I was both for a time. Now I'm American."

"How could you be both?"

"A matter of papers."

"Documents?"

"Yes."

"Ahhh."

The Emperor-President closed his eyes and seemed to nod off for a moment or so. He was a chunky man in his early fifties with a big stomach that bounced and rolled around underneath a long white cotton robe. The robe resembled a nightgown, and Citron thought it looked both cool and eminently practical. The Emperor-President opened his eyes, which seemed a bit inflamed, picked his nose, wiped his finger somewhere on the throne, and then beckoned Citron. "Come closer."

Citron moved closer.

"Closer still."

Citron took two more steps. The Emperor-President looked around suspiciously. They were alone. He beckoned Citron with a single finger. Citron leaned forward until he could smell last night's gin. Or today's.

"I wish to send a secret message to the Presidents of France and the United States," the Emperor-President whispered. "No one must know. No one." He waited for Citron's reply.

"I'm not sure," Citron said carefully, "how soon I will be seeing them."

The Emperor-President nodded his big head, as if that were exactly what he would expect a spy to say. "My message is brief. Tell them—tell them both that I am ready for reconciliation—on their terms."

"I see."

"Can you remember that?"

"Yes. I believe so."

"Here." The Emperor-President fumbled into the folds of the long white gown, found the pocket, and brought out a clenched fist. "Hold out your hand."

Citron held out his hand.

"Palm up."

Citron turned his palm up. The Emperor-President unclenched his fist. A two-carat diamond dropped into Citron's open palm. He automatically wrapped a fist around it.

"A token," the Emperor-President said. "A gesture."

"A token gesture."

"Yes. For your trouble."

"I see."

"You are free to go."

"Yes. Well. Thank you."

Citron turned and started toward the tall double doors, but stopped at the sound of the Emperor-President's voice. "Wait." Citron turned.

"I understand they fed you monkey today."

Citron only nodded.

"Did you like it?"

"I ate it."

"So did I," the Emperor-President said and began to chuckle —a deep bass chuckle that seemed to rumble up from his belly. "We both ate monkey today," the Emperor-President said and then went back to his chuckling. He was still at it when Citron walked through the tall double doors.

Miss Cecily Tettah counted three hundred French francs onto the plain table, picked them up, and handed them to Citron. He put them into the envelope that contained his Air France ticket to Paris and his American passport.

"How was he?" she asked. "You never said."

"He laughed a lot."

"Nothing else?"

"He still thinks I'm a spy."

"Really? I thought we'd got that all sorted out. Are you still quite certain there is no one you wish us to notify in the States?"

"No. No one."

"Not even your mother?"

Citron shook his head. "Especially not her."

2

It was almost a year to the day after Citron sold his diamond in Paris that Draper Haere, the money man, flew into Denver from New York. He arrived late, just before midnight. Because Haere had experienced a couple of uncomfortable rides with Denver taxi drivers in recent years, he carefully examined the man behind the wheel of the taxi at the head of the rank and was pleased to discover that he was Mexican and apparently a very sunny fellow.

Two years before when Haere had caught a taxi at Denver's Stapleton Airport, the driver had turned out to be a disgraced lieutenant governor from Louisiana who had taken to drink, but was now on what he called his rocky road to recovery and wanted to tell Haere all about it. The second time, almost a year later, another taxi driver had been a former Teamsters business agent from St. Louis who had been caught with his hand in the till. The former business agent was philosophical. "What the hell, Draper," he said. "I took a chance and I got caught." Haere sometimes wondered if taxi driving in Denver was a mystical restorative experience that somehow helped the fallen to climb back up onto the stool of redemption.

Before flying to Denver, Haere had been staying in New York at the Pierre, talking to a man who was toying with the idea of running for President—provided it didn't cost too much —and provided his mother gave him permission. But when the man who would be President seemed incapable of making up his mind, Haere had made a date with the mother.

They had tea at the Plaza. Or rather she had a vodka martini and Haere had tea. It took only five minutes, perhaps four, for them to agree that forty-three-year-old Sonny wasn't quite ready to be President, at least not in 1984, and probably not even in 1988. After that they spent another pleasant half hour or so talking politics.

Haere discovered she had one of those shockingly brilliant political minds that sometimes crop up in such places as Texas and Wisconsin and even Nebraska (Norris came to mind), but rarely in New York and not quite never in California. She was from West Virginia and had married steel. Big steel. When Haere told her it was too bad she couldn't run for President herself, she had shrugged and smiled, more than a little pleased. Haere didn't bother to call Sonny, who, he decided, would probably rather get his bad news from Mommy.

When the Mexican driver in Denver wasn't smiling about some nice secret, he hummed to himself and seemed to feel that all conversation was superfluous. So while the driver hummed, Draper Haere stared out the cab window and remembered the Denver of his childhood and early adolescence when it had been a quiet, sleepy, strangely green town content to nestle at the base of the Rocky Mountains under the collective thumb of the banks and Colorado Fuel and Iron and Great Western Sugar. Back then, Haere recalled, lungers from the East were still coming to Denver for its air. Now nobody came for the air. If they wanted clean air, they stayed in Pittsburgh.

As always, Haere was pleased to see that nothing much had happened to the Brown Palace Hotel in the past ninety years or so—other than the new west wing they had added on in the sixties. The room prices had changed, of course, and Haere still felt uncomfortable about paying $100 or $125 or $150 a night for a room. But Haere was one of those who still compared the price of everything with what he had paid back in the economic benchmark year of 1965—a silly, unbreakable habit that he often found extremely depressing.

The Brown Palace even had a bellhop on duty, an elderly one, who took Haere up to his room and accepted a $5 tip with polite thanks. Twenty seconds after the bellhop left, the phone rang. Haere knew it had to be the Candidate. It could be no other.

The Candidate was actually the forty-one-year-old governor-elect of California, calling from his Santa Monica house, working his phone calls west. It was now 2:00 A.M. in Washington, midnight in Denver, and 11:00 P.M. in Santa Monica. Soon the Candidate would have no one left to call but his fellow Californians.

Haere always thought of the governor-elect as the Candidate because no sooner was he elected to one office than he began lusting after the next. His name was Baldwin Veatch—which rhymed with wretch, as Haere was fond of pointing out—and beginning in his twenty-third year he had been elected in rapid succession from Los Angeles's suspiciously liberal west side to the state assembly, the state senate, the U.S. House of Representatives, and finally the governorship of the nation's most populous state. The White House was the only conceivable next step up, and Baldwin Veatch, not yet sworn in as governor, was already taking his first cautious preliminary soundings.

After Haere picked up the phone and said hello, the governor-elect said, "Well?"

"She doesn't think he should run."

"Really?"

"Really."

There was a pause. "Is she as bright as they say she is?"

"Brighter."

Another pause. "Well, that's one down."

"And a half-dozen or so to go," Haere said.

"Replogle will meet you in the lobby at nine tomorrow," Veatch said. "He wants to go up to his lodge in Breckenridge."

"Okay. How'd he sound?"

"Like a man dying of cancer, and cancer of the prostate at that, which is not exactly the most pleasant way to go."

"He still thinks that what he has is . . . interesting?" Haere said, choosing his ambiguous words carefully.

"He thinks it'll blow them out of the water in 'eighty-four," Veatch said.

Draper Haere sighed. Despite repeated efforts, he had never been able to convince Baldwin Veatch that the telephone was not a private means of communication. Veatch loved to call people, all sorts of people, and offer praise, encouragement, and chatty, surprisingly sensible advice. Just before the fall campaign began in earnest, he and Haere had spent the Labor Day weekend up in Veatch's summer shack in French Gulch. Among those Veatch had called and talked to (if briefly) had been Schmidt of Germany, de la Madrid of Mexico, Hussein of Jordan, and Rose of Philadelphia, who was in a slump.

"Baldy," Haere said, "you know something?"

"What?"

"You talk too much," Haere said and hung up. He turned to his bag, took out a bottle of Scotch, poured some into a glass, added water from the bathroom tap, crossed to the window, and gazed out across Broadway at the tall bank building, which now stood on the site of the long-demolished Shirley-Savoy Hotel, an old pols' hotel in whose rooms Haere recalled more than a few sexual and political adventures. For some reason, sex and politics for Haere had always gone hand in hand.

Deciding he didn't really need or want any old memories that night, Haere finished his drink, brushed his teeth, and got into bed with his illicit bedtime reading, which had been flown to him in New York by Purolator Courier from Sacramento.

It was a special bootleg copy, fresh off the Xerox machine, of a precinct-by-precinct breakdown of the voting in California during the just-over election. It was also nothing but a long, long list of names and figures, although to Draper Haere it was a wonderful tale of glorious victory and ignoble defeat, which he read avidly until he fell asleep just before he reached Ventura County.

Draper Haere awoke at 6:30 the next morning, which was when he always awoke regardless of jet lag and changing time zones. At forty-two, Haere was a deceptive-looking man who wore a martyr's face atop a natural athlete's body. The face he found useful, but the body had gone largely unexploited because Haere had long since decided that all vigorous physical activity, other than sex, was by and large a waste of time. It had been at least twenty years since he had last shot a gun, mowed a lawn, washed a car, painted a wall, caught a fish, or hit a ball of any kind. However, Haere did walk, often as much as seven or eight miles a day. He walked because it was a sensible way to get somewhere, because it gave him time to think, and because he was one of life's great gawkers.

The sad brown eyes, the weary mouth, the delicate nose, and the sturdy chin had somehow melded themselves into a long-suffering look that many mistook for past tragedy, but that was actually chronic exasperation. Because of his almost saintly looks, Haere was the first person trusting strangers turned to with their tales of despair and their questions about how to get to Disneyland. Haere could have been a world-class confidence man. He had instead gone into politics on the nuts-and-bolts side, and nearly everyone agreed that he was the best there was at his particular specialty, which was writing letters to people and getting money back in the mail.

After Haere awoke he noticed that it seemed strangely quiet until he looked out the window and discovered it had snowed during the night—not much, perhaps five or six inches, which was hardly anything in Denver because the sun usually came out and melted it by midafternoon. In New York, Haere knew it would have created chaos; in Washington, panic; and in Los Angeles, well, in Los Angeles five inches of snow on the freeways could only have signaled Armageddon. In Denver they didn't even bother to put on the chains.

Haere, still wearing the Jockey shorts he had slept in, got out the three-cup pot and the instant Yuban. The pot boiled three cups of water in less than sixty seconds and Haere had bought it at Marshall Field's in Chicago five years before after paying, for the first time, $12 plus tip for two cups of room-service coffee in the Ritz-Carlton. Although he realized that of such small economies are crotchety bachelors made, the pot now went with him everywhere. He also brought along his own mug, spoon, and sugar.

After the coffee, the three cigarettes, the shave, and the shower, Haere dressed in what he always dressed in, a blue three-piece pinstripe suit, and took the elevator down to the lobby, checked out, turned, and got his first shock of the day, which was a three-quarter profile of Jack Replogle as he stood in the lobby and did what everyone does in the Brown Palace—gaze up at the splendid hollow core around which the hotel is built.

Replogle had lost weight—at least twenty or thirty pounds. He seemed to huddle down in his Antartex coat. For a moment it also seemed as though he had lost two or three inches in height, which would have brought him down to Haere's own five eleven and a half. Haere then realized that Replogle was bent over, angled down and to one side, and apparently couldn't look up by throwing his head back, but only by twisting it around on his neck.

Replogle's deep-set green eyes had burrowed even farther back into his head, and under them were twin dark smears. His skin seemed to have the color and texture of newsprint. He was an obviously sick man, so Haere went up to him and tapped him on the shoulder. When Replogle turned, Haere said, "You look like hell."

Although the pain had etched itself across his face, Haere saw that Replogle's smile was still the same—the smile of a man who has long known some very funny secret he has finally decided to divulge to you and none other.

Replogle looked Haere up and down carefully, nodded as if satisfied, or at least reassured, and said, still smiling, "I don't need your fucking sympathy."

"Hurts, huh?"

"Yeah, it hurts. Let's go."

Replogle turned and started toward the west entrance of the hotel. Haere followed with his bag through the door and out into the street, where a Jeep station wagon was parked at the curb. Haere saw it was the four-wheel-drive kind, which he thought was called the Wagoneer.

Replogle got behind the wheel and fastened his seat belt. Haere didn't. He never did. And then Replogle did what he had always done whenever Haere had ridden with him—and this went back more than thirty years to when Haere had been only a child. Using one hand, his right, Replogle slowly pulled an imaginary pair of World War II flying goggles down over his eyes. Even after thirty years it still got a smile out of Haere.

Jack Replogle had been a hot navy pilot in that long-ago war. After it was over Haere's father and Replogle discovered they had once been only a thousand feet or so apart on a small island in the Philippines: Replogle up in the air in his Hellcat, Haere's old man down on the ground: both of them shooting at each other; Replogle by mistake, Haere's old man on purpose. Jack Replogle later swore that the infantry rifle fire had actually hit his plane that day. It was a charming lie and he told it often and Haere's old man always pretended to believe it, but it was still a lie, because, as the senior Haere later told his son, everyone in Company D had been an absolutely rotten shot. Haere was six years old when his father had finally come back from the war in 1946, and he remembered it was years after that before the overage former private first class had stopped referring to it as the fuckininfantry, not two words, but one, virtually inseparable.

The morning traffic was heavy, but Replogle drove quickly, expertly, apparently oblivious to the snow that was already turning to slush. They headed south and then turned west at Sixth Avenue, which would lead them onto Highway 6, which eventually turned into Interstate 70. The sun had come out and there was no smog. Ahead, there were the glittering mountains to admire.

Replogle lit a cigarette, which Haere noted was still an unfiltered Lucky Strike, and said, "I knew I had cancer at least two months before they cut me open down in Houston."

"How?"

"My plumbing started backing up. I figured it was the prostate. When they went in, they found out there wasn't much they could do, so they sort of patched me up and reamed me out and now I come backwards." He paused. "Except I haven't been doing much of that lately either, although there is this one lovely I've known for years who's got a lady friend, and once a week or so we all three get together and play a mild game of Lincoln logs. Very mild. Almost geriatric."

"Well, an orgy's an orgy, I guess," Haere said. "How's Maureen?" Maureen was Replogle's wife of twenty-seven years.

"Maureen," he said. "Let me tell you about Thanksgiving."

"Which Thanksgiving?"

"This one."

"It's still two weeks away."

"Not at my house. At my house they had Thanksgiving last Thursday on account of they don't think I'm going to last through Christmas, which sure as hell won't bother me too much."

Replogle paused and put his cigarette out in the car's ashtray. "Well, they're all there, Maureen's family, gathered around the table—her three brothers, already half in the bag, and their godawful wives, and maybe half a dozen assorted nephews, all of them nine feet tall and out of work, and Maureen's old man who's ninety-two and barking about how he's not going to eat any fucking turkey because what he really wants is Salisbury steak. That's what they always call hamburger in Maureen's family. Salisbury steak."

"Class," Haere said.

"So there we all are, the pot smoke so thick you could can it, my brothers-in-law shitfaced, my sisters-in-law arguing about what TV show they're going to watch, Maureen's old man complaining about his goddamn Salisbury steak being too rare, and suddenly Maureen announces that we're going around the table so everybody can say what they've got to be thankful for—starting with me."

"Norman Rockwell," Haere said.

"Exactly. Well, they're all looking at me and I just sat there and didn't say anything for a while. And then I said, 'What the fuck have I got to be thankful for? I've got cancer.' Well, you should've seen their faces." Replogle chuckled at the memory and then said, as though repeating a favorite punch line, "What the fuck have I got to be thankful for? I've got cancer."

After that he started to laugh, and he went on laughing until Draper Haere joined in out of what he later decided was self-defense.

3

HAD IT NOT BEEN FOR THE ACTRESS Craigie Grey, it is doubtful that Draper Haere would ever have found and retained the services of Morgan Citron, who, for the past year, had been living on the $6,000 he had realized in Paris from the sale of the somewhat flawed two-carat diamond.

Until the money ran out, Citron had lived the year in a converted two-car garage in Venice, California, only a block from the beach. The rent had been $300 a month for the one large room with its cement floor, toilet, sink, and the jerry-built shower that was rigged up out of a garden hose. For heat and cooking, there was a two-burner hot plate.

Citron spent much of his time during that year in the comfortable Santa Monica library reading old travel books, the older the better, and anything he could find on cannibalism, which was not very much. When not in the library, he was usually down on the beach, where he watched the people, but talked to virtually no one, and sipped carefully, even sparingly, from his daily bottle of cheap red wine. He talked to virtually no one because his disease was still in remission. It had gone into remission shortly after he was jailed and he often suspected that he was cured of it forever. The disease that Citron no longer suffered from was curiosity.

Citron's one meal a day was taken in the evening and usually consisted of a large bowl of what he still insisted on thinking of as *pot au feu*, which simmered sporadically on the hot plate and whose ingredients were suspect vegetables, meat and chicken bought on sale with blackmarket food stamps at Boys Market in the Marina del Rey. Sometimes Citron also bought day-old bread. He once estimated that he was living slightly more than $1,000 a year beneath the federal government's official poverty line, which that year was $4,680.

After the diamond money finally ran out and he was down to his last $32.64, Citron packed what little he owned into the trunk and backseat of his one luxury, a 1969 Toyota Corona sedan, and headed north to a spot on the Pacific Coast Highway about halfway between Malibu and Oxnard. It was there that the Cadillac People lived.

The Cadillac People into whose midst Citron settled were called that because that's what some of them lived in—old Cadillac sedans with savaged fenders and rust spots and backseats jammed with whatever their owners couldn't bear to part with. Other Cadillac People lived in equally old Lincolns and Chrysler Imperials and huge Ford station wagons and converted school buses and homemade campers that perched haphazardly on the beds of senile pickup trucks. It was a community of sorts, an anarchists' community perhaps, parked defiantly and illegally at the edge of the continent on land owned by the state. Occasionally, the highway patrol stopped by and halfheartedly shooed the Cadillac People away. But they almost always drifted back.

Some of the Cadillac People drank. Some didn't. Nearly all of them slept in their cars and used the ocean as their combination bathroom and TV set. They sat there in the mild sunshine, day after day, on the western edge of the American dream, listening mostly to country-western radio music because of the stories it told, drumming bored fingers on worn doorsills, and staring out through tinted windshields at the Pacific as they waited for something inevitable to happen—death perhaps; certainly not taxes.

For three weeks Citron had waited with them and listened to their stories, which, like the country-western lyrics they favored, usually involved cheating lovers, faithless friends, venal employers, and feckless offspring.

"You know what this is kinda like?" the Cadillac People's resident philosopher had once asked Citron. "This is kinda like a real bad double feature. You sit here waitin' for this one to end and the other to begin, except you know damn well the second one ain't gonna be no better'n the first. But you wait anyhow."

During what he sometimes later came to think of as Life's Intermission, Citron gambled four gallons of gasoline to drive into Venice and back to check out his post-office box. Another six months' rent would be due on the box in two weeks. Citron had no plans to pay it.

The post-office box in Venice was Citron's last outpost, his final link with civilization. It was where dunning letters could be sent; where strangers could implore him to buy their costly goods and services; where his oldest and dearest friends could send him money orders and entreaties to come and stay with them forever; where warmhearted foundations could offer him grants-in-aid; and where somebody, somewhere, could write to tell him that she loved him.

What Citron found in the post-office box were four letters from the Internal Revenue Service, which he tossed, unopened, into the wastebasket. There were also nineteen pieces of junk mail, which were also discarded, and two letters from the American Express Company, forwarded from Paris, which he assumed to be rude demands for payment and which he also tossed away unread, unopened.

The one letter Citron did open was prettily addressed to him by hand in brown ink. It was an invitation to an American Civil Liberties Union fund-raiser in Bel-Air. Citron assumed the ACLU had somehow got his name and address from Amnesty International.

Citron turned to look up at the clock on the post-office wall. He still owned no watch and sometimes doubted that he ever would again. The post-office clock read 4:32. The ACLU reception with its promise of free food and drink was from 5:00 to 7:30. Citron found the public washroom and inspected himself in the mirror. He had clipped his gunfighter mustache the day before, just after one of the Cadillac People had given his gray-streaked brown hair a free trim along with a fanciful story about having once been Sinatra's favorite barber in Tahoe.

As for clothes, Citron was wearing a clean blue button-down shirt, a worn but still good tweed jacket, faded jeans, and presentable brown loafers. It was a uniform that in Los Angeles would enable him to pass for either a sincere probation officer or a rich producer.

At the ACLU fund-raiser in Bel-Air, Citron managed to put away a quarter of a pound of assorted cheese, a half-dozen cocktail sausages, perhaps fifteen Triscuits, and two glasses of white wine before he was discovered by Craigie Grey, the actress, questioned sharply, and hired on the spot as the resident manager of her Malibu beach apartment building.

Upon turning thirty-two in 1971, Craigie Grey had taken a long bleak look at herself in a three-way mirror and a week later put every dime she could raise into a down payment on the two-story, eight-unit beach apartment on the Pacific Coast Highway a block or so from the pier in what was generally conceded to be one of Malibu's less ritzy sections.

The redheaded film actress bought the apartment building as both an investment and a hedge against what she called the three Fs—Fat, Fifty, and Forgotten. She also bought shrewdly and cheaply, bargaining the price down to less than three-quarters of a million. Eleven years later it was still worth four, possibly five times what she paid for it. Some said six.

On that unseasonably warm November evening when she hired Citron (despite his murmured protestations that his inability to fix anything broken, either mechanical or spiritual, just might border on criminal negligence), Craigie Grey raised a glass of white wine to her broad, grin-prone mouth, sipped it, and stared at him over the glass' rim with her bluebonnet-blue eyes. A native of Longview in East Texas, which she had left thirty years ago when she was twelve (or six to hear her tell it now), her birthplace could still be detected in the softly twanged vowels that glided in and out of her speech.

"How long were you in there, all in all?" she said, lowering her glass.

"All in all, not quite thirteen months," Citron said.

Her next question was predictable—at least to Citron. But first there was to be the inevitable hesitation while the battle with prurience was fought. As usual, prurience won.

"Was he *really* a cannibal like they all said?"

Citron shrugged his answer, or lack of it, as he almost always did when asked that particular question. He reached for another Triscuit on which he placed a large chunk of cheese that turned out to be Monterey jack. They were standing next to the table where the wine and cheese were being served. Craigie Grey was there to make the fund-raiser's principal speech. Citron, of course, had come for the grub.

"You don't like to talk about it," Craigie Grey said in a tone that mingled sympathy with disappointment.

"It's not my favorite topic," Citron admitted.

Craigie Grey nodded and changed the subject. "You used to move around a lot, didn't you?" she said. "Overseas, I mean."

"Yes. A lot."

"Why'd you come back here? I mean to L.A. You're not from here."

32

"No."

Craigie Grey waited for him to answer her latest question. Citron seemed to be thinking about it. "The weather," he said finally, as though the answer came as a surprise even to him. "I got used to a warm climate. I don't much like the cold anymore."

The answer seemed to satisfy her, because she raised the wineglass to her mouth again, drank, put the glass down, and turned back to Citron, her attitude suddenly crisp and businesslike.

"I'll tell you what it pays," she said.

"All right."

"It pays four hundred a month and you get the grungy downstairs back unit free—that's the one on the highway."

Citron decided he should at least appear to consider it. He counted to five and said, "Okay. Fine."

"If something goes kaput, call a plumber or a carpenter or an electrician. Whatever. I'll give you a list of numbers. It's cheaper in the long run. Professional maintenance, I mean."

"All right."

"I've only got two rules. Maybe three. Don't rent to any coke dealers or whore ladies. And anyone who doesn't come up with their rent by the tenth of the month is out on their ass. No exceptions. Okay?"

Citron nodded. "Okay."

"Then you're hired," she said.

Out of loyalty and gratitude to his new employer, Citron sat through her speech, which turned out to be predictably gloomy and uncommonly trenchant. When the pledge cards were passed around, he pocketed his and told a vaguely familiar-looking young television actress that he'd mail his check in.

4

THE NAME that Jack Replogle signed to checks and contracts was John T. Replogle. The T stood for Townsend. He built things. Or rather Replogle Construction, Inc., did. With its headquarters in Denver and offices in Jidda and Rome and Singapore, it built things all over the world—roads, docks, airfields, hospitals, pipelines, virtually anything. Replogle was the firm's president and chief executive officer. He was both very rich and very smart, and if he had a hobby, it was politics.

Over the years Replogle had come to specialize in political fund-raising, which he always called "shaking down the flush-bottoms back East"—although back East to Replogle could mean Dallas or Tulsa or Kansas City or Chicago. Over the years he had shaken them down for close to forty million dollars.

It was around 10:00 when he and Draper Haere stopped in Idaho Springs for breakfast, a meal Haere had never been able to do without. Although he regularly skipped lunch, Haere could never deny himself breakfast, which was invariably the same: two eggs over easy; bacon or sausage; toast and hash browns, or—if he was in the South—grits. He had grown fond of grits in Birmingham.

Haere noticed the big high-sprung dark-blue pickup truck when they pulled into the café. It was a Dodge. He noticed it because of the angle parking that made it almost impossible not to read the sticker plastered across the pickup's tailgate. The sticker read: "Is There Life After Death? Fuck with This Truck and Find Out."

Replogle ordered only coffee, which he scarcely touched. He told Haere he didn't eat much anymore and that the drugs he had to take made everything taste like brass. For some reason, however, the drugs didn't affect the taste of liquor, so he was drinking more than he probably should, although at this point in his life he didn't think anyone was bothering to keep score.

Back in the station wagon, Replogle again buckled his seat belt, and again Haere didn't. But this time Replogle failed to go through the fighter-pilot-goggles business, either because he forgot, or because he thought that once a day for the old joke was enough.

They drove in silence for five minutes or so admiring the scenery. It had also snowed the night before in the mountains, and there was a seasonal accumulation of three or four feet on level ground and much deeper than that in the drifts. The snowplows had already been through that morning, and the highway was clear and even dry in places where the sun had managed to get at it.

Replogle lit another of his cigarettes and said, "When they told me they were going to have to cut, I decided to take a little trip."

"How little?"

"Not so little. Around the world. I started in Jidda, where I fired a couple of guys and brought in three more. Then I doubled back to Rome, where I didn't fire anybody because you can't beat those Italians for hot-weather construction. I even hired a couple of real finds there and then flew on out to Singapore. That's where it happened. In Singapore."

35

"What?"

"What I'm going to tell you about, which is the reason you're here."

"Okay."

"You know about me and Langley." It wasn't a question.

"No," Haere said. "I don't."

"At least you suspected."

"All right. I suspected."

"You never said anything."

Haere shrugged. "It wasn't any of my business."

"When's that ever bothered you?"

"Okay," Haere said. "I presumed."

That seemed to mollify Replogle. "Okay, let's say you also presumed that before anything gets built in some country where the weather's hot and the people're poor there's going to be some graft—some dash, baksheesh, whatever you want to call it. Otherwise, the poor folks aren't going to get their shiny new doctorless hospitals, or their four-lane highways going nowhere, or their brand-new international airports where they can go out every Sunday, Tuesday, and Friday and watch a twenty-year-old DC-8 drop in—maybe. At least none of these things—without graft—is going to be built by Replogle Construction. Instead, they're all going to be built by the British or the Italians or those fucking Koreans, who're getting to be a real menace. So. I've spread a little money around—right?"

He seemed to be expecting some sort of answer, so Haere said, "Right. Absolutely."

"And the first thing you know the Permanent Secretary for the Ministry of Works and Progress, who's been getting to work in his five-year-old VW, if he's lucky, suddenly starts showing up in his brand-new chauffeur-driven BMW that he thinks nobody's going to notice the way they would a new Mercedes, which is what he and his wife and his girlfriend really had their hearts set on. I'm making myself clear, I take it?"

"I thought Congress made them tax-deductible. Bribes, I mean."

"Not if it's against the law in the country where you hand out the grease. And I'm not talking about tipping the headwaiter. I'm talking about corruption. Big bucks."

"You're also exaggerating."

"A little. But not much. Not much."

"It's an old story anyway," Haere said.

"Old as the Pyramids—and the Acropolis and El Tajin and the fucking hanging gardens of Babylon. Nothing public ever got built clean. Not even by the WPA. I'm convinced."

"So what happens?"

"So what happens is that I'm awarded the contract. And maybe four or five months or even a year later, I'm back out there where it's hot in my air-conditioned suite at the Inter-Continental—it's almost always the Inter-Continental, for some reason—and I'm trying to find out why my cement is still a little soupy, or why my steel I-beams are maybe a touch brittle —and the phone rings."

"The phone rings," Haere said.

"If it's working that day, yeah. And on the phone is the second secretary or maybe the commercial attaché at the embassy who wants to know if he can drop by for a minute."

"Whose embassy?"

"Ours."

"Right. Ours."

"Well, he shows up in his Haspel seersucker and his black knit silk tie and his lace-up cordovans and no, he doesn't think he'll have a drink because it's still a tiny bit early for him, but I should go right ahead, if I really want one, and he'll just have a Perrier, if I have it, but if not, no problem, club soda will do just fine. Well, already I'm a morning lush. So he talks about this and that for a while and then wants to know if there's anything the embassy can do for me, because if there is, all I need to do is holler, except he doesn't say holler because he went to Princeton or Yale or Harvard, like you, and Harvards don't say holler much."

"I say it all the time."

"Yeah, but you're weird. Anyway, there's a little more tiny talk and then right at the end, almost like a throwaway, he says, by the way, isn't it delicious about old Iskander Soedibio, or Mohammed al-Harbi, or whatever the name is of the poor sap who's driving around in the new BMW. Well, the Yalie's got it all, of course—dates, time of day, and how much the juice was down to the dime."

"You mean the spook from the embassy?"

"Yeah. The spook. And, of course, he claims Langley is just terribly sympathetic and fully understands and appreciates the problems of doing business in the hot countries, but frankly they're rather concerned that neither Justice nor the SEC nor Congress—especially Congress—would understand quite so readily. That's how they all talk. Well, not really, but something like that."

"Then what?" Haere said.

"Then the quid pro quo, what else? I know damn well what would happen if some of Langley's trained seals in the Senate or the House got hold of the fact that Replogle Construction was bribing permanent secretaries and ministers and their various cousins and brothers-in-law. What would happen is that I wouldn't be rich anymore and you and me couldn't shoehorn maybe one or two ugly but halfway honest guys into Congress every two years or so. I might even be poor like you. How'd you ever manage to stay so poor?"

"It's a knack—like anything else."

"It must be. Well, what they always wanted me to do—"

"Langley."

"Yeah. Langley. What they always wanted me to do, and this has happened, with variations, maybe five or six times over the past fifteen years or so, is to put one or two of their guys on my payroll in some country where the weather's hot. It's not going to cost me anything because they're going to feed it all back to me, the money, through the Somesuch Corporation in, let's say, Liechtenstein. And the Langley guys on my payroll might even do a little work—maybe empty the pencil sharpeners or something."

"You're their cover, then?"

"Replogle Construction is."

"How many?"

"On my payroll now? About fourteen."

Haere turned it over in his mind for a moment or two and then said, "Then what's the problem?"

"With Langley? None. Well, not yet anyway. I stumbled across something out in Singapore. Something really shitty. Something that could blow those fuckers out of the White House in 'eighty-four." Replogle paused, and then went on. "If things were normal, I might just sit on it—to cover my own ass. But then I thought, what the hell, you'll be dead soon, so what can they do? So I waited until the elections were over and then got in touch with Veatch. I figured Veatch and you'd know how to run with it best." Replogle glanced at Haere as if expecting encouragement.

"Go on," Haere said.

"Well, it was in Singapore, like I said, and this time I was staying at Raffles instead of the Inter-Continental. You ever stayed at Raffles?"

"I've never been to Singapore."

"Well, I sometimes stay there because it's old and it's nice and I keep hoping I'll run into some gorgeous Eurasian beauty I can run off to Bora Bora with, or at least bump into somebody tragic and seedy with stories to tell, but all you bump into at Raffles nowadays are the Japs and the blue-rinse set from Santa Barbara, because they're about all who can afford it."

"Except this last time," Haere said.

"Right. He knocked on the door and there he was, right out of Maugham—shabby old suit, three-day beard, gin for breakfast—everything."

"Who?"

"Meade."

"*Drew* Meade."

Replogle nodded.

"Jesus."

Draper Haere had been barely twelve years old when Drew Meade, revealing himself for the first time as an undercover FBI agent, appeared as the star witness before an investigating U.S. Senate subcommittee. Meade swore that Haere's father, the overage former private first class in the Americal division and, prior to that, a youngish lieutenant in Spain with the Lincoln Battalion (not brigade, kid, battalion), had been then and was indeed even yet a card-carrying, dues-paying member of the Communist Party (U.S.A.).

Out of more than mild curiosity, Draper Haere had kept track of Drew Meade over the years, finally losing both interest and Meade's trail in the late sixties.

"I heard he went with Langley," Haere said. "I heard he crossed over in 'sixty-one or -two—around in there."

" 'Sixty-one," Replogle said. "He wound up in Laos in 'sixty-nine and by then he was maybe four or five years away from retirement, but he went into dope instead and Langley dumped him, very quietly."

"He was *dealing*?" Haere said, unable to keep the surprise out of his tone.

Replogle nodded. "In a big way. But when I talked to him he was flat broke."

"Where was this?"

"Up in my room. He knocked on my door, I opened it, and there he stood—just what I was hoping for: somebody to tell me a story."

"How much did he want for it?"

"His story? Fifty thousand, but I knocked that down to ten grand pretty quick."

"It still must be some story."

"Yeah," Replogle said, "it is." He paused for a moment and then continued in his most precise engineering manner. "Meade came to me because, one, he remembered how close your dad and I always were; two, because he knew I could use what he was going to tell me; and three, because I could pay for it. Pay pretty good, in fact. That was the most important. Well, I had to give him the money first, and that meant a trip to the bank. Then he had to have a few drinks before he'd finally sit down and tell me how it all began six months ago down in Miami when Langley—"

Replogle never finished the secondhand story because the big blue Dodge pickup honked and pulled up on the left. Haere looked over. There were two persons in the pickup. Both wore ski masks. The pickup and the station wagon had reached a sharp curve in the deep canyon. On the station wagon's right, some fifty or sixty feet below, was a frozen creek.

The pickup swerved, and its right front fender slammed into the station wagon, which went into a skid on a patch of ice. Haere later thought they must have been counting on that—the ice. Replogle did everything he was supposed to do. He kept his foot off the brake. He steered into the skid. He swore.

The station wagon plunged over the side. On either the first or second roll the right-hand door popped open and Draper Haere popped out. He landed in a snowbank. The station wagon somersaulted two more times, end over end, and smashed against some immense boulders at the creek's edge. Two seconds later the gas tank exploded.

Haere got up and made himself stumble through the snow down to the burning car. He tried to open its front left door, but it was either jammed or locked. Haere burned his hands trying to get the door open. He finally could stand neither the heat nor the pain, so he moved backward, tripped over something, and sat back down in a snowbank. He jammed his scorched hands down deep into the snow and sat there watching Jack Replogle burn to death if, indeed, he wasn't already dead. In either event, there was nothing Draper Haere could do about it.

5

AFTER HIS HANDS WERE TREATED by a doctor in Idaho Springs, Draper Haere talked to a trio of policemen that consisted of a fiftyish Clear Creek County deputy sheriff and two mustachioed, look-alike investigators from the Colorado Highway Patrol.

Haere described the blue Dodge pickup and its two masked occupants as best he could. He also said he didn't think it was an accident: that as far as he could tell it had seemed intentional. The policemen nodded somberly, looked thoughtful, and marked it down as hit-and-run. Haere didn't mention Jack Replogle's tale about the CIA and Singapore and Drew Meade, because he could see no purpose it would serve.

Since Haere no longer went to funerals, he didn't stay for Jack Replogle's. Instead he called Maureen, Replogle's wife, to express his condolences. Maureen was appropriately tearful and, as always, excessively dramatic.

"Tell me he didn't suffer, Draper," Maureen Replogle said.

"He didn't suffer, Maureen."

"That man was my life—my entire life. How can I live without him? How can I possibly go on living without him? I'm thinking of killing myself, Draper. I've got some sleeping pills. I'll just take those and when I wake up I'll be with Jack."

"I don't think Jack would really want you to do that, Maureen. He'd want you to go on living for as long as possible."

There was a silence and then Maureen said in a very small voice, "Do you really think so?"

"I'm sure of it."

There was another silence and then the tears started again. "Do you know what I am, Draper? I'm—oh, my God—I'm a *widow*."

Maureen hung up without saying goodbye, and Draper Haere went aboard the United flight to Los Angeles. There, in the first-class section, even before the plane took off, he asked for and was served a martini, which he drank through a couple of straws because of his lightly bandaged hands.

During the two-hour flight to Los Angeles, Haere stared down at the occasional lights six miles below and thought about death and dying and the last funeral he had attended, which had been that of his father twenty-five years before in Birmingham, Alabama.

Father and son had moved to Birmingham from Denver in 1954, when the senior Haere had managed to secure a job on the copy desk of the *Birmingham News*. The *News* didn't seem to care whether the senior Haere was a communist or not as long as he was a competent journeyman who would work cheap. Haere was just finishing his junior year in high school when his father—on his day off—started going down to Sylacauga on the bus. Haere at first thought his old man had found a lady friend, until father invited son to go along. They got off the Trailways bus at the combination depot and five-and-dime and walked three miles out of town to a small farmhouse, where they sat on the front porch with a man of about the same age as Haere's father. Haere drank lemonade. The two men drank beer. Nobody said much. The other man had also served in Spain, and his left leg was gimpy. They sat there in the warm spring afternoon in a not uncomfortable silence that seemed both to separate and embrace what surely were the only two veterans of the Abraham Lincoln Battalion in Alabama. A Sunday or so later, when Haere's old man asked him if he'd like to go down to Sylacauga again, Haere said no.

On March 25, 1957, Haere was summoned to the office of the high school principal and informed that he was being offered a full four-year scholarship to Harvard. "That's in Cambridge," the principal said. "In Massachusetts." Haere told the principal he would have to think it over.

It wasn't until years later that Haere learned that it wasn't his straight-A average that had won him the Harvard scholarship. Instead, it had been Jack Replogle calling in a political debt. Replogle had called Big Ed Johnson of Colorado, who had called Big Jim Folsom of Alabama, who had called a Birmingham banker who had earned both his B.A. and M.B.A. at Harvard. Big Jim as governor kept large sums of the state's money interest-free in the banker's bank. The banker was one of Harvard's unofficial scholarship scouts. It took only a few minutes for the banker to decide that Draper Haere would do wonderfully well at his alma mater.

When Haere told his old man about the scholarship offer, the senior Haere had grinned and said, "No shit? You going to take it?"

"I don't know," Haere said.

"I don't see why not."

"I'll think about it," Haere said.

He reached his decision four weeks later when his father died from heart failure, seated in front of the radio listening to the detested Fulton Lewis, Jr. He also would have detested anyone's calling it heart failure. "Heart *failure* kills everybody," he sometimes told Haere, quoting one of his favorite copy-desk

45

maxims. "But people die from heart *attacks* and heart *seizures*. Remember that."

There was just enough money to bury him in a cemetery called Memorial Park. There were no services of any kind. The man from Sylacauga came up for the burial. He and Haere rode out to the cemetery together in the funeral-home car behind the hearse. No one from the paper came. Haere never did know why. Perhaps, he told himself, they just forgot.

There were two funeral-home attendants in the hearse. They, along with Haere and the man from Sylacauga, were to carry the casket, the cheapest available. At the last moment another car, a 1949 Hudson, pulled up and a man in his late forties got out. Wordlessly, he took hold of one of the handles and the five of them carried the casket to the open grave, into which it was lowered by a pair of gravediggers.

The man who came late turned to Haere. "I knew your father," he said. "I admired him." The man had a European accent of some kind. He didn't say anything to the man from Sylacauga. Haere thought they might not have known each other, or it might have been that they did know each other but the man from Sylacauga simply ignored the stranger the way he ignored almost everyone.

"Would you like me to say a few words?" the man with the accent said.

"Sure," Haere said. "If you want to."

The man with the accent reached down, picked up a clod or two of red clay, and tossed the earth down on the casket.

"I knew this comrade," said the man with the accent. "He was steadfast in the pursuit of justice all his life."

The man from Sylacauga snorted in disgust, turned, and walked away. Draper Haere never saw either man again.

At virtually the same time that Draper Haere and his bleak thoughts were passing over the Grand Canyon on their way to

Los Angeles, Morgan Citron was parking his 1969 Toyota sedan on the edge of the Pacific Coast Highway in Malibu.

From the highway, Craigie Grey's apartment building didn't look like six million dollars to Citron. Or five million. Or even four. It was only two stories in height and a bare fifty feet in width. Its architecture was mineshaft modern, and it was protected from Valley marauders by a seven-foot-high redwood fence that had a locked gate. Citron tried the key Craigie Grey had given him in the gate's lock and was mildly surprised to find that it worked.

He went through the gate and into a small bricked patio. The bricks were used and divided into squared-off sections by old railroad ties. The patio also boasted a small green jungle of potted succulents and ferns illuminated by an outside floodlight that was mostly focused on the gate. From the light Citron could determine that the apartment building was constructed of redwood and shingle, which would burn quite merrily when one of the periodic fires swept down from the Santa Monica mountains and hopped the highway. If the place was really worth upward of four million dollars, Citron decided it must be because of the sound caused by the bang and crash of a heavy surf, which was so loud he could scarcely hear the highway traffic.

The grungy downstairs back apartment seemed to be Unit A. Using the same key he had used on the gate, Citron unlocked the apartment door and went in. He felt for the light switch, turned it on, and found himself in a one-room studio with a large single window overlooking the patio. The furnishings were sparse: a phone, a couch that he assumed pulled out into a bed, a round Formica-topped table with four chairs made out of bent iron and molded plastic, a shabby armchair that seemed to be of the reclining variety, and an old seventeen-inch black-and-white General Electric television set. The floor was covered with linoleum of the speckled-white-and-gold kind. It was almost worn through in the space in front of the Pullman kitchen. On the walls there was nothing. Not even a calendar.

It took Citron only two trips out to the Toyota to bring in everything he owned. As he was storing away the last of his three aluminum cooking pots, a woman's voice said from the still-open door, "Can you fix a running toilet?"

Without turning, Citron said, "No."

"What about a broken heart?"

"Not that either," he said and turned.

His first impression was that although she was not very old, she was not nearly as young as she looked, which would have made her around nineteen, possibly twenty. Twenty-one at most. Somehow Citron knew she was at least thirty. It might have been the melancholy that peered out through her eyes, which were large and almost the color of woodsmoke. She had a beach dweller's careless sun-streaked hair and an oval face with a rather interesting nose and a wide mouth set above a quite small chin that nevertheless looked defiant—or perhaps only stubborn. She was effortlessly pretty and with a little artful makeup might even have been beautiful in a vulnerable sort of way.

"I'm in Apartment E—in front," she said. "My name's Keats. Velveeta Keats."

"Velveeta."

"Sort of tips you off, doesn't it? I mean, about my family. You're wondering what kind of folks would name their youngest daughter Velveeta."

"Am I?"

"Sure. The answer is: my kind of folks. The Keatses. The Florida Keatses. Or to pinpoint it: the Miami Keatses. My family was very big in the drug trade down there in the sixties and seventies."

"But no more," Citron said.

"They cashed out and went into T-bills. At least, that's what

48

they were in a year or so ago. They may be in municipal bonds by now. You ever notice how fast things move nowadays? The Keatses went from dirt-poor to hog-rich to banker-stuffy in one generation. But when I was born back in 'fifty-two they named me Velveeta because back then they thought it sounded pretty and tasted good."

"They still like Velveeta?"

"The name?"

"The cheese."

"They don't like either one anymore. Mama calls me Vee now and they switched to Brie. Mama puts it on crackers with slivered almonds and sticks it in the microwave for a few seconds. If you're wondering what I'm doing out here, I'm a remittance woman. Are you the new super?"

"Caretaker really."

"What's your name?"

Citron told her.

"That's nice. French, isn't it?"

"French."

"Well, I've got this running toilet."

"Jiggle it."

"The handle?"

"Right."

"I did that."

"Try taking the top off. There's a round ball in there that floats. Bend the rod that holds the ball. Bend it down. That sometimes works."

"I did that, too."

"Have you got a radio?"

"Sure."

"Well, put the radio in the bathroom and turn it on. If you play it loudly enough, you won't hear the toilet."

She came farther into the apartment and looked around curiously. "Mind if I ask you a personal question?"

"Not at all." He gestured toward the recliner, but Velveeta Keats chose instead one of the bent-iron-and-plastic chairs. Citron took a half gallon of Gallo red out of one of the two cardboard cartons he had carried in from the Toyota and poured wine into a pair of mismatched Kraft cheese glasses. He handed one of them to Velveeta Keats and then sat down opposite her at the table.

She examined her glass. "I remember these. Pimento cheese used to come in them. The Keatses always drank out of these and jelly glasses. Back when we were poor. Are you poor?"

"Extremely," Citron said.

"What'd you do—before you got poor?" she said. "That's my personal question."

"I wrote and traveled."

"You mean you were a travel writer? What's doing in Omaha? Beautiful, unspoiled Belize. Tierra del Fuego on twenty a day. Stuff like that?"

"I guess I was really more of a writing traveler."

"What's the difference?"

"Well, I'd travel to someplace where not too many people go, live there awhile, maybe six months, sometimes longer, and then write about what it was like."

"Is that what you're doing here—in Malibu?"

Citron shook his head. "No."

"What happened?"

"I think I ran out of places."

"How long've you known the landlady?"

"Craigie Grey? Not long."

"How long's not long?"

"About five hours."

"You're right. That's not long."

Velveeta Keats finished her wine, put the glass down, and cupped her face in her palms. "I was married to a Cuban for three years."

Citron waited for the rest of the tale. When there was nothing but silence for almost fifteen seconds, he said, "Well. A Cuban."

"His family used to own all the milk in Cuba."

"Before Castro."

"Uh-huh. I don't know how anyone could own all the milk in Cuba, but that's what he always said. When I married him, he was in the dope business. That's really why I married him, so the Keatses and the Manerases could combine operations. It worked out okay. Sort of, I reckon. For a while. You ever been married?"

"No."

"Why not?"

"The usual reasons."

"Name two."

Citron thought for a moment. "Well, one died and the other one said no thanks."

"Then you're not gay?"

"I don't think so."

"The guy who was here before you, he was gay. I mean, he was gay gay. I'd be feeling low and he'd pop over with a plate of fudge and the latest gossip and have me in stitches in no time." She examined Citron carefully. "Somehow, I don't think you're the type to pop over with a plate of fudge."

"Who can tell?" Citron said.

Velveeta Keats rose. "Well, thanks for the wine and the plumbing advice."

"You're welcome."

She moved to the still open door, stopped, and turned. "I'm a good cook," she said.

Citron smiled. "I'll keep that in mind."

"Yes," she said. "You do that." She then turned and went through the door.

After Velveeta Keats had gone, Citron continued to sit at the table with his almost empty glass. He felt it stir then, almost uncoil, the first faint signs of the disease that had killed a billion or so cats. Curiosity. He began to wonder how it would all turn out and where he would be a year later. He was not accustomed to thinking of the future in terms of more than a day or a week—a month at most. The thought of a year was unsettling. It seemed like infinity. For a moment he thought of repacking his two cardboard cartons and returning to the comforting hopelessness of the Cadillac People. Instead, he rose, rinsed out the two glasses, transformed the couch into a bed, brushed his teeth, and got between what seemed to be a pair of reasonably clean sheets. After fifteen minutes or so, the sound of the surf put him to sleep. He dreamed of Africa.

6

FOR THE PAST FOURTEEN YEARS home to Draper Haere had been a two-story red brick commercial building on Main Avenue at the northern fringe of Venice, almost in Ocean Park, a community that helps spell out the difference between Venice and Santa Monica.

It had been a cheap neighborhood back in 1968, a blowzy, end-of-the-line kind of place with dim prospects and depressed real estate prices, which was why Haere had moved there: It was all he could afford. He had paid $27,500 for the old building with ten percent down. Less than thirteen years later an Iranian offered him $425,000 for it, cash, thus convincing Haere that property, after all, was indeed theft.

In the seventies, speculators discovered Venice. The usual pattern followed. Out went the old retired Jews, the aging Beats, the students, the artists, the radicals, the dopers, the crazies, the pool cleaners, the professional tire changers, and in came the trendy young moneyed whom Haere often suspected of existing solely on cheese and chablis.

The Haere Building was forty feet wide and one hundred feet long, and ran from the sidewalk to the alley. The downstairs was vacant when he bought it, the last tenant having been a paint store that went broke. The upstairs was divided into small offices occupied at the time by a bail bondsman, an answering service, a collection agency, a couple of jobbers, and a free-lance bookkeeper, all of them on a month-to-month basis. When Haere hinted he might have to raise their rents by ten dollars a month, they promptly moved out.

With the last tenant gone, Haere had all the partitions knocked down. That gave him one enormous room, forty by a hundred, four thousand square feet. Since much of his life had been spent in furnished rooms, including those in some ex-tremely pricy hotels, he decided, perhaps perversely, to create the most enormous room of them all. The only enclosed space would be a rather indulgent bath.

Haere started at the rear on the alley and installed an elab-orate kitchen. The kitchen lurched into the dining area, which jumped or fell into the living-work area, which more or less wandered into the sleeping area. He also built a great many bookcases, cabinets, and closets. Or had them built. It took four years to get everything just right, because Haere kept running out of money. When at last all was done, he found it magnifi-cent. Nearly everyone else thought it monstrous.

Haere lived over the shop. Downstairs in the former paint store were the leased IBM computers that stored the names and the elaborate machinery that printed the God-ain't-it-awful letters that were sent to the names pleading for money to rescue the Republic from ruin. Haere employed a staff of twenty-three direct-mail and computer specialists, whom he overpaid and who were fanatic in their loyalty. Ten years after he began the Haere Company, his employees had presented him with an oil portrait of himself, dressed in his usual three-piece blue pin-stripe, standing with one hand resting formally on an ancient mimeograph machine. The small brass plate on the portrait's oak frame read: *Our Founder*. Haere hung the portrait in the company's small reception room.

54

Haere was a bachelor not only by choice, but also by misadventure. For nearly ten years now he had been in love with a married woman. It was a hopeless affair that he felt was doomed to grow even more so. There had, of course, been others along the way, at least seven women that he had been fairly serious about. Possibly eight. One had died. Four had married. Two had fled, one to Rome, the other to Costa Rica, and one had simply disappeared—suddenly, mysteriously, absolutely. Late at night Haere often worried about her.

Finally, Haere did what all bachelors are said to do: he got a cat. It cost $10 at the local animal shelter and it came to live with him at about the same time that, in a last gesture of vanity, he had his teeth capped. That had cost $2,355 back in 1975, and for a while Haere spent considerable time marveling at them in the mirror.

The cat was an extremely garrulous castrated half-Siamese tom that Haere named Hubert. When Haere traveled, he boarded Hubert at the Musette Hotel for Cats in Santa Monica, where Hubert seemed to like it, possibly because he could talk endlessly to a captive audience.

On the night that Haere flew in from Denver, he took a taxi from the airport to the cat hotel, ransomed Hubert, and tipped the driver ten dollars to lug the cat carrier up the stairs, which was something Haere didn't want to attempt with his bandaged hands. After freeing Hubert, Haere got into pajamas, robe, and slippers. Next year, he thought, a tasseled nightcap.

His wondrous refrigerator's automatic icemaker and coldwater dispenser enabled him to mix a Scotch and water without too much difficulty. He had just taken the second long swallow when the downstairs buzzer rang. Haere crossed to the intercom, pressed the button, and asked: "Who is it?"

"This is the FBI, Mr. Haere," said a man's voice made thin by the small speaker. "We'd like to talk to you."

"Who's we?"

"I'm Special Agent Yarn. Special Agent Tighe is with me."

"How do you spell Tighe?"

The voice spelled it for him.

"What do you and Special Agent Tighe want to talk to me about at eleven o'clock at night?"

"We'd rather not discuss that down here on the street."

"Who's in charge of your San Francisco office?"

A name was offered promptly. It meant nothing to Haere, but because there had been no hesitation he pushed the button that sounded a buzzer and unlocked the downstairs street door. A moment later he could hear the footsteps on the uncarpeted stairs that led up to his apartment.

FBI agents were no novelty to Haere, not since the early fifties when they had started coming around to investigate his father's old friends. In the sixties they had come around wanting to know if some of Draper Haere's older friends were really fit to serve in the higher reaches of the Kennedy and Johnson administrations. By the early seventies the agents were back wanting to know about the bomb-throwing tendencies of some of the children of those older friends.

But back in the fifties, FBI agents to Haere had seemed stern elders of the law, sober-sided, grim, forbidding. They grew younger over the years, of course. The two who appeared on Haere's doorstep that night were mere tykes, neither a year over thirty-two. One was blond, the other brunette.

"Mr. Haere?" the blond one said.

Haere nodded, and they whipped out their folding ID cases and offered them for inspection. Haere reached for both with his bandaged hands and took his time examining them.

"There was a man I knew in Washington once," Haere said, still examining the credentials. "Back in the late sixties. A psychologist. He was hired by the FBI to put agents through sensitivity training. It seemed that when some of you guys got home, instead of kissing the wife, you'd whip out your ID at her and say, 'Carson, FBI.' "

Special Agent Tighe looked at Special Agent Yarn. "I do that all the time, don't you?"

"Sure," Yarn said. "Every night."

Haere handed back their ID cases and told them to come in. The blond one was Yarn, John D. Tighe's first name was Richard. He had no middle initial. Their hair was neither short nor long. Yarn wore a suit and tie, Tighe a gray herringbone jacket, dark-gray slacks, and no tie. Haere noticed that both wore loafers with rubber heels. Yarn was a little over six feet tall, Tighe a little under. Neither was handsome, neither was ugly. Only their eyes were alike: steady, watchful, and curious. Extremely curious. All four eyes, two brown and two blue, were now taking in Haere's enormous room.

"Just the one big room, huh?" Yarn said.

"That's all."

"Interesting."

"Different," Tighe said.

"Sit down," Haere said.

Yarn sat down on the leather couch that had once graced the Washington office of Senator Wayne Morse of Oregon. Tighe chose the padded walnut armchair that had been in Henry Agard Wallace's Capitol office when Wallace was Roosevelt's Vice-President. Haere sat in the old high-backed easy chair he almost always sat in, the Baton Rouge chair, which a dealer in Opelousas had sworn was the last chair Huey Long ever sat in before he was gunned down in 1935. Haere collected political furniture. Political mavericks' furniture, to be precise. For a year now he had been dickering with a man in Tulsa for a brass spittoon that the almost forgotten Alfalfa Bill Murray of Oklahoma was said to have been partial to.

Yarn took out a black notebook and a ballpoint pen. Hubert jumped up into Tighe's lap and screamed in his face. Tighe scratched Hubert's ears absently with the air of a man who knows all about cats. "Lot of Siamese there," he said.

57

Haere nodded. "Half."

"We'd like to talk to you about Mr. John T. Replogle," Yarn said.

"He's dead."

"We know. Tell us about him."

"Tell you about him?"

"Yes. Please."

"Well, sir," Haere said, "he was a hardworking, industrious citizen, and probably the most steadfast and patriotic son of a bitch I ever knew. As for politics, he never belonged to any political party. He was a Democrat."

Yarn wrote none of that down. Tighe, still scratching the cat's ears, said, "Mr. Dooley?" without looking up.

"Will Rogers," Haere said.

"Oh."

Yarn frowned slightly. "You were with Mr. Replogle—when he died?"

"Yes."

"Tell us about it."

"You must have the Colorado Highway Patrol's report by now."

"We've got it," Tighe said, "but we'd like you to tell us about it, if you don't mind."

"Why?"

"You said it was no accident," Yarn said. "That it was intentional. If so, Mr. Replogle could have been murdered. If he was murdered, then there's the possibility that his civil rights were violated. If so, the Bureau is interested—definitely, officially."

"Your instructions are coming out of Washington?"

Yarn nodded. "Out of Washington."

Haere told them about the drive from the Brown Palace to Idaho Springs, where he had first noticed the blue Dodge pickup. He then described the drive into the mountains and

58

estimated they had gone approximately fifteen or sixteen miles when it happened.

"It was actually fourteen point three miles," Tighe said. "Past Idaho Springs."

It was Yarn's turn again. "What'd you and Mr. Replogle talk about on the way up?—if you don't mind us asking."

Haere shrugged. "Death and dying. Thanksgiving. Old times. He had terminal cancer. Of the prostate."

"We know," Yarn said.

"Was he despondent, apprehensive?" Tighe said.

"Well, he wasn't exactly looking forward to it."

"What I mean is, did he seem to think that anyone was trying to kill him?"

"No."

It was again Yarn's turn. "Did he mention Singapore?"

"He said he'd been there recently."

"Did you ever know a Drew Meade?"

"A long time ago."

"Mr. Replogle also knew him."

"That's right."

"Did Mr. Replogle tell you he had seen Mr. Meade in Singapore?"

"He mentioned it."

"What did he say?—exactly, if you can."

"He said Mr. Meade looked like something out of Somerset Maugham."

" 'The Casuarina Tree?' " said Tighe.

"He wasn't quite that specific."

"What did they talk about?"

"Money."

Yarn looked interested. "Can you give us a little more detail?"

"Sure. Meade didn't have any and he wanted Jack Replogle to lend him some."

"Did he?"

"Probably. Mr. Replogle was not only an extremely industrious and patriotic citizen, he was also a very soft touch."

"So he lent or gave Meade some money?" Tighe said.

"I didn't say that. I said probably."

There was a brief silence. Tighe scratched Hubert's ears some more. Yarn wrote something in his black notebook. When he was finished, he looked up at Haere and said, "Is there anything else you can remember about what Mr. Replogle and Mr. Meade discussed?"

Haere lied as a matter of course. "No."

Yarn nodded, as if that were the answer he had expected. "Tell us a little about yourself, Mr. Haere, what it is you do."

"You're serious?"

Again, Yarn nodded.

"Well," Haere said, "I try to shape the events that alter and illuminate our lives."

"Politics."

"Politics," Haere agreed.

"But you're not a politician?"

"I'm more of a shadowy figure who moves behind the scenes, a faceless manipulator grasping at the levers of power. If you want more, there's a fat FBI file on me nearly four inches thick that goes back almost thirty years to when I was a kid."

"We know," Yarn said. "It's been coming in over the telex all evening."

"So long, pussy," Tighe said as he gently dumped Hubert to the floor, rose, and gave Haere's enormous room another curious glance. "Much money in politics?"

"Not if you're halfway honest."

Still looking around, Tighe nodded as if what he saw spoke of total probity as well as dubious taste. Yarn was also up now, and they both moved toward the door after thanking Haere for his cooperation. When they reached the door, Yarn turned.

"About Mr. Meade," he said.

"What about him?"

"He seems to have disappeared."

"Vanished," Tighe said.

"Into the usual thin air, I suppose," Haere said.

Yarn nodded. "Where else?"

"Well," Haere said and for some reason looked down at his bandaged hands. Tighe noticed.

"They still hurt?" he asked.

"No," Haere said, "not much."

After they had gone, Draper Haere stood by the door, still staring down at his bandaged hands. He then turned, crossed to the phone, looked at his watch, picked up the phone, and dialed the number of Baldwin Veatch, the governor-elect.

7

THEY MET FOR BREAKFAST the next morning at 7:30,
the three of them: Draper Haere, Baldwin Veatch, and his wife,
the former Louise Guidry of Crowley, Louisiana, where in
1967 at age eighteen she had been crowned queen of the an-
nual rice festival. Two years later at Berkeley she had been one
of the firebrands leading the march on People's Park. After
being graduated in 1972, she had gone to work in Sacramento
for Baldwin Veatch, then a newly elected state senator. They
were married later that same year. In the fall of 1973 she and
Draper Haere had begun their long, hopeless, and often
acrimonious affair.

Louise Veatch sipped tea and her husband black coffee in the
booth at Kenny's delicatessen-restaurant on Wilshire Boulevard
in Santa Monica. Across from them, Draper Haere mopped up
the last of his two fried eggs with a piece of rye toast. Two
booths away sat a pair of state policemen who were the
governor-elect's bodyguards. Both were in their late twenties
and neither ever drank anything stronger than orange juice.

Draper Haere liked working breakfasts because he had found
that most people were not at their best in the morning. It some-

times proved to be a slight, useful edge. He also liked Kenny's for its eavesdropping. Haere was particularly fond of psycho-babble, and there was a lot of it at Kenny's after 10:00 at night when the evening group-therapy sessions let out.

"They want it then—whatever Replogle had," Veatch said.

"Who?"

"The FBI."

"I think they've already got what he had," Haere said. "What I suspect they're trying to do is put the lid back on and make sure nobody else gets it."

Louise Veatch looked at her husband. "Draper's right."

Veatch nodded. "Perhaps."

"The question is," Haere said, "what do you want to do about it?"

The Veatches continued to stare at each other. They were an unusual political couple, Haere often thought, even remarkable. Louise Veatch had kept all of her beauty-queen looks: still a blue-eyed, black-haired Cajun lovely with a touch of the wild about her. Veatch himself was a tall lean angular blond with calculating gray eyes, a disarming, lopsided grin, and the perfect political personality that all its life had struck up conversations with strangers at bus stops. She was the smarter of the two, Haere felt, but Veatch was the wilier. Their ambition was evenly matched in that it was limitless. She often brooded, but he went to bed optimistic and woke up feeling even better. She had unassailable convictions, while her husband had to make do with mere principles. They were colleagues, even friends, but rarely lovers. Sex to Baldwin Veatch was an occasional afterthought. To Louise Veatch it was a primary reason for living, which is why she so long ago had jumped into Draper Haere's bed.

Haere had never once even bothered to ask Louise Veatch to leave her husband. It wasn't that Haere didn't love her. He did so desperately. Sometimes when they had been separated for a month or so, he would enter a room where she was and something strange happened to him. Something adolescent. He temporarily lost the power of speech. He had minor palpitations. He sweated. He suspected that he even blushed, although no one had ever said anything. But all Draper Haere had to offer Louise Veatch was love, politics, and a room over the store. If Louise Veatch had to live over the store, he realized she would just as soon do it in the White House.

The Veatches were still staring at each other, engaged in some kind of wordless communication, when Louise Veatch finally turned to Haere and said, "Okay. Let's do it."

Haere nodded. "All right."

"Can you handle it?" Veatch asked.

Haere shook his head slowly. "I don't know how."

"Who would?"

"A trained investigator, maybe a smart reporter, someone like that."

Veatch frowned, obviously running a list of unacceptable candidates through his mind. "We don't want to share this though, do we?"

"No."

"Anyone in mind?"

"Not offhand," Haere said.

Louise Veatch turned to her husband. "Give me some change."

"Who're you going to call?" he said, digging into a pants pocket.

"Craigie Grey. If somebody like we're looking for's around, she'll know. Craigie knows everything."

Veatch rose to let his wife out. "Just don't tip her off about—"

Louise Veatch interrupted him. "Baldy. Have I ever?"

"No," he said. "Of course not. Never."

The two men watched Louise Veatch head for the pay phone

in what a feature writer had once called "a rhythmic slither."
They turned back to look at each other, and again Haere wondered if Baldwin Veatch knew he was being cuckolded. And as always, Haere came up with the same answer: Probably, but he doesn't really care as long as it's discreet. Better me than someone else.

"How was he?" Veatch said. "Replogle."

"I guess you'd have to say he was cheerfully resigned. The pain was getting to him."

"You two went back a long way, didn't you?"

"Ever since I was a kid. He and my old man were good friends. When they went after him for being a red back in 'fifty-two, Jack was about the only one who stuck with him. He was like that. Jack, I mean."

"You know," Veatch said, "I could never understand all this nostalgia for the fifties. Talk about a low and dishonest decade."

"I think it was Gable mostly."

"Clark Gable?"

"Right," Haere said. "If you closed your eyes when Eisenhower talked, he sounded exactly like Clark Gable. That must have been awfully reassuring to most people."

They both looked up when Louise Veatch returned to the table wearing a pleased smile. Veatch rose to let her in. She slid into the booth, looked at both men, said, "Morgan Citron," and waited for their reaction.

Haere was first. "The *Chicago Daily News*. A long time ago."

"Not so long," Veatch said. "Eleven years. Ten maybe."

"How old is he now—fifty?" Haere asked.

Louise Veatch shook her head. "Craigie says forty or so—if that."

"I thought he was older," Haere said.

Baldwin Veatch looked up at the ceiling, his expression thoughtful. "There was something," he said slowly, "something about a Pulitzer, wasn't there?"

"He was nominated," Louise Veatch said, "and everyone thought he was going to get it, but then they changed their minds, or something like that."

"Why?" Veatch said.

"I don't remember."

"I remember his stuff, though," Haere said. "There was this one long piece he wrote for *The New Yorker* about Togo and Dahomey—about four or five years back. Very sad, funny stuff."

"That's not quite what I had in mind," Veatch said.

"Wait a minute," Louise Veatch said. "I recollect now. About the Pulitzer. He was in Vietnam. It was a series he did on corruption. They threw him out of the country."

"You're right," Haere said. "So where is he now?"

"You know Craigie's place down on the PCH in Malibu?"

Haere shook his head.

"Well, that's where he is. He's Craigie's new super."

"Jesus," Veatch said.

They kept the governor-elect out of the approach to Morgan Citron. They kept him out for the usual reasons: so that he could deny he knew anything about it, so that he could attend yet another breakfast meeting with his transition team at the Beverly-Wilshire, and so that Haere and Louise Veatch could steal an hour to thresh around in bed together. Veatch at first was not at all sure he wanted his wife in on the approach to Morgan Citron until she crisply reminded him of her admittedly uncanny ability to spot hidden defects of character, faith, and morals.

"Remember that banker up in Redding—the one you were going to make chairman of your campaign finance committee?"

Veatch nodded glumly. "The child molester."

"Well, who spotted him right off?"

Veatch sighed. "Okay. Go ahead. You and Draper size him

up and if he looks good, hire him." He turned to Haere. "But he'll be working for you—not me. Understand?"

"Perfectly," Haere said.

Morgan Citron was slicing some carrots into his new batch of *pot au feu* when they knocked on the door of Unit A. Still carrying the knife and the carrot, he crossed to the door and opened it. Louise Veatch stood there, smiling. Draper Haere was just behind her.

"Mr. Citron?" she said.

Citron nodded. "Somehow," he said, "I don't think you two're the Jehovah's Witness folks."

"My name's Mrs. Veatch," she said, extending her hand. "Mrs. Baldwin Veatch."

"I know," Citron said, accepting her hand.

"And this is my friend and associate, Mr. Haere."

Citron looked at Haere, who moved his still-bandaged right hand in a small apologetic gesture.

"Draper Haere, right?" Citron said. "The money man."

Despite himself, Haere was pleased by the recognition. He smiled and said, "We were wondering if we might talk to you."

"All right," Citron said. "Come in."

Louise Veatch and Haere entered the apartment and looked around. What they saw made them keep their expressions carefully neutral. Citron smiled. "Not exactly your basic Malibu sybaritism."

"Not exactly," Louise Veatch said.

"Sit down," Citron said, waving them to the Formica table and its molded plastic chairs. "Coffee?"

"If it's no bother," Haere said.

"It's instant," Citron said and moved to the Pullman kitchen's small stove, where a pot of water was boiling. He spooned instant coffee into three mismatched mugs and poured the water. "I've got sugar, but no cream."

Louise Veatch said she drank hers black; Haere asked for sugar. Citron served the coffee, sat down at the table, leaned back in his chair, smiled slightly, and waited for the pitch to begin.

"Craigie Grey told me you were looking after her place," Louise Veatch said. "Have you known Craigie long?"

"Not long."

"Craigie's—well, Craigie's unique."

"She seems to be."

Haere took up the indirect interrogation. "You were in Africa not too long ago."

"It's been a little more than a year now."

Haere nodded as if grateful for being corrected on some minor point. "I remember reading about it—when you got back to Paris. It was a wire-service story, I think. AP."

"They all moved it," Citron said. "AP, UPI, Reuters. And then it died. Thank God."

"You never wrote anything about it yourself though, did you?" Louise Veatch said. She looked around the room again. "This looks as if it would be a good place to write. Maybe even a book."

"I'm not writing a book, Mrs. Veatch."

Haere nodded, this time sympathetically. "It must've been a lousy experience—being in jail there, I mean."

"Yes," Citron said. "It was."

"My father was a newspaperman," Haere said, wondering why he even mentioned it. He then uncharacteristically tacked on yet another autobiographical note. "Down South. In Birmingham."

Citron smiled pleasantly.

It was Louise Veatch who asked the question Citron had been anticipating. "Was he—well, was he really a cannibal?"

Citron shrugged. "That's what a lot of people say, anyway."

Louise Veatch leaned back in her chair. She looked at Citron and smiled slightly. Haere took it to be her stamp of approval and decided to get to the point. "You don't have anything scheduled right now, then?"

"No," Citron said. "Nothing much."

"Would you be interested in taking something on?"

"It depends."

"Of course. But what I mean is, are you free to take on something?"

"I'm free."

Louise Veatch leaned her elbows on the table and dropped her voice down into a lower register. It made her tone throaty and confidential. It sounded to Citron something like a born conspirator's voice. "A friend of ours got killed up in the Colorado mountains just outside of Denver yesterday." She paused and looked at Haere. "Was it just yesterday?"

Haere nodded

"We think he was murdered."

"Well," Citron said because she seemed to expect him to say something.

"His name was Replogle. Jack Replogle."

"Replogle Construction?" Citron said.

Haere looked surprised. "You knew him?"

Citron shook his head. "I used to see his signs in some of the countries I moved around in."

"The hot countries."

"Right," Citron said. "The hot countries."

Louise Veatch looked at Haere. "Tell him what happened, Draper."

Haere again repeated everything Jack Replogle had told him about Singapore and Drew Meade and how Meade, according to the two FBI agents, had gone missing. Citron listened, made no notes, but asked Haere to repeat the names of the FBI agents. When Haere had finished, there was a silence, which was broken when Citron shoved his chair back, rose, and moved to the stove, where he picked up the knife and resumed slicing the remainder of the carrot into the *pot au feu*.

"Smells good," Haere said. "What is it?"

"Stew," Citron said, put down the knife, turned, and leaned against the sink, his arms folded across his chest as he examined the attractive, well-dressed woman and the man with the despairing face. Citron sensed that they were more than mere political colleagues. They spend a lot of time in bed together, he told himself, and was mildly surprised to find that he approved of the notion. It had been two years at least since Citron had last approved or disapproved of anything.

"What you want then is just the political stuff—the dynamite this guy Meade said he had."

"That's right," Haere said. "Just the political stuff."

Citron looked at Louise Veatch. "Who'd I be working for—your husband?"

"For me," Haere said.

Citron continued to stare at Louise Veatch. "But for your husband really—at one remove."

"My husband, Mr. Citron, knows nothing about this."

"I don't believe that."

"If you believed it," she said, "Mr. Haere wouldn't hire you."

Citron smiled. "Deniability, I think they're calling it."

"Or covering our ass," Haere said.

Citron looked at Haere. "You don't care who killed him?—Replogle, I mean."

"I care," Haere said. "I care very much, but Jack Replogle was dying of cancer, so whoever killed him put him out of his misery. We'll let the cops and the FBI do their job and we'll do ours. And if the stuff that he bought from Drew Meade does what he hoped it would do, it can be his memorial."

"You're sure it wasn't just a hit-and-run accident and nothing more?"

Draper Haere looked down at his bandaged hands. "I'm sure."

Citron moved back to the table, sat down, picked up his cup, and drank the rest of his coffee. There was another silence as he felt his worm of curiosity stir again. He wondered what he would say next and was faintly surprised to hear himself say, "How much?"

"Five hundred a week?" Haere said.

"Cash?"

"Sure. Why not? Cash."

"I'll need an advance—to buy some things."

"What?"

"A typewriter. A small tape recorder." He paused. "Maybe a suit. I don't have any clothes. Or a bank account."

"Two thousand do it?" Haere said, adding, "Cash, of course."

"Fine," Citron said. He looked first at Haere and then at Louise Veatch. "You know what you're getting, don't you?"

"I think so," she said.

"What you're getting is a little unused, maybe even rusty. I'm not sure it even functions anymore."

Louise Veatch smiled, then nodded contentedly, as if what she saw was little short of perfection. "Mr. Haere and I have been in this peculiar business for some time, Mr. Citron—do you mind if I call you Morgan? Mr. Haere is very good at sizing people up, but I'm even better, and what I see sitting across the table from me I like, probably because there seems to be almost no bullshit about you. Anyone who tells me he'll take the job provided I buy him a new suit can't be much of a bullshitter, and in this town that's as rare as green snow. What I'm really trying to say is that we're glad you said yes—right, Draper?"

"Right," Haere said, marveling as always at how Louise Veatch by tone and gesture, if not by the words themselves, could convince people of their own immense self-worth and the enormous esteem in which she seemed to hold them.

Citron smiled again, but only slightly, and looked at Haere. "How many political due bills have you people got in Washington?"

"You mean the three of us?" Louise Veatch said.

Citron nodded.

She turned to Haere for the estimate. He thought for a moment and then answered carefully. "Would plenty be enough?"

"Maybe," Citron said.

An hour later, Draper Haere's secretary called Citron and told him she was, to use her participle, "messengering" him out $2,000 in cash. Citron thanked her, hung up the phone, picked it back up, dialed information, and asked for the number of the FBI.

The number was 272-6161. When the woman operator answered with "FBI," Citron said, "May I speak to Agent Richard Tighe, please."

There was a brief hesitation and then the operator said, "Let me give you verification."

After another pause, another woman's voice said, "Verification," and then gave her name, which Citron didn't catch.

"Agent Tighe, please. Richard Tighe."

This time there was no hesitation. "We don't have an agent by that name," she said.

"I see," Citron said. "What about Agent Yarn—Y-a-r-n, first name John, middle initial D?"

"We don't have an agent by that name either," the verification woman said.

Citron said thank you and hung up with the conviction that he was already earning his money.

8

HE HAD DECIDED to cross at Mexicali. The long bus ride up from Mexico City had tired him and made him look much older than his sixty-three years until he found a barber who gave him a shave, a massage, and a haircut for less than $2. On the way to the border entry, he bought a cheap sombrero, the kind a tourist might buy, and settled it firmly on his head. From his reflection in a plate-glass window he saw that it made him look ridiculous, which pleased him because that was exactly how he wanted to look.

He strolled up to the U.S. immigration official, who gave him the quick practiced glance of an experienced sorter. "Business in Mexico?"

"Just rubbernecking."

"Place of birth?"

"Ohio," he said, lying automatically. He had been born in Indiana. In Terre Haute.

The immigration official nodded and Drew Meade walked across the border into his native land, the country which he felt had betrayed him, although he never thought of it in quite those terms. When he railed to himself alone at night in cheap hotel rooms, he railed against having been handed the shitty end of the stick, which, arguably, is a form of betrayal.

The first thing Drew Meade did upon returning to the United States after an absence of thirteen years was to seek out a Mc-Donald's and order two Big Macs, a chocolate shake, and an order of French-fried potatoes. After gobbling it all down he talked one of the sullen sixteen-year-olds behind the counter out of a couple of handfuls of change and then spent an hour walking around Calexico looking for a pay phone that worked.

It took several conversations with various operators, but Meade finally got the number he wanted. While it was ringing he dropped in $2 worth of quarters against the long-distance operator's stern advice. The number was answered on the fourth ring by a hollow hello. It was a woman's voice.

"Mr. Replogle, please."

"Oh my God," said the hollow voice that belonged to the newly widowed Maureen Replogle.

"Is Mr. Replogle there?"

"You don't know, do you?"

"Know?" Meade growled. "Know what? Is he there or not?"

"Jack's . . . gone."

"Gone? Gone where?"

"Jack is . . . dead." The news was followed by a sob.

"Well, shit," Meade said.

Maureen Replogle refused to hear that. "The funeral was early this afternoon," she said. "This very afternoon. He had a host of friends. They've been so very kind. I'm all alone now, of course. All alone."

"When did he die, Mrs. Replogle?"

"It was only yesterday. Yesterday morning. He and Draper were driving up to Breckenridge. We have a lodge up there. Jack likes to ski, but I've never really cared for it. There was an accident. Poor Jack. Dear Jack."

74

"What kind of accident?"

"You know, in the car."

"You said Draper was with him. Is that Draper Haere?"

"Do you know Draper? Draper didn't stay for the funeral. He doesn't go to funerals, you know. I've always found Draper rather strange, even as a child."

"Where's Haere now?"

"He flew back to California."

"Frisco, L.A., where?"

"No, not Los Angeles. Santa Monica. Well, Venice actually, I suppose. The air is ever so much better there."

"Okay. Thanks."

"It was very kind of you to call. So many people have been so very kind."

Drew Meade hung up. The phone rang. He picked it up and cautiously said hello. It was the long-distance operator, advising Meade that he owed an additional sixty-five cents. Meade told her to fuck off and hung up again.

At the Calexico bus station, the first Trailways out was bound for Redlands. Meade bought a ticket. From Redlands he would bus his way up and over to Santa Barbara and then come down into Los Angeles from the north. With any luck he would be there late that evening or, at the outside, early tomorrow morning. The bus to Redlands would leave in ten minutes. Meade bought provisions for the trip. They consisted of two packs of Camels, a giant-size Mr. Goodbar, and a pint of Jim Beam. The sombrero he shoved into a waste bin.

They had performed their early-afternoon sexual acrobatics in the Sir Galahad, a beachside motel on Ocean Avenue in Santa Monica just south of Pico. They had giggled for a while at an X-rated film the motel supplied for $3.50 over its closed-circuit television system. The film involved a threesome, and while it was still running they had made love for almost thirty minutes. Now both lay naked on the bed, watching the film with a kind of clinical detachment.

"You want to see how this shit ends?" he said.

She shook her head. "Not especially."

Draper Haere rose, crossed to the TV set, and switched it off. He turned and smiled down at Louise Veatch. "You are, without a doubt, the best-looking naked lady I ever saw in my life."

"Pretty just happened."

"Pretty and smart with it."

Louise Veatch smiled. "They used to say that down home. 'She's pretty and smart with it.' "

"I know," Haere said, sat back down on the edge of the bed, and lit one of his occasional cigarettes.

"How'd it go in New York?" she said, reaching down for her panties on the floor. "All I got out of Baldy was a satisfied grunt."

"The guy was a toe tester."

"You mean he stuck his toe into the political waters and found them lukewarm?"

"He thought they were lukewarm, but Mommy thought they were ice-cold. If he'd jumped in with a big splash, she would've said wonderful and whipped out her checkbook. But he didn't, and she won't."

"Then he's out."

"He's out."

As they talked, they dressed slowly, unhurriedly, as if it were morning and they had risen early and had been married for twenty years.

"You mean out in 'eighty-four or all the way out?"

Draper Haere tucked in his shirttails. The shirt was a white oxford-cloth buttondown. It was almost the only kind of shirt Haere ever wore except for exact copies in blue. "Out in 'eighty-four," he said. "After that, who can say?"

"You still think Baldy's got a real no-shit chance?" Louise Veatch asked as she buttoned up the simple silk cream-colored blouse that went nicely with the simple straight-line light-gray skirt that was complemented by the simple dark-gray double-breasted cashmere jacket. Haere estimated that all that simplicity cost three or four times the price of one of his blue pinstripes, and Haere spent $550 on his suits at Lew Ritter's.

"Baldy's got a chance," Haere said, after giving it some thought. "Not much of one, but a chance—provided things break just right for him, and provided he turns out to be just one hell of a governor."

"But you're talking about 'eighty-eight, aren't you? Not 'eighty-four."

"I figure 'eighty-four is the jinx year."

"Oh, hell, Draper."

"Look. 'Eighty-eight's his best shot. Four years as governor, and then he gets re-elected in 'eighty-six. He's got a record he can point to with pride. The old hacks will have dropped out from exhaustion and Baldy'll be what by 'eighty-six—forty-six?"

"Forty-seven," she said.

"Not too young and certainly not too old. He starts out after it in 'eighty-six and leaves you behind to run the state."

"Draper," she said, "he's not going to wait."

"He'd better."

"Okay, what would it take to get him the nomination in 'eighty-four—besides money and luck? You can get him the money and he's got all the luck in the world. So what else would it take?"

"I don't know."

"Bullshit," she said. "What about this Replogle stuff that Citron's going after? This dynamite that could blow them out of the White House? Isn't that what Jack Replogle said?"

Haere sighed. "He said it could blow those fuckers out of the

White House in 'eighty-four. An exact quote. Almost, anyway."

"And you believed him?"

Haere started knotting his tie. "Jack Replogle, when it came to politics, was a man much given to understatement. Hyperbole in almost everything else, but not in politics."

"Then it is dynamite, isn't it?"

"Maybe."

"Which is just what Baldy needs."

"It wouldn't do him any harm," Haere admitted as he crossed to the bathroom and looked behind its door to see if anything had been left hanging there. He did it out of sheer habit, for they had checked into the room empty-handed. After his inspection, he looked down at his still-bandaged hands and said, "Funny thing about dynamite, though." He looked up at her. "Sometimes when it gets old it gets unstable."

"It could blow up in our faces, right?"

He nodded. "Right."

"Well, that's the chance we're all willing to take, isn't it?"

Haere again looked down at his hands and then back up at Louise Veatch. "Sure it is," he said.

Morgan Citron came through the redwood gate carrying a large sturdy shopping bag that held a used Olivetti Lettera 32, a new Sony hand-held tape recorder with various attachments, and a box containing a $159 light-brown mohair suit that he had bought on sale at Henshey's department store in Santa Monica.

Citron noticed the envelope lying on the floor when he entered Unit A. It was a square, off-white envelope, and when he picked it up he saw that it was made by the Crane people out of some very expensive paper. On its front his name had been written in black ink by someone with a broad-nibbed pen and a sound knowledge of the Palmer method. The carefully written message inside said: "Come to dinner tonight at 7 or I'll throw myself in the ocean." It was signed "Velveeta."

Citron was hanging up his new suit in his one closet when the knock came at the apartment's door. He went to the door and opened it. The man who stood there was slender, graceful, more pretty than handsome, and not much more than twenty-four.

"My name is Dale Winder," he said, "and I work for your mummy."

"Christ," Citron said.

"She wants to see you."

"No thanks."

"Don't you love your mother, dear boy?"

"No," Citron said. "I don't love anybody."

Dale Winder actually clapped his hands once in apparent joy. "Oh, you *can* quote it! I just somehow knew you could. May I come in?"

"Sure," Citron said. "Come in."

Winder glided into the apartment and looked around, hands on hips. He wore a white cashmere pullover, but no shirt, very tight jeans and Gucci loafers, but no socks. Citron had the feeling that Dale Winder thought anyone who would wear socks with his loafers was hopelessly out of it.

"Wonders—just wonders could be done with this place with so little effort," Winders said regretfully and even clucked a couple of times when he noticed the worn linoleum in front of the Pullman kitchen.

"How'd you find me?" Citron said.

"It wasn't hard."

"What does she want?"

"Just to say hello. After all, it's been a while, hasn't it?"

"Not long enough."

"But you will see her?"

"She's not sick or anything?"

"Oh, heavens, no. Fit as a fiddle. You know Gladys. Well?"

Citron was not at all sure that he really did know Gladys, and even less sure that he wanted to. His mother had always

79

been a remote figure, almost the Mysterious Stranger that parents were said to warn their children about. Two months earlier he would have refused to see her. A month earlier he would have hesitated. Now he shrugged and said, "Okay. Let's go."

"She'll be so pleased. Shall we go in my car? I'll drive you there and back. It's such a nice day and I've got the top down and I do so love Malibu, don't you?"

Citron didn't bother to answer as he followed Winder out into the patio. At the gate, Winder turned and smiled. He had a good tan and nice white teeth and a dimpled cheek and a left eye that was slightly bluer than the right. "I've just been *dying* to ask you. Was he *really* a cannibal?"

"Sure he was," Citron said. "Missionary stew every day."

"Oh, my *God*, I can't *stand* it!" Dale Winder said and shivered with delight.

9

THE WEST COAST BUREAU of *The American Investigator* occupied half of the twelfth floor of a three-sided building that rose up out of the old Fox back lot in Century City, but it resembled no newspaper or magazine office Morgan Citron had ever seen.

What surprised Citron, perhaps even saddened him, was certainly not the walnut paneling or the thick taupe carpet or the beautiful blond twin sisters who held down the antique partners' desk in the reception area. Nor was he overly impressed by the wonderfully faked Miro and Chagall and Braque that hung on the reception area walls, or even the signed Daumier engravings (authentic) that lined the corridor leading to the West Coast bureau manager's office. Rather, what really bothered Citron was the cryptlike silence as he followed Dale Winder down the corridor. There were no ringing phones. No typewriters. No teletypes. No voices. There were only closed doors behind which Citron suspected perfectly god-awful fibs were being carefully concocted. He even thought up one himself: TOT LOCKED IN FRIDGE GNAWS OFF TOES, although he wasn't at all sure he hadn't cribbed that one from a copy of the

Investigator he had scanned once while standing in line, food stamps in hand, at the checkout counter of Boys Market in the Marina del Rey.

It was a long corridor, and when they neared its end, Dale Winder smiled reassuringly over his shoulder. "We're almost there," he said and pushed through a door. It led into a small reception room that had only a brilliant copy of a blue Picasso clown on its walls. There was also another antique desk with nothing at all on it but the folded hands of a striking young Chinese woman.

"The prodigal," Dale Winder said.

"Really." She smiled at Citron. "Please go in, Mr. Citron. She's expecting you."

"I'll run you home whenever you're ready," Dale Winder said. "Just give me a shout."

"Right," Citron said, moved to the door, put his hand on the knob, sighed, turned it, pushed the door open, and entered the office of Gladys Darlington Citron, who, he immediately saw, had changed scarcely at all.

She still wore her Chanel suits, he noticed. She had more than a dozen of them, and several were at least twenty or twenty-five years old. The one she wore that day was a dusty pink. And as always in the lapel was the red ribbon of the Légion d'Honneur, which de Gaulle himself had presented her in late 1946 for her remarkably bloody service in the Resistance. Citron knew it was why she almost always wore suits: so she would have someplace to display the decoration.

At sixty-two her hair was the color of silver. Old expensive silver. She wore it looped down near one cool green eye, her left, and then back and up into what was supposed to be a careless chignon. Yet not a strand was out of place. Citron could not recall when one ever had been.

Gladys Citron had kept her figure through diet and exercise: no more than 1,350 calories a day with no exceptions and thirty minutes a day every day devoted to the Canadian Air Force exercise regime. She was blessed with those facial bones that helped keep her flesh from sagging. There were a few lines, of course, and wrinkles, especially around the corners of her eyes, but her chin was firm, her long dancer's neck still fairly good, and she remained all in all very much the beauty.

"You may kiss me, Morgan," she said, "unless you feel it would be overly demonstrative."

She offered her cheek. Citron kissed it lightly and said, "How are you, Gladys?"

"Splendid," she said. "Absolutely splendid."

She was sitting behind an almost bare two-hundred-year-old desk that might have come from the cabinetmaker yesterday, or possibly the day before. She opened a drawer and took out a small gray box. She pushed the box toward Citron.

"Do sit down, Morgan. Please."

Citron sat down. She examined him thoughtfully. "You look well. A bit thin, but well. And, dear God, you do look like him. Your father." She tapped the small box. "For you. A present for your fortieth birthday."

Citron didn't touch the box. "I'm forty-two and my birthday was in June."

She dismissed the discrepancy with a graceful wave. "Go on. Open it."

Citron opened the box. In it lying on a bed of black velvet was a gold Rolex Oyster, almost exactly like the one he had traded, bit by bit, to Sergeant Bama for supplemental rations. Citron stared at the watch for a long moment, then removed it from the box and slipped it over his left wrist. Before he could thank his mother, she asked, "How long has it been now—five years, six?"

"Six, I think."

"You could've written."

"I could have."

83

"I was worried."

"I'm sorry."

"I don't suppose I've really been much of a mother to you, have I?"

"No," Citron agreed, "not much, although at forty-two I don't see how that's particularly important."

"You never forgave me, though, did you?"

"For what?"

"For dumping you with the Gargants during the war."

Citron shrugged. "You had all those Germans to kill, and by the time I was five and old enough to be aware of anything, I was very fond of the Gargants. They had a lot of cows."

"But afterwards, when you were seven."

"You mean England."

"It was supposed to be a very good school."

"It was, but I had sort of a French waiter's accent, and I also missed them."

"The Gargants?"

"The cows."

"I'd like to make it up to you, Morgan."

"Now?" He paused, the wonderment on his face mingling with suspicion. "Whatever for?"

She smiled. "Atonement."

"What's the real reason, Gladys?"

"You're my son."

"I'm just somebody you met a few times over the years. How'd you find me, anyway?"

"Were you trying to hide?"

"No."

"Craigie Grey mentioned your name to someone who mentioned it to someone else who mentioned it to us. I'd been trying to locate you for more than a year—ever since those wire-service stories moved out of Paris. I even talked to a Miss Tettah with Amnesty International in London, but all she had

84

was a post-office-box number in Venice. Then we tracked down that young man in Provo."

"The Mormon missionary."

"He told us about your watch. He said you were a saint."

"The Mormons always were saint-happy."

"He said you saved his life."

"He exaggerated."

She picked up a gold-plated letter opener and experimentally pressed its sharp point against the ball of her thumb. "Was he really a cannibal like they all said—or was it just French propaganda?"

"Why?"

She shrugged again. "It's our kind of story."

" 'Dictator Dines on Human Liver and Lights,' right?"

She put the letter opener down. "We cater to our readers," she said. "We have to compete with television for their wandering attention. Therefore, our features need to be a trifle provocative."

Citron looked around the large office. "You seem to be prospering."

"They pay me one hundred and twenty-five a year, if you're curious. That young man I sent to fetch you?"

"He's sweet."

"He's also the most junior on our editorial staff. I pay him sixty a year, mostly for his absolutely devastating sources."

"I can imagine."

She rose, walked around the desk, leaned against it, and stared down at her son. "I'll pay you fifty thousand for your story, your by-line."

"It's not worth that."

"We'd fancy it up a little."

Citron smiled and shook his head.

"I could come up with another five thousand. That's tops."

"Sorry."

She moved back around her desk and sat down. "We've already spent a fortune on it, Morgan. It has some interesting angles. For instance, we managed to get someone into the prison about three months ago. A warder there in the *section d'étranger* was about to retire on a ridiculously low pension. He sold us a fascinating rumor—all about how the Emperor-President had fed foreign prisoners on human parts."

"I'm speechless," Citron said.

"No you're not. Confirm it and I can up the offer to seventy-five thousand."

"For 'My Son, the Cannibal,' *n'est-ce pas*?"

When she didn't reply, Citron rose, went around the desk, leaned down, and kissed her lightly on the cheek. "Gladys, you really never should've left the spooks."

She stared up at him. The stare was cold now. "They paid for your rather expensive education."

"And I'll always be grateful."

He turned and moved to the door, but stopped when she called to him.

"Morgan."

He didn't turn back. He merely waited with his hand on the doorknob.

"We've got too much invested not to run with it."

"You could kill it." When she didn't reply, he said, "Well, goodbye, Gladys," and then frowned as if trying to remember something else he had forgotten to say. "Oh, yes," he said finally, "and thanks for the watch."

Citron left the offices of *The American Investigator* and rode the elevator down to the ground floor. He didn't bother to give Dale Winder a shout. Instead, he walked a couple of blocks, went down into Harry's Bar, and ordered a bottle of Beck's.

10

DRAPER HAERE WAS in his downstairs cubicle-like office working on one of his diseases when Morgan Citron finally reached him. To keep his staff occupied and the payroll met during slack political seasons, Haere handled the direct-mail solicitations of a half-dozen organizations that were trying to cure, or at least alleviate, diseases of the heart, the lungs, the eyes, the mind, and the nervous system. The mailer he was editing when Citron called was for an organization that claimed to be easing the suffering of disabled children whom Haere always thought of as the crippled kids. It was his favorite disease. Haere rendered his services at cost and over the years had raised substantial sums. He was not at all sure that the money was being well spent.

When his secretary told him Mr. Citron was on the line, Haere picked up the phone and said hello.

"I've been trying to get you," Citron said.

"I was in a meeting," Haere said, remembering with much pleasure and no guilt his meeting in the Sir Galahad Motel. "What've you got?"

"Something I think we'd better talk about."

"Right. Where are you?"

"Harry's Bar."

"Give me fifteen, maybe twenty minutes."

"Fine," Citron said.

It took Haere thirty-five minutes to reach the underground parking garage in the Century City complex that housed Harry's Bar. He would have made it sooner except he had trouble finding his car. Because he walked so much, Haere sometimes didn't use his car for days and frequently forgot where he had parked it. The car was an immense sixteen-year-old dark-green Cadillac convertible that Haere had accepted in lieu of a fee from one of his first clients, a Congressional candidate who had tried vainly to swim against the Republican tide in 1968. It was only the second car Haere had ever owned, and because it ran faultlessly with minimum maintenance, other than the new batteries he had to keep buying, Haere saw no reason to replace it. Haere was really not much interested in cars, although he had once dickered for a Model T Ford of doubtful provenance that supposedly had been purchased in 1923 by William Jennings Bryan.

Most of the lunch trade was gone when Haere entered Harry's Bar and joined Morgan Citron at a table near the entrance. Citron had a cup of coffee in front of him and also an empty sandwich plate.

"Sorry I'm late," Haere said.

"I had something to eat. You want anything?"

Haere shook his head. "I usually skip lunch." He looked around. "Shall we talk here?"

"I don't see why not." Citron signaled a waitress, who brought a fresh pot of coffee and a cup and saucer for Haere.

When she had gone, Haere said, "Well?"

"Those two guys who dropped by to see you last night?"

Haere nodded. "The FBI agents."

"Well, they're not."

"Who says so?"

88

"Their verification section."

"Here in L.A.?"

"Right."

"You called?"

"Yes."

Haere smiled his appreciation. "You've got one suspicious mind, haven't you, friend?"

Citron smiled back, but said nothing.

"I checked their ID," Haere said. "Carefully. Over the years I must've checked a hundred of them. They've been popping in on me since I was sixteen."

"Did these two have all the right moves?"

"They were perfect."

Citron poured them both more coffee. "What'd they want to know—most of all?"

"They wanted to know a little about me and a lot about Jack Replogle, and whether he'd said anything to me before we cracked up."

"What in particular?"

"Drew Meade. They wanted to know if Replogle told me what he and Meade had talked about."

"Did they want that more than anything else?"

Haere thought back to the night before. "I'd say they bore down on it pretty hard." Haere took out a pack of cigarettes and offered Citron one. Citron shook his head. Haere lit his with a match from a small box supplied by the bar.

Citron waited until the cigarette was lit. "I guess I'd better spend some more of your money."

Haere nodded his assent. "What on?"

"Long distance."

"Singapore?"

"Singapore," Citron agreed. "I thought I'd call this afternoon. If you can drop me off on the PCH, I can catch a bus or hitch a ride from there."

Haere signaled for the check. "Where's your car?"

"Somebody gave me a ride into Century City. To see my mother. He was supposed to run me back, but it didn't work out."

Haere almost had his American Express card out of his wallet when he stopped and looked at Citron. "Jesus. Not *Gladys* Citron?"

Citron grinned. It was a brief, wry grin. "I'm not sure if that's a question or an accusation. But you're right. She's my mummy."

"Jesus," Haere said again.

"You know her?"

"We've met a few times." Haere tried to make the tone of his next question casual, but he could hear his voice betraying him. "Somebody didn't tip her off on the Replogle thing, did he?"

Citron shook his head. "No, she just wanted to say hello, give me a birthday present, and find out if I'd ever been a cannibal."

"That sounds like Gladys."

"Yes," Citron said. "Doesn't it?"

Because he had a thirty-five-minute wait between buses, Drew Meade took a twenty-minute survey stroll around Santa Barbara and reconfirmed his impression of it as a candy-ass town. He found its people either too tan or too old, its weather too nice, its architecture too hokey. There was no hustle. Everybody seemed to have just got up from a nap, or about to go take one. Still candy-ass all right, he thought, looking up State Street, then turned and went back to the bus station.

The thing to do, he decided, is to stay out of towns named after saints. St. Louis, St. Paul, San Diego, all horseshit towns. Even San Francisco, now that the fags have taken over. But when his ship came in (and Meade's ship had remained hull down on the horizon for forty years now), he'd go live in New York or Chicago or even Cleveland. Someplace without suntans. Someplace with suits and ties. Someplace civilized, for God's sake.

Meade went into the bus station's men's room and had two quick drinks from his pint of Jim Beam. Back out in the waiting room he sat down in a plastic seat, took out a box of gumdrops, and ate them one by one as he surveyed his fellow passengers, not at all liking what he saw.

Time was, he told himself, when people going somewhere could be divided up into three classes: bus guys, train guys, and plane guys. Bus guys wore coats and pants that didn't match and tieless shirts buttoned up to their necks. Train guys dressed a little better, if not much, and carried shoeboxes filled with fried chicken, hard-boiled eggs, and potted-meat sandwiches. Plane guys all wore $100 suits with vests and if they couldn't think of anything else to do, they'd climb up on a shoeshine stand and let some nigger play with their feet. Nowadays, though, you couldn't tell the plane guys from the bus guys. They had leveled it all out. It's like they'd gone over it all with a grader.

If someone had suggested to Drew Meade that at sixty-three he might be considered a senior citizen, or even elderly, he would have stared contemptuously at them with his chilly hazel eyes and demanded to know what the fuck they were talking about. If he'd had a drink or two and was feeling expansive, he might even have tried to explain how you can't get old until you've got it made. Until then, you just can't afford old age. This was Drew Made's faith, his dogma, his creed. It kept him young.

They called the bus to Los Angeles just as Meade finished his last gumdrop. He rose and headed for the bus, a six-foot-two, wide-shouldered man with a shambling gait of deceptive quickness. Because he was also a totally suspicious creature, Meade turned his lined, big-jawed face up toward the destination sign on the front of the bus to make sure it really was going to Los

Angeles. Satisfied, he used his 223-pound frame to shoulder a smaller, younger man out of the way and entered the bus, heading toward the rear and, if possible, a seat all to himself.

Meade now had $19.47 in his pocket, which meant he couldn't afford to feel any older than thirty-three. He was on his way to Los Angeles to seek his fortune, a quest that had taken him almost around the world. When he pulled this deal off, he could afford to feel older—as much as forty-five or so. But until then, thirty-three. Maybe thirty-four tops.

He took a slip of paper from his pocket and studied the address again. It was in Beverly Hills on the wrong side of Wilshire—down in the flats where the original planners had intended the servants and tradesmen to live. Beverly Hills, he thought. Queen of the candy-ass towns.

11

MORGAN CITRON WAITED until a little after 5:00 P.M. before placing his call to Singapore, where he estimated the time to be around 8:00 in the morning. The call went through with surprising ease, and less than five minutes after he picked up the phone, Citron was listening to the ripe Cambridge tones of Lionel Lo of the Singapore CID.

"Morgan! It's been years. I read in one of our local rags how you'd been eaten by cannibals or something equally bizarre. Didn't believe it for a second, of course."

"How've you been, Lionel?"

"Mustn't grumble, can't complain. What're you working on? —something naughty, I trust."

"I'm just fooling around with a piece that may or may not pan out."

Lo giggled. It was the only incongruous thing Citron had ever noticed about the man. It was a high-pitched giggle that sometimes turned into a titter.

"I think," Lo said, "no, in fact, I'm almost positive that was exactly what you said to me—when? ten years ago?—after they kicked you out of Saigon and you wound up here on my doorstep with all of those oh-so-innocent questions. What a lot of bother the answers turned out to be."

"You got promoted, Lionel."

"How kind of you to remind me."

"I need to ask you about someone."

"Ask away."

"What, if anything, can you tell me about a guy called Drew Meade?"

There was only silence. Citron could picture Lo sitting at his well-ordered metal desk with the tape running; the phone clamped to one neat ear, the left; the thick black hair precisely parted—two inches long on the right, three on the left; two pens and one pencil in the pocket of the short-sleeved white shirt that was starched and ironed just so: the dark tie; the carefully pressed, very dark gray slacks; the oval face with its wide nose, thin, dubious lips, and those black eyes that seemed to snap at you. Forty-five now at least, Citron estimated, and maybe even a touch of gray in the hair, but probably not. And that mind, that slippery remarkable mind that made even the quick and the clever feel dull. That mind was working now, Citron knew, because there was only silence. Citron was about to say something when he heard Lo sigh.

"You Americans."

"Think of me as French, if it'll help any."

"I don't like the French either." Lo sighed again. "What long ears you have, *Grand-père*."

"Tell me about it."

"Where are you anyway, Morgan?"

"L.A."

"I know, but where in L.A.—Bel-Air, Beverly Hills?"

"Malibu."

"Of course. Where else. Well, there you are on the beach in Malibu and there's just a whisper of something in Singapore and suddenly you're on the phone."

94

"Am I the first?"

"Well, yes and no."

"Who else?"

"Your Langley chaps. A swarm of them all over the place."

"Just them?"

"There're others. One of the Langley lads described them as the crosstown rivals."

"The FBI."

"A gaggle of them, at least. Rather a rare bird in these parts. And the strangest thing of all, they're not even speaking to each other."

"The CIA and the FBI?"

"Precisely."

"How do you know?"

"This is my town, Morgan. I'm *paid* to know."

"Did they come to you?"

"Not at first. So I went calling on the station chief and politely asked if we could possibly assist them in their inquiries. I mentioned, in passing, of course, that we do have a certain amount of expertise in such matters and so forth and so on."

"What'd he say?"

"He grew quite testy and said that it was none of my fucking business."

"My."

"So I decided to find out what their romp through my patch was really about. I think it took about an hour. Both were looking for this Drew Meade." He paused. "Now the next thing I'm going to tell you, Morgan, I probably shouldn't, but I was really quite miffed. Still am."

There was another brief silence. Citron broke it with, "Go on."

"Well, they offered a reward for this Meade chap."

"A reward?"

"Yes."

"Publicly? I mean, did they send out fliers?"

"Oh my, no. It was all rather sub rosa. They just passed the word around."

"How much?"

"The reward? Seventeen thousand five hundred. American, of course. Why the odd amount I have no idea. Perhaps they've fallen on hard times."

"When was all this?"

"About two weeks ago."

"Did they find him?"

"No, but we did. Or so they say."

"You've just lost me."

"There was an anonymous call. In poor Cantonese. One of my chaps took it. He was given an address down on the docks. When we got there, we found a body floating in the water. It was very badly decomposed. The fish had been at it, naturally. But the passport and the Maryland driver's license were perfectly preserved in a wallet all neatly wrapped up in an airtight plastic bag that was tucked away in a hip pocket that was buttoned. Now I ask you."

"Drew Meade, huh?"

"Both the CIA and the FBI swore to it. Separately."

"But you don't believe them?"

"Hardly."

Citron's hand tightened on the phone. "What do you believe, Lionel?"

There was another of Lo's long silences followed by yet another sigh. "I do owe you, don't I, Morgan?"

"A little."

"Well, what I believe is this. First of all, they bought themselves an Anglo body somewhere. Secondly, they soaked it in the ocean for a time. And thirdly, they salted it with the Meade passport and driver's license and the other pocket litter. That's what I believe."

"Why'd they go to all the bother?"

"Why? Because they wanted him thought of as dead."

This time it was Citron who created the silence. At least five seconds went by before he said, "Whatever for?"

Lo giggled and then said, "I really must go now, Morgan. Do keep in touch."

The phone went dead. Citron slowly replaced the handset and wondered how long he had talked to Lionel Lo. Then he remembered his new watch, looked at it, and found the conversation had lasted nine minutes. He wondered how much it had cost. After that he started wondering about Drew Meade.

After five minutes of wondering and a glass of red wine, Citron called long-distance information, was given the number he asked for, and then dialed New York directly. He was calling what arguably was the World's Finest Newspaper. When the switchboard answered, Citron asked to be connected with a man he had once known fairly well in such backwaters as Lagos, Belfast, Addis Ababa, and Tananarive. The man had spent twenty-five years as a journeyman foreign correspondent, and Citron remembered him as a very intelligent reporter, if not quite brilliant, who wrote crisp, clear copy very quickly.

The man would have remained a foreign correspondent of the utility infielder type until retirement if—as he always put it—"the legs hadn't given out." He now lived in Connecticut, raised Jack Russells, commuted to work, and wrote the obituaries of famous foreigners he had known and whom he expected to die soon. Or relatively soon. He himself had four years to go until retirement, and when Citron called he was working on the obituary of the still-vigorous Chief Obafemi Awolowo of Nigeria.

"Not calling your own obit in, are you, Morgan?" he said after they said hello.

"No. Not yet."

"Some guys do that, you know. They retire and the phone

doesn't ring anymore and they start brooding about how they're going to be remembered, so they call it in—just to make sure we've got the facts right. But what they're really worried about is that we'll forget who they were and what they did on the Federal Power Commission back in 1947. They also get garrulous, like me. What can I do for you?"

"Drew Meade. Does it ring a bell?"

"Meade. Meade. I-led-nine-lives Meade, you mean?"

"Was it that many?"

"Close. He never did cash in on it like Philbrick did, though. Philbrick only led three lives, if you recall, which few do except for ancients like me. What're you working on, a feature?"

"Thinking about it. Is he still alive?"

"Philbrick or Meade?"

"Meade."

"Let's see what the trusty computer has to say."

There was the sound of the phone being put down, then being picked up again. "Died in Singapore the day after the election. That would be election day our time. We used it in the first edition as a filler and then dropped it to make room for the election stuff. So all Meade's nine lives got was two graphs from AP."

"Can you read it to me?"

"Sure. 'The body of Drew Meade, sixty-three, a former employee of both the FBI and the CIA, was found here Wednesday by Singapore police. A spokesman for the police said Mr. Meade apparently had drowned.'

"Second graph: 'A member of the Office of Strategic Services during World War Two, Mr. Meade joined the FBI in 1947 and later transferred to the CIA in the early sixties, according to a U.S. Embassy spokesman here. Funeral arrangements are pending.' That's it. No mention of his nine lives. No kith or kin either. It sounds like an embassy handout."

"So he's dead, huh?" Citron said.

"So AP claims. You know, Morgan, if I really gave a shit anymore, which I don't, I'd say you were working on more than just a feature."

"I'm just fooling around."

"Uh-huh. Let me ask you another one. Was old what's-his-name really a cannibal?"

"Sure he was."

"You've made my day."

"The least I could do."

At 6:07 P.M., Citron resumed his role as building superintendent and changed a light bulb in a ceiling fixture in Unit C for Miss Rebecca Clay, a very pert and very short twenty-nine-year-old senior copywriter who worked for J. Walter Thompson in Century City. Miss Clay invited Citron to have a glass of white wine, which he accepted. While they drank their wine, Miss Clay told him about some of her adventures in the advertising business and about the screenplay she was writing, which was based on these same adventures. Citron listened politely, thanked her for the wine, and went back to his own apartment. It was 6:37.

At 6:57, Citron was shaved, showered, and dressed in his newly purchased suit. He picked up the bouquet of carnations he had bought from the young blond woman who sold them out of the back of a pickup at the intersection of Sunset Boulevard and the Pacific Coast Highway. They had cost $1.50. He had asked Draper Haere to pull over and stop so he could buy the flowers. Haere asked if he had a date, or if he just liked flowers. Citron replied that he had a date with Velveeta Keats for dinner.

"Velveeta—like the cheese?"

"Like the cheese."

"Who's she?"

"A remittance woman, she says."

"Malibu," Haere had said.

At 6:59 P.M., Citron—who was seldom late and often early —knocked at the door of Unit E, his bouquet of carnations in hand. When there was no answer he knocked again. Because he could hear loud music coming from either a radio or a stereo unit, Citron tried the door. It was not locked. He went in.

There were two of them. Both wore black wet suits and diving masks that obscured their faces. They were holding Velveeta Keats. One of them had a hammerlock on her right arm. The other had a hand, his left, clamped over her mouth. Without thinking, Citron threw the bouquet of carnations at them. They ducked. Velveeta Keats bit down on the hand over her mouth. The hand went away from her mouth and she started to scream. She screamed once and then stopped when the .38 caliber revolver was jammed up under her chin.

"Not a sound," said the man with the revolver. "Understand?"

Velveeta Keats nodded.

"You either," the man with the revolver said to Citron.

"Right," Citron said.

The two men backed carefully toward the large sliding glass doors that opened onto the balcony. The man without the gun slid the door open. Both backed through it onto the balcony. The man without the gun jumped over the railing of the balcony and down to the sand. The man with the gun followed him.

Citron moved cautiously to the balcony and watched the two men enter the surf. He saw that they wouldn't have a long swim. Anchored a hundred yards out was a small cabin cruiser. The two men were already swimming toward it.

"Thank you for the flowers," Velveeta Keats said.

Citron turned. Velveeta Keats had gathered up the carnations from the floor. "Want me to call the cops?" he said.

She shook her head. "I wish you wouldn't."

"What was all that about?"

"Something to do with Papa, I reckon."

"Want me to call him for you?"

"No."

"Are you hurt?"

"No, they didn't hurt me."

"Any idea about who they were?"

"No. None. I guess they're just mad at Papa about something."

"Maybe I should call him for you."

She gestured toward the small round table that was placed in front of the sliding doors. It was set for two. The plates, Citron saw, were gold rimmed. The wine goblets were lead crystal. The silver place settings were laid out exactly. The white napkins had been carefully folded and twisted into the shape of giraffes. They stuck up out of the wine goblets. Two red candles were still to be lit. Velveeta Keats had gone to no little trouble, so Citron turned to her and said, "It looks very nice, but I still think you'd better call someone."

"We're having veal," she said. "Do you like veal?"

"Very much."

"I thought we'd eat first, and then maybe fool around a little, and after that, well, maybe I'll call somebody. How does that sound?"

"That sounds fine," Citron said.

"Hold me, will you?"

Citron put his arms around her. She was trembling.

"Hold me real tight," she said.

12

IT WAS A LITTLE PAST 7:00 P.M. when Drew Meade
got off the Los Angeles RTD bus near the Beverly Wilshire
Hotel and walked two and a half blocks south until he came to
the small mission-style, tile-roofed bungalow with a metal sign
that claimed it was guarded night and day by an "armed response" private security service. The small round sign glowed
in the dark.

Meade stood across the street under a sycamore and studied
the bungalow. Lights were on in what seemed to be the living
room. A dark-blue or black Mercedes 450 SEL sedan was
parked in the drive. Meade wondered if there was a second car
in the detached garage at the rear of the house.

He watched for another three minutes, then ran a hand
through his thick gray hair, felt the stubble on his face with the
same hand, shined his shoes one after the other on the backs of
his trouser legs, hitched up his belt, and crossed the street. He
went through an iron gate and up a cement walk that curved
back and forth for no reason that he could see. On the small
porch he found a button and pressed it. He could hear two-tone
chimes ring inside. He waited, but the door didn't open. He
would have been disappointed if it had. Only dopes opened

their doors at night. Meade had not come calling on any dope.

Meade rang the doorbell again. A woman's voice from behind the still-closed door said, "Who is it?"

"Me. Drew."

"Good Lord," the woman's voice said.

He could hear the chain being removed and the deadbolt being turned back. The door opened a crack. An eye peered out. The door then opened wide.

"Good Lord," the woman said again. "Come in."

"How the hell are you, Gladys, anyway?" Meade asked as he went through the door and into the living room.

Gladys Citron was wearing an ivory raw silk robe with a high Chinese collar. She backed up as Meade came into the room. "They say you're dead."

Meade nodded and looked carefully around the room. "Yeah, well, I'm not." He smiled appreciatively at what he saw in the room. "You're doing all right. You renting this place, or what?"

"I bought it—five years ago."

"Well, shit, Gladys, aren't you gonna ask me to sit down, take a load off, have a drink? You're looking good, by the way. Real good."

"Well, shit, Drew, sit down. Take a load off. Have a drink. Bourbon?"

"Bourbon."

Drew Meade picked one of the two wing-back chairs that were drawn up before the unlit fireplace and sat down. Gladys Citron turned to a tray that held bottles and glasses, and poured two drinks: bourbon for Meade, white wine for herself. She moved over to Meade, handed him his drink, and sat down in the opposite wing-back chair.

"So," she said. "I heard you got rich."

"Yeah, I did. For a while there." He drank two large swallows and lit one of his Camels.

"What happened?"

"A couple of things fell apart."

"And they kicked you out."

"Who says they kicked me out?"

"Don't try that, Drew," she said. "Not on me."

"Okay, so they kicked me out."

"Heroin, I heard."

"Some heroin, but a lot of hash. Mostly hash. I got set up by the slope generals."

"Of course you did."

"I took the fall."

"Pity."

"It was a long way down. The fall. You know what I've been doing for ten years now?"

"What?"

"Nickel-and-diming it, trying to come up with two bits. Singapore, Hong Kong, Bangkok, Djakarta—the circuit. Opals, a little gold, some blue-sky shares. Hell, I was even a tour guide in Bángkok for a couple of months. The *real* Bangkok, know what I mean?"

"I can imagine," she said. "Then what?"

"Then—well, then I got lucky."

"Tell me," she said. "I like happy endings."

"What happened is I ran into one of the Maneras brothers. Remember the Manerases?"

She nodded. "At the Bay. They were to have gone in on the first wave, except they were no-shows."

"The Manerases always were pretty smart—for Cubans."

"Which one did you run into?"

"Bobby—he's the oldest, isn't he?"

Again, she nodded.

"Well, Bobby'd got himself into a mess. They were all looking for him. The narcs, some hard cases, the feebies, not to mention a whole bunch of other people. I mean, he was in a real mess. And what's more, he was broke. When I ran into him in Singapore he was living off an American Express gold card he'd dipped off some tourist. So what the hell, Gladys. You know me. I got a heart as big as a house. I took him in."

"Why?" she said.

"You got any more of this bourbon?"

"Help yourself."

"I will."

Meade crossed to the liquor and made himself another drink. On the way back to his chair he gave the living room another calculating inspection, and then sank down into his chair with a long pleased sigh.

"Why'd you take him in?" she said.

"Bobby? Because he had something to sell. Cheap."

"What?"

"A story."

Gladys Citron leaned forward in her chair, caught herself, and leaned back. Drew Meade grinned. She noticed that he still seemed to have all his teeth. They were big teeth, nearly square and absolutely even. They were also a strange shade of very pale yellow, although she now remembered that they had always been that peculiar shade ever since she had first met him in France thirty-what?—dear God, thirty-eight years ago.

"What kind of story?" she said.

"Interested, huh?"

"Perhaps."

"That's some sheet you help put out, Gladys. I've seen a couple of copies. One had a story about this little girl who was swooped up by a flying saucer and flown to the moon or someplace and had a talk with Jesus. Hell of a story. People really buy that crap, huh?"

"Six million copies a week."

"You pay for some of those stories, right?"

"We pay."

"You pay pretty good?"

"We can be generous."

Meade looked around the living room again, much as a bank appraiser might have looked. "How much does a house like this go for?"

"Three-fifty to three-seventy-five now. I paid three-twenty-five."

"Seems like a hell of a lot to me."

"It's in Beverly Hills."

"Jacks up the price, right?"

"Right."

"I oughta buy a place. Maybe a condo in New York or Chicago. Settle down, you know? Maybe write my memoirs. I've even got a title. 'More Lives Than a Cat.' What d'you think?"

"They'd never give you clearance."

"Maybe," he said. "Maybe not."

"Tell me about Bobby Maneras and his story."

Meade lit another cigarette from the one he was already smoking. He tossed the finished butt into the fireplace. "I'd like to, Gladys, but I've got a little problem."

"You're broke."

"That's part of it."

"I could fix that."

"I wanta put my feet up, know what I mean? I'm tired of the hustle. In New York, Chicago, I'd need fifty a year just to get by. That means I'd need half a million, doesn't it? Put it into municipals maybe."

"You're dreaming, Drew."

"I'm talking about cash, of course."

She shook her head slowly. "Impossible."

"I was thinking maybe I could tap you for around a hundred thousand. Secondary rights, I think they call it."

"Who's your principal buyer?"

"Lemme tell you about Bobby first, okay?" She nodded. "Bobby was in a real jam and flat on his ass and all he had to sell was this story of his. Well, shit, I didn't have any money and he wouldn't tell me the story until I came up with some. So what I did is, I got him to tell me just part of the story, and I'll tell you this much, it's some story. So then I had to figure out who'd pay for what I had. It just so happened there was this guy in Singapore I'd known a little, back in the fifties. I got ten thousand out of him."

"For just part of the story?"

Meade nodded. "That's how hot it is."

"Who is he?"

"We'll get to that. Lemme get back to Bobby. Now Bobby's problem was he had to disappear. So what I did was, I got him a Filipino passport and offered him that and seventy-five hundred for the rest of the story. He grabbed it and for all I know Bobby's in Manila now, probably getting rich all over again."

"But he told you the rest of the story?"

"Oh, yeah. All of it."

"Then what?"

"Then I figured I'd better get out of Singapore."

"Why?"

"They came looking for Bobby."

"Who?"

"Everybody." He paused. "And then they started looking for me." He paused again. "Well, I had just enough money for a ticket to Santiago and then on to Caracas and from there to Mexico City. I crossed over at Mexicali."

"Walked across?"

He nodded. "I figured I could sell the whole story for a bundle to this same guy who'd paid me ten thousand for just the taste. So I called him from a phone booth in Calexico and guess who I got?"

"I don't guess. Who?"

"His widow."

It was a long stare. The cool green eyes locked on the cold hazel ones. Neither gaze wavered. It was Gladys Citron who spoke first, asking a question whose answer she was fairly sure she already knew.

"Did he die in bed?"

Meade shook his head. "It was an accident. They say. A car wreck."

She rose and reached for Meade's glass. When she was at the liquor, pouring two more drinks, she asked her next question casually, her back still to him.

"Who was he?"

"Replogle. Jack Replogle. John T. Replogle."

"Replogle Construction," she said.

"Big bucks, Gladys."

"An accident, you say," she said as she turned, moved back to the fireplace, and handed him his drink.

"So his widow claims, but what does she know?"

"What do you do now?"

"There was a guy with him."

"With Replogle?"

"When the wreck happened. A money guy. He wasn't hurt."

"I see. You think he'll buy."

"I know he will."

"And he's here—in L.A.?"

Meade nodded. "He gets first crack; you get second."

"What's his name?"

Meade swallowed some of his drink and then frowned. "I've been trying to decide if I oughta tell you."

Gladys Citron smiled—a small, slight, confident smile.

"Well, why the hell not? His name's Haere."

The smile went away. "Draper Haere?"

"Yeah. You know him?"

"We've met a time or two."

"He's a money man," Meade said. "Politics."

"I know."

"What I've got is sort of a political shoot-'em-up."

"I see. Do you know Draper Haere?"

"Sure, I know him. Not well. I used to know his old man pretty good, though. He was a commie."

"How do you know that?"

"How?" Meade asked with a cold grin. "What the hell, Gladys, I turned him in."

"To the subcommittee," she said. "Back in the fifties."

Meade nodded, still grinning his cold, almost mechanical grin that contained, as far as Gladys Citron could detect, neither regret nor apology. Nor humor, for that matter.

"I want in, Drew," she said.

"I figured you would." He frowned as though in warning. "It's big bucks though, understand?"

She shrugged. "I'll have to make a few calls. You want to spend the night here? There're a couple of spare rooms."

"What's wrong with yours?"

"I go for younger men these days."

"What the hell," he said, "I'm only thirty-three." He paused and frowned again. "Maybe thirty-four."

At three that morning, Gladys Citron rose quietly from her bed, turned to inspect the sleeping Drew Meade, and walked barefoot into the living room. In the bedroom Meade opened his eyes. It was absolutely quiet in the house and he could just make out the woman's low voice as it spoke into the telephone.

"That's right, he's here with me," she said. "He wants a hundred thousand—for what he calls secondary rights." There was silence as she listened. "He says he's going to give first crack at it to Draper Haere, that's H-a-e-r-e." She listened again. "He wants it in cash." Another brief silence and she said, "I'll see what I can do."

In the dark bedroom, Drew Meade stretched and smiled up at the ceiling.

13

Morgan Citron awoke and turned his head to inspect the left side of the king-size bed that took up most of the space in the small room. Velveeta Keats was no longer there. Citron looked at his new watch and saw that it was a few minutes past four. They had gone to bed around 11:00 and made love—or fooled around, as Velveeta Keats would have it—for forty-five minutes or an hour. Citron hadn't kept precise track of the time. Velveeta Keats had proved to be a passionate, inventive, even amusing lover much given to acrobatics and experimentation. Despite nearly four hours of sleep, Citron still felt slightly ravaged, but pleasantly so.

He located some of his scattered clothing—his shorts and shirt—put them on and went into the living room, where he found Velveeta Keats standing before the large sliding glass doors, a mug of coffee clutched in her hands. She was wearing a light cotton robe and staring out at the pale moonlight on the ocean. She was also crying, although she made no sound.

Citron put his arms around her. "Still scared?" he said.

He felt her nod against his shoulder. "I reckon . . . I reckon I'd best call him."

"Your father."

There was another nod against his shoulder. "He oughta at least know, hadn't he?"

"I think so."

She looked up at him. "What time is it back there?"

"Miami? About seven. Is that too early?"

She shook her head. "He won't talk to me, though."

"Not at all?"

Again, she shook her head no. "I suppose I could talk to Mama, but she'd just go into a tizzy. Mama doesn't much like scary news."

"Is there anyone else you could talk to—a brother, maybe a sister?"

"I had a brother, but Jimmy killed him."

"Jimmy?"

"My husband. My late husband. I told you all about him, didn't I?"

"You mentioned him. That's all."

"Jimmy found me in bed with Cash."

"Cash was who?"

"Cash Keats. My brother. He was two years older'n me. I." She turned away from Citron and resumed her inspection of the moonlit ocean. "Sounds like one of those sorry tales all about Southern decadence and incest, doesn't it?"

"It happens."

"Did you ever wanta go to bed with your sister or mama?"

Citron smiled. "Certainly not my mother. I don't have a sister, so I can't really say."

"But you can imagine it?"

"Sure. It's not hard."

"Well, Papa couldn't. He quit speaking to me, packed me up, and sent me out here. I call Mama now and then, or she calls me, and she says he hasn't budged—Papa, I mean."

"You want me to talk to him?"

She chewed her lower lip before answering. "I—I'd appreciate it."

"What do you want me to tell him?"

"Just tell him what happened and that I'm okay, but that I thought he oughta know about those two kidnappers or whatever they were."

The number in Miami rang six times before it was answered with an "allo." It was a male voice.

"I'd like to speak to Mr. Keats, please."

"*Je ne comprends pas.*"

Citron switched to French. "I would like to speak with Mr. Keats. My name is Citron."

"Ah, Citron. You are French?"

"Is Mr. Keats there?"

"You speak very good French. Are you from Paris?"

"Just tell him I wish to talk to him about his daughter."

A deep voice boomed over the line. "What about my daughter, mister?"

"Are you Mr. Keats?"

"I'm Keats. Get off the fuckin' phone, Jacques."

Citron could hear an extension phone being put down.

"My name is Citron."

"I heard all that. I'm getting so I can *parlez-vous* a little bit, but it's sure as shit harder'n Spanish. Hell, anyone can learn to *habla español*, but you gotta talk way up there in the front of your mouth and move your tongue around real quick to *parlez-vous* French. Now what's all this about somebody claiming to be my daughter?"

"Velveeta Keats."

"Never heard of her."

"I must have the wrong number."

"No, you ain't got the wrong number. Why don't you just go ahead and tell me about this daughter I'm supposed to have."

Citron could hear a woman's voice in the background. And

112

then Keats was yelling at her. "Goddamnit, Francine, I'm gonna find out what's wrong. Just lemme do it my way." Keats then resumed his conversational rumble. "Now go on with what you were saying, Mr.—uh—"

"Citron. Morgan Citron."

"Citron. That's 'lemon' in French, ain't it?"

"Right."

"Okay. Let's have it."

"I'm a friend and neighbor of your daughter's—"

"Where?"

"In Malibu."

"What's the address?"

Citron reeled off the five-digit number on the Pacific Coast Highway.

"Okay. That checks. What number you callin' from?"

Citron read off Velveeta Keats's number.

"Hang up and I'll call back. Just make sure it's you who answers."

The phone went dead. Citron hung it up and looked at Velveeta. "He said he'll call back."

She shrugged. "Papa's sort of, well, suspicious, I reckon."

A moment later the phone rang. Citron picked it up and said hello.

"Okay, buddy, let's hear it."

"As I was saying, Mr. Keats, I'm a friend and neighbor of your daughter's."

"So?"

"Last night she invited me to dinner. At seven o'clock, I knocked on her door. There was no answer. The door was unlocked so I went in. Two men dressed in wet suits were holding Velveeta. I threw something at them."

"What?"

"Flowers."

"You mean like—like pansies or something?"

"Carnations."

"You must have clabber for brains, brother."

"You may be right. Anyway, they pulled a gun."

"They shoot her?"

"No."

"Then what?"

"They left. Velveeta has a balcony facing the beach. They went over that, down to the surf, and swam out to a small cabin cruiser."

"You call the cops?"

"No."

"Why?"

"Velveeta said not to."

"This happened last night?"

"Yesterday evening. Around seven."

"And you've been fuckin' her ever since, huh?"

Citron sighed. "She just wanted to let you know."

"Hell, I don't mind. She's thirty, going on thirty-one. She can do any goddamn thing she wants to. But you say you're a friend of hers, huh?"

"That's right."

"Okay. I'm gonna take the next flight out to L.A. I want you to meet me at the airport. You. Not her. My missus will call back and tell you what flight it is. I want you to rent a limousine with a driver and a Hertz Ford. A big Ford."

"I don't have a credit card."

"Goddamn, she sure can pick 'em. Use her credit card. She's got credit cards coming out the kazoo."

"Why two cars?" Citron said.

"Because I never travel alone."

"Who's coming with you?"

"Who?" Keats said. "My two French niggers, that's who."

It was 7:15 A.M. when the phone rang at the crucial moment during Draper Haere's ritualistic preparation of his breakfast.

He picked up the kitchen's yellow wall telephone, said, "Call back in five minutes," hung up, and used the stainless-steel spatula to flip his two frying eggs over gently.

At 7:20 the phone rang again. Haere rose from the table, again picked up the long-corded yellow phone, this time in his left hand, sat back down, cut into one of the eggs with a fork, and was pleased to see it had been cooked to perfection. He then said, "Hello."

The man's voice said, "Is this Draper Haere?"

"Himself."

"What?"

"Yes, this is Haere," he said and forked some grits mixed with egg yolk into his mouth.

"How soon can you get to a pay phone?"

Haere clamped the phone between his left shoulder and ear, put down the fork, picked up a biscuit, broke it open, and spread both halves with butter. "I don't know," he said. "An hour. A day. Maybe a week. Why?" He took a large bite of the buttered biscuit and chewed it with pleasure. Haere rarely found anything to fault in his cooking.

"Well, fuck it then," the man said. "I'll just have to risk it."

"Risk what?"

"Telling you who I am."

"Okay. Who?"

"Drew Meade."

Haere had a square inch of homemade sausage about halfway to his mouth. He put the fork down, then picked it up again, examined the morsel of sausage carefully, put it into his mouth, and chewed it thoroughly before speaking. "Let's talk."

"Fine," Meade said. "Where?"

"My place in an hour."

"What's the address?"

Haere told him.

"You remember me, huh?" Meade said.

"I remember you."

"Yeah," Meade said. "I figured you would."

After the connection was broken, Haere rose and placed the yellow wall phone back on its hook. He turned, looked down at his partly eaten breakfast, picked up the plate, and started to dump its contents into the sink, but paused. On the plate was an untouched biscuit and a leftover sausage patty. He sliced the biscuit open, placed the sausage patty between the two halves, and wrapped it up in wax paper. He knew he would be hungry later, and cold biscuit and sausage would be not only good, but also comforting. It had often been his lunch or even dinner in Birmingham. My heritage, he thought, as he turned on the faucet, again picked up the plate, scraped its contents into the sink, and switched on the garbage disposal. As he watched what was left of his breakfast being ground up and sluiced away, Haere thought about his dead father and the man who long ago had accused him of political heresy. Haere discovered there was no anger left, or even any bitterness. Nothing now remained other than a kind of cold curiosity. It would be interesting to see how Drew Meade had survived the years. It would be even more interesting to find out just what it was he had for sale. If anything. Haere decided a witness to the meeting would be both useful, and, indeed, necessary. He turned back to the wall phone, picked it up, and called Morgan Citron.

Citron answered on the first ring. "I was just about to call you," he said after Haere identified himself.

"What've you got?" Haere said.

"I called Singapore yesterday. Also New York. Then I tried to call you, but couldn't get you."

"I was in a meeting," Haere said.

"The guy I talked to in Singapore can be described as either a highly reliable source or an authoritative spokesman. Take your pick."

"I like authoritative spokesman."

"Right. Well, according to him both the CIA and the FBI were looking all over hell for your Drew Meade in Singapore. When they couldn't find him, they bought themselves an Anglo body, dumped it in the ocean, let it be found, and then swore it was the late Mr. Meade."

"Why?"

"That my authoritative source wouldn't say—or didn't know. Anyway, Meade's supposedly dead and buried. AP made it official with a two-paragraph story they filed election day—or the day after, Singapore time. My authoritative source didn't believe a word of it."

"He's right," Haere said. "I'm meeting with Meade at my place in about forty-five minutes."

"I'll be damned."

"I need a witness."

"Me."

"Right."

"Fine," Citron said, "but I have to meet someone at the airport at noon."

"Anything to do with this?"

There was a long pause before Citron answered. "I don't really know," he said.

Gladys Citron turned from the medicine cabinet and handed Drew Meade her razor. He had already brushed his teeth with one of her spare toothbrushes. "Didn't you bring *anything*?" she said.

"Just me, darlin'."

She leaned against the bathroom doorjamb and watched as Meade soaped his face and began shaving with quick, impatient strokes. She was wearing one of her Chanel suits, the dark-gray, almost black one. The Légion d'Honneur ribbon was in place on the lapel. Meade was bare to the waist. She could detect no flab—not even at sixty-three.

"What do you do, work out?"

"Me? Christ, no."

"How do you stay in shape?"

"I don't sit around on my butt, that's how. People get out of shape because they sit around on their butts. You gotta keep moving. That's one thing you can say about me: I've kept moving."

"When're you going to move out of here?"

Meade looked back over his shoulder at her and grinned. The white soap made his teeth seem more yellow than they really were. "What's the matter, Gladys, not used to a man around the house?"

"Younger men, usually."

"We didn't do too bad last night for a couple of old crocks. I mean, you still know how to wiggle pretty good." He pressed up his nose with a thumb and shaved under it. When he was done, he rinsed off the razor, put it back in the medicine cabinet, and turned. "You know, I was just thinking about the first time you and me made it—back in 'forty-four just outside Dijon. Remember?"

"Vaguely."

"They'd just co-opted you into OSS to liaise with the Resistance and I was your new wire man."

"I remember."

"We stayed at that farm, that dairy farm, the one where you'd stashed that kid of yours. Whatever happened to him, anyway?"

"He's around."

"I remember he was only four or five then and didn't speak anything but French. He went on to become some kind of reporter, didn't he? A hotshot, I heard."

"Something like that."

"Back then, in 'forty-four, he didn't even hardly know who you were."

"He knows now," she said and turned to leave.

"Gladys," he said.

She turned back.

"I'm going to need a little cash to go see Haere."

"I can let you have a hundred. It's all I've got unless you can cash a check somewhere."

"No checks."

"When do I get a sample of what you're peddling, Drew?"

Meade thought about it. "Three o'clock?"

"Where?"

He reached for his shirt, which was hanging on the bathroom doorknob. "What's wrong with right here?"

"Nothing," Gladys Citron said.

14

DREW MEADE DIDN'T MUCH LIKE what he saw. Instead of one, there were two of them. There was the tall skinny one in the cheap new tan suit, and the other one, not quite so tall, wearing the banker blue suit and looking as if somebody had just run over his dog. Both were about the same age: forty, maybe even forty-one. He stared at each of them separately, memorizing them, and then gave a quick, careful examination to his surroundings.

"Just the one big room, right?" he said.

"Right," Draper Haere said.

"You're Haere."

Haere nodded.

"You got older. I don't even think I'd've recognized you. Who's he?" Meade nodded at Morgan Citron.

"A friend."

"The witness, huh? He got a name?"

"Mitchell."

"What's Mitchell's first name?"

"Mitch."

"Mitch Mitchell," Meade said, still staring at Citron. "Middle initial probably M. Okay, I can live with that. Let's get the other thing out of the way."

"What?" Haere asked.

"Your old man. I wanta clear the air about him."

"Go ahead. You want to sit down?"

"Yeah. Sure."

Meade chose the walnut armchair. He patted its left armrest appreciatively. "Nice old chair."

"It used to belong to Henry Wallace," Haere said, taking his usual seat in the Huey Long chair.

Meade was unimpressed. "Wallace, huh? Old bubblehead."

Citron chose the leather couch. He sat, leaning forward, arms on his knees. Hubert, the cat, jumped up on the couch and inched his way onto Citron's lap.

"About my old man," Haere said.

"He was a commie."

"Was he now."

"Sure. And I nailed him. It's what they paid me to do. It was a living, that's all, and not much of one at that. They offered me the job back in 'forty-nine, I took it, they paid me, and I did it. I didn't have anything against your old man. Not personally. In fact, he was a pretty nice guy. We used to have some laughs and a few beers together."

"While you were setting him up."

"Him and the others. You gotta remember I nailed him and six others out of that old Mine, Mill bunch. By rights, your old man should've gone to jail with the rest of 'em for contempt, except Replogle jerked hard on a few wires and got him off. You know it and I know it, but what the hell, it's all ancient history now. But if you wanta get steamed about it, well, go ahead. I just wanta get it over and done with."

There was only silence as Draper Haere examined the big gray-haired man who now sat slumped in the old chair, one long leg, his left, stuck straight out in front, the other, the right, dangling over the chair's padded arm. A mercenary, Haere decided, forever reenlisting on life's losing side. And a believer yet in all the old recruiting lies and tired blandishments, but perhaps a bit puzzled now by why the war is still not won. Of course, there's always the one big battle to come, the decisive one, the last one, the one that'll win the war and then, afterward, there'll be loot, booty, and spoils for all.

Haere had long wondered how he would feel upon seeing Drew Meade and now, sorting through his emotions, he was surprised that all he could come up with was a touch of pity.

"You want a breakfast beer?" he said.

"Sure," Meade said. "Thanks."

Citron gently dumped Hubert to the floor and rose. "I'll get them," he said, and headed for the splendid refrigerator.

"You saw Jack Replogle in Singapore," Haere said.

"That's right. He tell you about it?"

"He told me. I was with him when he died."

"That's what his wife said."

"He also said he paid you ten thousand dollars. You started out at fifty, but settled for ten."

"He tell you what it bought?"

"No," Haere said, and accepted a can of Budweiser from Citron. "He was just about to tell me when it happened."

"I'd like to hear about that," Meade said as he opened the top on his own can.

Haere drank some beer first. "He was just about to tell me when a blue Dodge pickup ran us off the road about fifteen miles past Idaho Springs. I got thrown out. Replogle didn't. The gas tank exploded and he burned to death. Or maybe he was already dead."

"You weren't hurt?"

"I scorched my hands. They just took the bandages off last night."

"Replogle didn't say anything at all?"

"He said it could probably blow them out of the White House in 'eighty-four."

Meade nodded thoughtfully. "Well, he was right about that. You say he was just about to tell you what he got from me when they ran you off the road?"

Haere nodded.

"They might've had you guys wired. The car anyway. But maybe not."

"Who?" Citron said.

Meade looked at Citron steadily for several seconds, then shifted his bleak gaze back to Haere. Meade jerked his head at Citron. "Mitch here doesn't talk much, does he?"

"He's a listener."

"Well, that question Mitch just asked brings us around to the meat of the thing."

"Money," Haere said.

"I'm thinking," Meade said, "I'm thinking of around four hundred and fifty thousand."

"Think again," Haere said.

Meade took out his Camels, lighted one, blew some smoke out, and smiled. "What I gave Replogle was just a taste— because that's all he'd pony up for. What I'm offering you and, of course, Mitch here is the full course. Is Mitch the money man?"

"No," Haere said. "I'm the money man."

Hubert, the cat, wormed his way back onto Citron's lap. Citron stroked him under the chin and the cat purred. Citron smiled at Meade and said, "They buried you in Singapore."

Meade looked at him and grinned. "Been checking me out, huh?"

Citron nodded. "They offered a reward for you, seventeen thousand five hundred dollars, but when nothing happened, they found themselves a body, buried it, and claimed it was you."

"Not much of a reward," Meade said.

"No."

"Dead or alive?"

"I forgot to ask." Citron smiled. "They gave you two paragraphs in the *New York Times*."

"No kidding. I'd sort of like to read that."

"You only made the first edition."

Meade shrugged. "Better'n nothing. How many guys get that?" He turned to Haere. "You want what I got, right? And no matter what price I set, you're gonna try and jew me down. I don't blame you. I'd do the same thing. And maybe I might come down a notch. I'm not saying I will, I'm just saying maybe. But first I'm gonna give you a smell. If you like it, we can start talking serious money. If you don't, I'll go peddle it somewhere else. Fair enough?"

Haere nodded slowly.

"Okay," Meade said. "About six months back, Washington fought a secret mini-war down in Central America there. Four guys got killed on one side, five on the other. The war was over a ton or two of cocaine and thirty-five to fifty million bucks in cash money. When the shooting was over and the smoke blew away, one side found out it had been suckered. I can give you time, place, dates, and names. All you gotta do is come up with four hundred thousand in cash."

There was a long silence. Finally, Draper Haere said, "One question."

"Maybe I'll answer it; maybe I won't."

"Whose money was it—the thirty-five to fifty million?"

"Didn't I say? Uncle Sam's."

"Cash?" Citron said.

"Cash."

"How much of this did you tell Jack Replogle in Singapore?"

"Not a hell of a lot more than I just told you. I gave him some names is all, and he forked over ten thousand without a blink and thought he'd made the buy of the year. But Replogle was one smart son of a bitch, although I don't have to tell you that."

"He's also dead," Haere said.

Meade shrugged. "What more do you need?" he asked. "I mean, I could sit around here all day selling you on the quality of my goods. But I don't have to. You were there. You saw him get it. Hell, you almost got it yourself. I don't know how you could want a better fuckin' testimonial than that."

"Now we get to the key question," Haere said. "Just who are they?"

Meade only smiled and slowly shook his head. Haere rose. "Let's have another beer," he said, collected the empty cans, and headed for the refrigerator. While Haere was getting the beer, Meade studied Citron.

"You look like somebody," he said. "Somebody I used to know."

"Who?"

Meade gave his head a small irritated shake. "I can't quite put my finger on it."

Haere came back with three more cans of beer, which he handed around. As he held out the can to Meade, he said, "You might as well forget about four hundred thousand, or three fifty, or even three hundred. We might—and I'm stressing might—well, we just might come up with one hundred, and then we'd only buy it in twenty-five-thousand-dollar chunks. If you started running dry or making it up toward the end, we wouldn't pay. That's our offer and it's take it or leave it."

Meade popped open his can, drank from it, wiped his mouth, belched softly, frowned, and said, "Cash?"

"That'll be a problem."

"Checks don't do me any good."

"Okay. Cash."

"When?"

"I don't know," Haere said. "I'll have to check around. It'll be tomorrow at the earliest."

"Tomorrow morning?"

"Afternoon."

"Where?"

Haere looked at Citron. "What about your place?"

"That should do," Citron said.

Meade frowned. "Who else?"

"Who else what?" Haere said.

"Who else will be in on it—when we talk, I mean?"

"Nobody else. Just you, me, and—uh—" For a moment Haere couldn't remember the alias he had given Citron.

Meade grinned coldly. "Mitch here."

"That's right," Haere said with a small smile. "Mitch."

15

THE FIRST BLACK, the tall lean one with the cast in his right eye, stumbled and seemed to trip over his own feet. With hands outstretched he fell hard against Morgan Citron and knocked him backward across the hood of the rented Cadillac limousine. The second black, the squat one with the build of a fat fireplug, bustled over and helped the tall lean one raise Citron back up onto his feet. They brushed him off, apologizing for their clumsiness in soft liquid French, and as they brushed he could feel their expert hands explore for hidden weapons.

The rented limousine, its uniformed driver still behind the wheel, was parked in front of the Eastern Airlines terminal at Los Angeles International Airport. Behind the limousine was the black Ford LTD sedan Velveeta Keats had rented from Budget in Malibu with her Visa card. The limousine-rental people had preferred American Express.

"A single apology is sufficient," Citron said in French as the two blacks still tried to rid him of some imaginary dust. "Too many tend to make me suspicious."

"Did I not say it?" the fireplug demanded of the cockeyed beanpole. "Does he not possess a perfect Parisian accent?"

"It is as you claimed," the beanpole agreed, turned, and said, "*Rien*," to the fifty-three-year-old man with the narrow sun-baked face who stood waiting ten feet away.

"*Rien*," the man said to Citron. "That means 'nothing.' It also means you're not gonna pull a knife or a gun on me. I'm Keats. B.S. Keats, B for Byron, S for Shelley. My mama married beneath her raisin' and I seem to have taken after Pap. He was a cracker, damn near white trash. That my limo?"

"That's it," Citron said.

"That my Ford?" Keats said, giving the black LTD a nod.

"Right."

"You *parlez-vous* better'n I do," Keats said. "Tell Jacques and Cecilio to follow us."

Citron told the two blacks what Keats wanted. Jacques, the beanpole, smiled. "We know. We understand far more than he thinks."

"That's what I thought," Citron said and gave him the keys to the Ford.

Before the uniformed driver could make it around the limousine, Keats had the door open and was climbing into the rear seat. Citron followed. Back behind the wheel, the driver turned and said, "Where to, Mr. Citron?"

"Nowhere," Keats said. "Just sit tight until my niggers get the luggage. You can also roll up that divider and turn on the air conditioner."

"We can't park here too long, sir. The airport cops are very strict."

"You get a ticket, I'll pay for it," Keats said. "Now roll up that divider."

The driver started the engine and pushed buttons that raised the divider glass and turned on the air conditioning. Keats took two plump cigars from his pocket and offered Citron one. Citron shook his head.

"Mind if I do?" Keats said.

"Not at all."

Keats lit his cigar carefully with a kitchen match that he took from the pocket of his tan cashmere jacket. Beneath the jacket was a pale-yellow polo shirt that was worn outside a pair of linen slacks the color of milk chocolate. On his feet were brown-and-white saddle shoes with red rubber soles. Yellow socks matched his shirt. Citron thought the saddle shoes made Keats look vaguely collegiate.

Keats got his cigar going, blew out some smoke, and turned his faded blue eyes on Citron. "Where'd you learn your French?"

"In France."

"You live there?"

"I was born there."

"I reckon I could speak it if I was born there. The reason we didn't take the bag on the plane is because it's got the niggers' pieces in it. Cecilio carries a thirty-eight. Old Jacques likes a magnum."

"Somebody going to kill you?"

"A few folks'd like to see me dead. What d'you think of 'em—Cecilio and Jacques?"

"They seem competent."

"They're Haitian. Boat people. Guess how much Cecilio made year before last?"

"When he was still in Haiti?"

Keats nodded.

"I have no idea."

"He made two hundred and sixty-eight dollars—the whole fuckin' year. You know how much I'm payin' them a week?"

"Two hundred and sixty-eight dollars."

Keats smiled. His teeth were almost an oyster white, and his smile stayed in place several seconds longer than necessary, as if he sometimes forgot it was there. His thinning hair was so sunbleached it was hard to tell whether it was blond or gray, and he combed it straight down over his forehead in short ragged bangs. The faded blue eyes squinted even in the shade, as if wary of any sudden light, and the long nose that poked out and up was separated from the thin bitter mouth by a well-clipped mustache. Beneath all that was a pointed chin with a scar that meandered across it like a white river.

"That was a pretty good guess—two hundred and sixty-eight dollars—but a softy's guess. I pay 'em one thousand bucks a week. Each. Now guess how much loyalty that buys."

"All there is?"

"That's close," Keats said, paused, and puffed on his cigar. "You know what Haitians are? They're ambitious. I never saw anybody, white or black, who'd work as hard as they do. You want a ditch dug? Shit, they'll dig it—just tell 'em how wide and how close to China. I don't hire anybody but Haitians anymore, although goddamn, I do wish they'd learn to speak American." He paused again. "How's Velveeta?"

"She seems all right," Citron said.

"She tell you about fuckin' her brother yet?"

Before Citron could reply, there was a tap on the window. Both men turned. Jacques was bent down, peering through the window, and smiling broadly as he pointed to the long, round buffalo-hide bag he carried in his left hand. Keats nodded and Jacques disappeared, heading back toward the Ford LTD. Keats pushed the button that lowered the glass divider.

"Let's go, son," he said to the driver.

"Yes, sir. Where to?"

"They got a scenic drive out here?"

The driver tried to think of someplace scenic. "Well," he said finally, "we could go up the coast."

"Sounds good," Keats said and rolled the divider back up. The driver put the limousine into gear and eased it out into the heavy airport traffic.

"She had a brother all right," Keats said, "and like she probably told you, he's dead. He died when she was seven and he was nine. He died of polio in the summer of 'fifty-nine. They had polio licked by then, but he caught it and died anyway. Maybe Cash and Velveeta played doctor once or twice, but the rest she just makes up. Incest. It turns some people on—did you know that?"

Keats didn't seem to expect an answer, and Citron gave none. Instead, he said, "She also mentioned a husband. Or did she make that up too?"

"No, she didn't make that up. She was married to Jimmy. Jimmy Maneras. Jaime, really. He was older'n her. A Cuban. The Manerases and me were in bidness together. She tell you about that?"

"Yes."

"Figured she would. That lady does like to talk. We ain't speakin', you know, her and me. Damn fool situation for a man to get himself into, but it happens. It happens." He sighed and sucked on his cigar. "Who were they?"

"I don't know," Citron said.

"Kidnappers, you reckon?"

"If they were, they weren't very determined."

"Because they took off after you threw the pansies at 'em."

"Carnations."

"Carnations. Why'd you do a damn fool thing like that?"

"Reflex."

"Before you thought, huh?"

Citron nodded.

Keats looked out the window. The view was of some gray-looking marshland. "Not much of a scenic drive," he said.

"It gets better."

"What'd they look like? I mean, were they white, black, brown, or what?"

"White. They had diving masks on. Wet suits. From the way they moved, I'd say they were in their late twenties, early thirties."

"Voices?"

131

"Standard American."

"What'd they say?"

"They said, 'Not a sound' or 'Don't make a sound.' I don't remember which, but they said it to your daughter. And then they said, 'You either,' to me. I think I said, 'Okay' or 'Right.' Nothing very memorable. Oh, one more thing. She bit one of them on the hand."

"Bit him, by God!" Keats beamed. "You didn't tell me that."

"I forgot."

"What'd he do?"

"He yelled."

"Bit him, by God!" Keats nodded and smiled to himself for a few moments, then turned and gave Citron a careful inspection.

"You married?"

"No."

"What d'you do for a living?"

"I'm a caretaker and a sometime writer."

"What kind of writer?"

"Travel articles."

"Pay anything?"

"Not much."

"Been to college?"

Citron nodded.

"Ever been in jail?"

"Once."

"How long?"

"Thirteen months."

"What for?"

"I was never quite sure."

"Where?"

"Africa."

"Shit, that don't count then." Keats again looked out the window, frowned at the urban clutter that lined Lincoln Boulevard, and turned, still frowning, to Citron. "I ain't gonna ask you if you've been beddin' Velveeta because I already know the answer to that, but I am gonna ask you this. What d'you think of her?"

"I think," Citron said slowly, "I think she's a bit . . . puzzled."

That seemed to satisfy Keats. He nodded as if confirming something and after a silence that lasted for nearly two blocks, said, "I'm rich. I mean, big rich."

"So I understand."

"Made it all off dope. Marijuana at first and then I went in early on coke, made a killing, and got out clean. You know what I'm in now?"

"No."

"Shoes. Automated, self-service, discount shoestores. I sat down and thought about what people gotta have, good times and bad. Well, I came up with shoes. Cheap imported shoes. I got a chain of stores going now, a dozen in Florida, five in Alabama, and we're moving into Mississippi and Louisiana next year. But, hell, you don't wanta hear about my shoestores."

"I can listen," Citron said.

"No, what you really wanta hear about is what I'm leadin' up to. And I'm gonna come right out with it. Velveeta, well, Velveeta's sort of pretty and halfway smart, even if she is six bricks short of a load, and four, five years back I set her up this irrevocable trust, so there's money there, but what I wanta know is if, for the next few weeks, you'd sort of be her fancy man."

Citron turned to stare at Keats, whose faded blue eyes had lost their squint. They were nearly round now and, Citron thought, almost honest. "Fancy man," he said. "Or do you mean keeper?"

Keats smiled. "Well, maybe a little of both."

16

WITH THE PLEASANT TASTE of the $32-plus-tip lunch
he had treated himself to in the elaborate Chinese restaurant on
Rodeo Drive still lingering in his mouth, Drew Meade used the
key Gladys Citron had given him to unlock the front door of
her house. Meade had lunched early and alone at straight up
noon. It was now only a little past one.

He did not go into the house cold. Meade wouldn't go into a
telephone booth cold. He had circled the block once on foot,
eyeing the cars parked at the curb and in the driveways. Most
seemed to be fairly expensive foreign makes—BMWs, Volvos,
and a sufficiency of Mercedeses. He also noticed the white Ford
van with the lettered sign that read "Cart's Custom Rug Clean-
ing" and below that the phone number to call and the address
on Santa Monica Boulevard. The van was parked four doors
down from Gladys Citron's house, and Meade made an automatic mental note of its license number. Using his own
mnemonic system, Meade could sometimes remember license
numbers for years and telephone numbers forever.

He pushed the door open, entered the small foyer, stopped
dead still, and listened. There was nothing to hear. He turned

back, closed the door, shot the deadbolt, and fastened the chain.

They were waiting for him when he entered the living room, the pair of them, their mouths open slightly for silent breathing, neither much more than thirty, if that, one with blue eyes, the other with brown. Both wore cheap tan cotton uniform-type jackets with their first names stitched in red thread above the breast pockets. The one with the blue eyes was John; the one with the brown eyes was Dick.

Meade stopped by the table with the Chinese lamp. "So how's the rug business?" he said, picked up the lamp, and threw it at Dick. While the lamp was still in the air, Meade launched himself at John. He feinted a crotch kick and when John turned his hip to it, Meade drove his left fist into John's lower abdomen, three inches below the belt. There was more muscle there than Meade had expected, but John nevertheless bent over, clutching himself and gasping. Meade had clenched his hands together to bring them down hard on John's bent neck when the gun muzzle was jammed into his ear and Dick's voice said, "Don't."

Meade spun, bringing his forearm up to knock away the gun, but it was no longer there. Dick was in a crouch now, more than a yard away, the gun held in both hands and aimed at Meade's chest just as somebody somewhere had taught him to aim it.

"Well, shit," Meade said, moved over and sat down in one of the two wing-back chairs in front of the fireplace, took out his Camels, and lit one with hands that shook only slightly.

John straightened up, still pressing both hands to his abdomen. "Moves pretty good for an old fart," he said.

"They said he might," Dick said.

"What're you supposed to be?" Meade said.

"What are we today?" Dick said, not taking his eyes from Meade or relaxing his aim. "I keep forgetting."

"We're the rug people today," John said. "Yesterday, or day

before yesterday maybe, we were Special Agent Tighe and Special Agent Yarn. I'm Yarn; he's Tighe."

Meade nodded thoughtfully. "The sweepers, huh? The ones they send out with the broom and the dustpan."

"Neateners, really," Tighe said.

"What happens to me?" Meade said.

"You?" Yarn said. "You're already dead. They wrote you up in the *New York Times*."

"So I heard."

"If you're already dead," Tighe said, "well, the worst has already happened, hasn't it?"

"Yeah. When you put it like that, I guess it has."

"You could just walk out the door and into a new life."

"Sounds good."

"Of course," Yarn said, "we've got to ask you a couple of questions first."

"I don't mind. Ask away."

"We noticed you talking to some people today—this morning," Tighe said.

"Yeah, now that you mention it, I guess I did."

"Who were they?"

"One guy said his name was Haere, Draper Haere, and the other one claimed to be Mitch Mitchell."

Yarn sighed and frowned. "See? We're already off to a bad start."

"You mean his name wasn't Mitchell?"

"No."

"Well, I'll be damned," Meade said.

"You know, maybe you'd better tell us something about yourself, Mr. Meade."

"Tell you about me?"

"Yes."

"Why?"

"Just to make sure we've got the right person," Tighe said.

"What I mean is, we don't want to wind up dealing with a ringer. You can understand that."

"Sure," Meade said. "How much do you want to know?"

"Just give us an outline," Tighe said.

"Well, I was born in Terre Haute, November nineteenth, 1919. My old man was in the AEF and he stayed on after the armistice and brought home a French bride. That's how I learned French—from her, my mother. When I got out of high school in 'thirty-seven, my old man got me a job with Western Union as an apprentice telegrapher. That's what he was. A telegrapher. Then I went in the army in late 'forty-one and because of my French and my trade, I wound up in the OSS in 'forty-two. This the kinda shit you want?"

"Exactly," Yarn said.

"After the war, I went to work for the telegraphers' union, first as an organizer and later as a business agent. That lasted until the Bureau got hold of me and I went to work for them." He paused.

"Undercover, right?" Tighe said.

"Right."

"You led quite a few lives for the Bureau, didn't you?"

"Four or five."

"Go on."

"Then I went to work for Air America. I was a scheduler."

"The spook line," Yarn said.

Meade nodded. "I did some pretty weird stuff for them here and there and they sent me over to Vientiane to do some more weird stuff. Flights into China, things like that."

"You didn't go into China, though, did you?"

"I flew in and out a couple of times—you know, turn-around."

"Dropped some people off, maybe?" Tighe said.

"Maybe."

"Then what?"

137

"Then I quit and went into business for myself."

"Where?"

"Hong Kong, Djakarta, Bangkok, places like that."

"Singapore?" Tighe asked.

"Yeah, sure. Singapore."

"Where you ran into our mutual friend?" Yarn said.

"Who?"

"Bobby Maneras."

"Oh, yeah. Him."

"Poor Bobby," Yarn said.

"Why poor?" Meade said.

"Not poor in the monetary sense," Tighe said, "but poor in the—what should I say? The temporal sense, I suppose. You know Boy Howdy's in Manila?"

"Yeah," Meade said, "I was in there a time or two."

"Well," Tighe said, "poor Bobby was in there having a drink or two or three, left, stepped off the curb, and got flattened by a great big truck. They say he was, well, you know, drunk. Poor Bobby."

It was then that Meade was sure he didn't have long to live. Five minutes maybe, he told himself, ten at the outside. He shook his head at the sad news about poor Bobby Maneras and said, "Mind if I have another smoke?"

"Go ahead," Yarn said.

Meade made his hands tremble on purpose this time as he lit one of his Camels with the box of matches he had taken from the Chinese restaurant. He waved the match out, turned, tossed it into the fireplace, and saw that the fireplace poker and tongs were just where he had remembered them. You'll never make it, he thought, turned back, smiled sadly, shook his head again, and said, "That's too bad about Bobby."

"What we want to know, Mr. Meade," Tighe said, "what we *have* to know, in fact, is how much of what Bobby told you, you told Draper Haere."

"Not much?" he said.

"How much?"

"A taste, that's all. You know, to get his attention."

"And did you?" Yarn said.

"Yeah, I guess so."

"What exactly did you tell him?"

"I told him they had a little war down there."

"Down there?" Tighe said. "You mean in Tucamondo?"

"I didn't tell him where."

"You're sure?"

"I'm sure. Hell, if I'd told him where, he could've gone down there and dug it up all by himself—or had Mitch or whatever his name is do it."

"Mitch," Tighe said. "I almost forgot Mitch." He paused. "You know what Mitch's real name is?"

"What?"

"Morgan Citron. You know, Citron—like the lady who owns this house."

"Aw, Christ," Meade said in a sad voice and turned to flick his cigarette ash into the fireplace. Instead, he threw away the cigarette itself, grabbed the poker, told himself he would never bring it off, and spun around only to find that Tighe now had a pillow from the sofa folded over what Meade thought of as the popgun, the .25 caliber Browning automatic. Not a chance, Meade decided as he rose quickly and brought the poker up anyway.

Tighe shot him twice in the chest. The shots of the small-caliber rounds were somewhat muffled by the pillow. Meade lowered the poker and stared down at the twin wounds in his chest. He realized with some surprise that he would never really have it made, and then consoled himself with the thought that he would never really grow old either. You can't grow old until you've got it made, he told himself, and you're not gonna do either.

He looked up at Tighe and Yarn, who were staring at him curiously, wondering when he was going to fall. "That goddamn

Gladys," Meade said, took a step backward, sat down in the wing-back chair, coughed once, breathed raggedly three more times, and died.

Seconds later Gladys Citron came into the living room from the hall, crossed to the wing-back chair, and stood staring down at the body of her quondam comrade-in-arms, infrequent lover, and occasional friend. Her left hand strayed up to the lapel of her suit where she fingered the Légion d'Honneur.

"They weren't very loud," she said. "The shots. I could just hear them in the bedroom with the door closed." She looked at Tighe and Yarn. "Did he say anything?"

"He claimed he just gave them a taste," Tighe said. "Haere and your son. He didn't know Morgan was your son, though. He's using the name Mitch Mitchell for some reason. Meade didn't believe that either, but he didn't know Morgan was your son until I told him."

"What did he say?" she asked. "When you told him."

"I think he said, 'Aw, shit.' "

" 'Aw, Christ,' " Yarn said.

"Anything else?"

" 'That goddamn Gladys,' " Tighe said. "That's the last thing he said."

She turned to look again at the dead man. "Poor old Meade," she said, crossed to the tray of bottles, and poured herself a glass of wine.

"Meade told him too much," Yarn said.

"Told who?" she said as she slowly raised the glass to her lips.

"Your son. And Haere, too."

Gladys Citron seemed to consider Yarn's assertion for several moments. Finally, she turned to look at Yarn, took another sip of her drink, and said, "Then I suppose we'll have to do something about that, won't we?"

17

THE MOST INTERESTING SIGHT B.S. Keats saw during the hour-long scenic drive up the California coast was the encampment of Cadillac People, which so intrigued him he had the driver turn around and go back for another look. The driver slowed the limousine as Keats stared fascinated at the collection of aging cars and campers and old school buses that were parked willy-nilly at the edge of the sea.

"What'd you say they call 'em?" he asked Citron.

"The Cadillac People."

"Not all of 'em have Cadillacs, though."

"They just call them that."

"What the hell do they do all day?"

"Listen to the radio and keep an eye on the ocean."

"None of 'em work?"

"Not anymore. They've more or less given up."

"How do they get by—on welfare?"

"No."

"What's gonna happen to 'em?"

"That's what they're waiting to find out," Citron said.

"You know what?" Keats said. "They make me kinda hungry. Any place to eat around here?"

"There's a place back at the county line. You like fish?"

"Sure."

"It's got good lobster and shrimp. You eat outside on picnic tables—with your hands mostly."

"Let's try it."

Citron rolled the divider down and told the driver where to go. After the divider was rolled back up, Keats gave Citron a long calculating look and said, "You given my proposition any thought yet?"

"About being a fancy man?"

"Maybe I shouldn't have called it that. About all I really want you to do is keep an eye on Velveeta. Take her to the picture show once in a while. Maybe to a museum. They got museums out here?"

"There's one just down the road," Citron said. "The Getty."

"Well, she likes things like that, so you could do those things and sort of look in on her, make sure she's eatin', listen to her jabber, maybe even take her to bed, if you all are of a mind to. What I reckon I'm really askin' you to do is be her best friend." Keats paused. "I'd make it worth your while."

Citron turned to examine the brown-faced man. The faded blue eyes had gone back into their round and almost honest shape. The expression was wholly ingenuous. Citron had seen such expressions before in places like Cicero and Marseilles and Montevideo. He had also learned to distrust them.

"Who were they, Mr. Keats?"

"Might as well call me B.S. Everybody else does."

"Who were they?"

"Those two fellas you run off? They were just hired hands, that's all. I still got me some enemies back home, Morgan. So after you called and told me about what happened, well, I made a couple of calls and now I got one less enemy than I used to."

Citron nodded slowly, as if the elimination of one's enemies was only to be commended. "So they won't be back?"

"No, sir, those two won't."

"What about others?"

"I'm workin' on that. Mendin' my fences, like the fella says."

"Why don't you just hire Velveeta a bodyguard?"

"She won't put up with it, that's why. I've tried, and her mama's tried, but she won't hear of it. So I gotta do it on the sly kind of, and you fit the bill." There was a long pause that lasted until Keats added, "Like I said, I'll make it worth your while."

"I'm not too interested in doing it for money."

Keats's eyes narrowed themselves back into their crafty squint. "But you're interested in something, right?"

Citron nodded.

"What?"

"Central America. You have any contacts there?"

"One or two maybe."

"I'm interested in finding out about a small secret war that broke out down there over cocaine and money. A great deal of money. I don't know where, though."

"A story, huh?"

Again, Citron nodded.

Keats made no attempt to keep the shrewdness out of his expression. "That's all you want—a story? You sure?"

"I'm sure."

"Well, shit, boy, get me to a phone after dinner and let's see what I can dig up."

The governor-elect put down his fork, picked up his wine-glass, drank, put the glass down, and said, "One hundred thousand dollars." His tone was reverent, as it always was when discussing any sum over $500.

"Cash," Draper Haere said.

"We haven't got it," Baldwin Veatch said.

"Or any way to get it," said his wife.

Louise Veatch and her husband were having lunch near their pool in the rear of the white two-story house with the sharp angles and too much glass brick that had been built by a Mexican movie actress in 1938. It was the last house on a dead-end street just off the Santa Monica Canyon. It was built on two acres of land and had a seldom-used tennis court to go with the pool.

Baldwin Veatch had bought the house on impulse in 1973 at a distressed price. Its value had subsequently soared, and the house was now the governor-elect's principal investment, indeed his only one other than the $5,000 he had in an E.F. Hutton money market fund. In the Veatches' joint checking account there was $1,452.26. Because politics was the only profession he had ever followed, Veatch was a relatively poor man. He had found his modest circumstances useful at the polls, if inconvenient at the end of the month when the bills came due. However, Veatch long ago had found a partial solution. Whenever he needed money, he asked Draper Haere to find him some. Haere always did.

Lunch that warm November day had been served by the Mexican maid. It consisted of hot dogs, canned baked beans, and a green salad. To drink there was an inexpensive, slightly acid red wine from the Napa Valley. The Veatches set what Draper Haere always thought of as a mean table, and he had declined their invitation to join them, citing his usual no-lunch rule.

"We don't need the entire one hundred thousand, Baldy," Haere said. "All we need is fifty, and I can get that."

"Where?" Louise Veatch asked.

"I don't want to know," her husband said.

"This time, darling," she said, "I think you'd better. Right, Draper?"

"It's the pig-fucker money," Haere said.

The governor-elect tightened his usually amiable mouth into a line of almost petulant disapproval. "I thought we'd agreed never to touch that except in extreme emergency."

"What do you call this?" Haere said.

The pig-fucker money was $50,000 in cash that Haere kept for Veatch in a safety deposit box. It was all in twenties and fifties—mostly fifties—and was to be used only for counter-attack against last-minute smears. It was untraceable, totally anonymous money and, if necessary, could be used to suborn and corrupt. It had lain unused for almost six years now. The name it bore stemmed from Draper Haere's only meeting with Lyndon Johnson back in 1970 when the former President had asked Haere about a close Congressional race in which Haere's candidate seemed to be trailing badly. Haere confessed that things did indeed look bleak and invited the sage's counsel. "Hell, Draper, it's simple," the former President had said. "Just call him a pig fucker and let him deny it." Haere's candidate followed the advice and lost by less than five hundred votes.

"I just don't like it," the governor-elect said. "I don't like it at all."

"We're only buying information," Louise Veatch said. "It's research, actually." She looked at Haere. "Although I don't understand how you're going to buy for fifty thousand what's advertised for a hundred."

"I'm cheap," Haere said. "I told Meade I'd only buy it in twenty-five-thousand-dollar chunks. He gives us the essential basic stuff for the first fifty and the rest is just details that Citron can dig up at five hundred a week."

"How's Citron working out?" Veatch said.

"Good. Very good. He's very quick, very bright."

Veatch looked at his wife. "Well?"

Again, they exchanged their silent confidences. Veatch turned back to Haere. "Okay. Do it. Just remember one item.

This whole thing is apparently a cover-up. If they find out we're trying to lift the lid off, they'll try to stop us. You understand that, don't you, Draper?"

"Whether we go ahead or not depends on just one thing, Baldy," Haere said.

"What?"

"How badly you want the nomination."

Veatch threw his napkin down on the table. "I want it, all right," he said. "I want it damned bad." He stood up. "It all seemed so simple at first."

"It's never simple," Haere said.

Veatch looked at his watch. "I've got a meeting with the transition committee." He looked at Haere. "Did you walk or drive?"

"I walked."

"You want a ride?"

"I need the walk."

"When will you be back?" Louise Veatch asked her husband.

"I don't know. Late. Around six, six-thirty." He again looked at Haere. "You might as well have some more coffee. Keep Louise company. She might think of something I forgot to ask."

"All right," Haere said. "I will."

The governor-elect nodded as if he had said all he had to say, leaned down, kissed his wife on the cheek, turned to leave, but turned back.

"Let me know what happens," he said.

Haere nodded. He and Louise Veatch watched the governor-elect turn, cross the patio, and enter the house. When he was inside, Louise Veatch filled Haere's coffee cup. He thanked her and said, "Let's go to bed."

"Yes," Louise Veatch said. "Let's."

B.S. Keats spoke his terrible Spanish with no trace of self-consciousness. He spoke it loudly, more or less bawling it into the telephone without regard for accent or grammar. He ignored both past and future tenses, and spoke only in the present. When his grasp for a Spanish word failed, he substituted an English one, sometimes tacking on an "o" or an "a" for harmony. He seemed to have absolutely no difficulty in making himself understood.

The calls, four of them, were all long-distance, international long-distance, and had been placed to numbers that B.S. Keats read into the phone from a small notebook. Two calls had gone to Bogotá, one to Costa Rica, and one to Panama. No names were mentioned, because Keats made all the calls station-to-station and charged them to his phone-company credit card.

The calls were made from Citron's telephone and they had not begun until 3:30 P.M. When the limousine pulled up outside the apartment building, Keats had made Citron go in first to make sure Velveeta Keats was nowhere around. "I just don't wanta see her, Morgan," he had said. "That may be hard to understand, but that's just the way it is."

When the last long-distance call was completed, Keats hung up the phone and turned to Citron. "Tucamondo," he said. "Got a fix on that in your head?"

Citron nodded.

"Well, that's where it happened—just outside the capital."

"Ciudad Tucamondo."

"Right."

"*Mucha muerte, mucho dinero,*" Keats said. "That means a lot of death, a lot of money. That's all they knew—or all they'd tell me, anyway."

"Did they say when it happened?"

"Five or six months back, give or take a week either way, but you know how the beaners are when it comes to time."

Keats rose, glanced at his watch, stuck his left hand down into his pants pocket, and brought out a thick roll of bills. Citron saw that they were hundreds. Keats peeled at least a

147

dozen of the bills from the roll without counting them. He offered the money to Citron. "It's gonna cost something to be Velveeta's best friend."

Citron stared at the proffered money and wondered where greed had gone. Maybe that's what the spur of poverty really does, he thought. It makes you indifferent instead of ambitious. Still staring at the money, he shook his head and said, "No, thanks."

"You sure?"

"Yes."

Keats glanced around the shabby studio apartment, shook his head as though unaccustomed to dealing with fools, and put the money back in his pocket. "You'll look in on her, like we talked about?"

"I'll look in on her."

"My plane's at six."

"You'd better go then. Do you want me to tell Velveeta hello?"

B.S. Keats thought about it and his faded blue eyes grew round and almost innocent. "Well," he said finally, "I don't reckon that'd do any harm, would it?"

18

THE MEXICAN MAID, a confidante and co-conspirator of Louise Veatch's, awoke the sleeping couple at 5:15 P.M. By 5:30, Draper Haere was dressed and out of the house and walking his long walk back to his enormous room in Venice. It was a walk of a bit less than four miles, and Haere made it in just under sixty minutes. The sun had set by the time he left Louise Veatch, and it had been dark for almost an hour when he inserted his key into the Haere Building's side entrance. Behind him, a car door slammed. Haere turned and saw Morgan Citron leave his Toyota and start walking toward him. "I've been waiting for you," Citron said as he drew near.

"I was in a meeting," Haere said, unlocked the door, pushed it open, and gestured for Citron to precede him up the stairs. At the landing, Haere used another key to unlock the door that led into the room. He went in first, found the switch, and turned on a lamp. When he saw Drew Meade propped up in the Huey Long chair, he said, "Shit."

"Is he dead?" Citron said from behind Haere. "He sure as hell looks dead."

"Hey, Meade," Haere said, raising his voice slightly. When

there was no answer, Haere said, "He's dead. They even left the rug."

Citron looked. A cheap eight-by-ten blue rug lay neatly rolled up by the Huey Long chair. Hubert, the cat, was on the rug, using it as a scratching post. When he was through scratching, he yawned.

"Not much of a watchdog, that cat," Citron said.

"He has no enemies," Haere said, turned back, closed the door, and moved slowly and cautiously over to the dead Drew Meade. Citron moved with him.

"I don't think your locks bothered them any," Citron said.

"Not much," Haere agreed and took a ballpoint pen from his vest pocket. He used the pen to move the lapel of Meade's jacket to one side. The two bullet holes made in the white shirt by the .25 caliber rounds were separated by less than an inch. A bloodstain, about the size of a saucer, had spread over the shirtfront.

"He didn't bleed a lot, which means he died fast," Haere said.

"There's no blood on the chair either, and what's on his shirt seems dry, so I'd say he's been dead awhile, and that's about the extent of my forensic knowledge."

"Mine, too," Haere said as he bent over and almost absently picked up the cat, who cried with delight in its loud half-Siamese voice. Stroking the cat, Haere circled the dead Meade, stepping over the rolled-up rug. "Ever search a dead body?" he asked Citron.

"Shouldn't we let the cops do that?"

"What cops?" Haere said as he and the cat started circling Meade once more.

"I see. No cops."

"He's already dead and buried in Singapore. We'll just prop him up against a lamppost somewhere, maybe over in Culver City. Dead bodies don't bother them much over there. See what he's got in his pockets."

"Me?"

"I've got to feed the cat."

Still carrying Hubert, Haere headed for the kitchen area, took down a can of 9-Lives from a shelf, and sliced off its top with his electric can opener. While Haere fed Hubert, Citron knelt by the side of the Huey Long chair and studied the dead man.

Drew Meade's eyes were still open and, for some reason, seemed focused on something off to the right. Despite himself, Citron glanced over his shoulder, but there was nothing to see but a wall of books. He looks as if he's reading the titles, Citron thought, and doesn't see much that interests him. If there was an expression on Meade's dead face, it was one of disappointment mingled with disdain. The mouth was slightly open in the beginning of what seemed to be a sneer. The head was tilted back, leaning against the large chair's padded rest. The lifeless hands lay palm up in the lap in a supplicant's helpless position that somehow Citron knew they had never once assumed in life. The big feet were firmly planted on the floor. Meade smelled of death, which meant that he smelled of urine and feces.

Citron sighed and reached into the inside breast pocket of Meade's jacket just as Haere rejoined him. He found a U.S. passport and handed it to Haere. In the outside jacket pockets he found a pack of Camels and a box of matches that bore the name of a Chinese restaurant. He passed both up to Haere. There was nothing in the shirt pocket or in the pants hip pockets. In a pants side pocket, the one on the right, there was a small roll of bills, which he also handed up to Haere. The other side pocket produced seventy-four cents in change. Citron put the change back and studied Meade for several moments, then lifted up the pants legs and rolled down the short black socks. There was nothing concealed beneath them, only eggshell-white, surprisingly thin ankles. Citron rose.

"That's it," he said.

"He had sixty-seven dollars and a passport made out to

someone called Donald B. Millrun. Has he got a watch?"

Citron looked. "Yes."

"Take it."

Citron removed the watch, an old self-winding stainless-steel Omega Seamaster. He gave it to Haere. "Robbery?" he asked.

"Why not?" Haere said. "It'll make the cops happy."

"What now?"

"Well, now we roll him back up in the rug, put him in your car, and dump him over in Culver City. Somewhere just off the freeway, I think."

"My car?"

"Sure."

"Why not yours?"

"I can't remember where I parked mine."

"Well, Christ," Citron said, knelt again, and rolled out the rug. He looked up at Haere. "What d'you want? The head or the legs?"

Haere frowned. "Did you look in the watch pocket? A New York cop I once knew told me some guys hide things in their watch pockets. Older guys especially. He said it was one of the first places he always looked."

"I didn't look there."

"Well, why don't you?"

"What do you expect to find—a folded-up thousand-dollar bill with the Swiss account number on it?"

"Just look, will you?"

Citron dug a forefinger down into the small watch pocket, felt something, and used thumb and forefinger to lift it out. It was a business card folded into a small square. Citron unfolded the card. On its front was printed: "Drew Meade, Investment Counselor." There was no address or phone number. On the back was written in pencil, "D. Haere," and then Haere's phone number. In ballpoint ink was written, "B. Maneras," and after that something illegible. Citron handed the card to Haere.

Haere read the investment-counselor side and then turned it over. "Well, Haere we know," he said. "Who's B. Maneras?"

"Maybe he's the one they want us to find out about."

"You think it was planted?"

Citron shrugged. "If we hadn't found it, you would've been talking to the cops."

Haere thought about that and then shook his head. "I can't decide whether it was planted or not." He turned to examine Meade thoughtfully, then turned back to Citron. "What d'you think we should do about B. Maneras?"

"We can stop where we are and call the cops—or I can find out who Maneras is, which I don't think is going to be too hard. You call it."

Instead of replying, Haere once more turned back to the dead Drew Meade and again seemed to study him thoughtfully. After fifteen seconds went by, Citron said, "Well?"

"I'll take the feet," Haere said.

They had no trouble getting Drew Meade down the stairs, but they did experience some difficulty in folding him into the rear of Citron's 1969 Toyota sedan. Either Meade or the rug wouldn't fold. They finally managed to fit him in by lowering the head end of the rug down onto the floor and letting the feet end stick up in the air, pointing at the rear window.

Haere slammed the rear door shut. "Well, that should do it," he said, taking a step backward to see how it all looked.

"You're coming, aren't you?" Citron said.

"Did you think I wouldn't?"

"It crossed my mind."

"Mine, too," Haere said as he opened the curbside front door and got in.

In Culver City they found an industrial side street with a vacant lot that contained six junked cars, and there they dumped Drew Meade. They left him, still wrapped in his cheap blue rug, lying between the remains of a 1970 Volvo and a 1973 Ford Fairlane.

Back on the Santa Monica freeway, Draper Haere said he could use a drink, and they decided on a bar in Venice they both knew, the Mainsail, a place that catered to serious drinkers.

After the waitress brought Haere his double Scotch on the rocks and Citron his double vodka, also on the rocks, they both drank and then waited for the other to begin. Finally, Haere lit one of his occasional cigarettes and said, "You've got something else, haven't you? That's why you were outside waiting."

"A place name. Tucamondo."

Haere nodded as he drew a mental map and pinpointed Tucamondo. "Is that where it happened—the small secret war Meade was going to tell us about?"

"Maybe."

Haere had some more of his Scotch. "How'd you find out—if you don't mind my asking?"

"There's a guy from Miami called B.S. Keats. The B.S. stands for Byron Shelley. He's got a remittance-woman daughter who he wants me to baby-sit. Mr. Keats was once very active in the cocaine trade. He wanted to pay me to baby-sit his daughter, who's a touch fey. I agreed, but instead of money, I asked him to make a few phone calls. He did and came up with Tucamondo."

"Just like that?"

Citron nodded.

Haere sighed and said, "I think you'd better tell me about Mr. Keats and his daughter."

"Yes," Citron said. "I think I'd better."

They were on their second drink, singles this time, when Citron finished his report. The report was delivered to an impressed Haere in short paragraphs, none more than two sentences long. Citron had spoken in a flat, almost uninflected voice, pausing at the end of each sentence, pausing even longer before a new paragraph began, and spelling out each name as if he thought Haere might want to write it down. The most important facts were grouped together first, and the rest were recited in their descending order of interest and importance. He's calling in a story, Haere marveled, as Citron ended his report with a precise accounting of how much of Haere's money he had spent thus far.

Draper Haere was silent for almost a minute as he digested what he had been told. "I rather liked the two Haitians," he said. "The two bodyguards." He paused. "And Keats, too. B.S. Keats. B for Byron, S for Shelley. I liked him, too. And all it took him was a couple of phone calls."

"Four actually."

"Four."

There was another silence. Haere finished his second drink and said, "That's it, then?"

"Not quite."

Haere nodded slowly. "I sort of expected there'd be something else. A kicker."

"Velveeta Keats."

"Velveeta. I like her, too. The name, I mean."

"She was once married to someone called Maneras."

"R. Maneras, maybe?"

"J. Maneras. J for Jimmy—or Jaime."

"Maneras. That's a pretty common name, isn't it?"

"About like, oh, say, Hansen or Nichols."

"Still a pretty common name."

"Not if you find it written on a card that's folded up and stuck down inside some dead man's watch pocket just a couple of hours after you agree to baby-sit a lady who was once married to somebody called Maneras. I'd say that makes it a rather unusual name."

Haere rattled the ice in his empty drink. "So where are we?"

"I think we're being pointed in a certain direction, don't you?"

"The right direction?"

"I don't know."

Haere rattled his ice again. "Velveeta Keats," he said. "It's a pretty name, if you forget about the cheese."

"I thought I'd take her to dinner tonight."

"Someplace nice."

"Yes."

"Buy her some wine."

"She likes wine."

"Maneras," Haere said. "I wonder who B. Maneras is."

"I'll try to find out."

"If you do, call me."

"No matter how late?"

"Anytime," Haere said.

19

AT 7:45 THAT NIGHT the two men who sometimes called themselves Yarn and Tighe parked their Oldsmobile 88 behind the Mercedes sedan in Gladys Citron's driveway. John D. Yarn was behind the wheel, Richard Tighe beside him. They examined the house briefly. A light was on in the living room. The porch light had also been turned on.

Without speaking, they got out of the car and walked through the iron gate and up the curving cement walk to the front door. Tighe rang the bell. The door was opened almost immediately by Gladys Citron. Nothing was said. The two men went inside, through the small foyer, and into the living room. Gladys Citron followed them.

Tighe headed for the tray that held the bottles and glasses. He spoke over his shoulder to Yarn. "What d'you want, Scotch?"

"Scotch."

"Gladys?"

"Nothing," she said.

Tighe mixed the two drinks, turned, and handed one to Yarn. Gladys Citron crossed to the wing-back chairs, hesitated, then sat down in the one where Drew Meade had died. She was wearing a long dressy robe of dark-blue silk. It went nicely with her hair. She leaned her head back against the chair, closed her eyes, and said, "Well?"

Tighe sat down in the chair opposite her and took a swallow of his drink. Yarn continued to stand, sipped some of his Scotch, and said, "I like that, Gladys. The way you plopped down in old Drew's chair."

"It's my chair," she said, her eyes still closed. "He merely died in it."

"Well, it went about like we thought it would," Tighe said. "They dumped him over in Culver City."

"And?"

"They found the card."

"You're sure?" she said.

"It was gone, anyway."

"I wonder which one," Tighe said.

Yarn looked at him. "Which one what?"

"Found it."

"Haere. I'd say Haere."

"Why?"

"I don't know," Yarn said. "Maybe just because he's foxier."

Gladys Citron opened her eyes. "I won't have him hurt."

Tighe smiled at her. "You should've thought of that before, Gladys."

"He's still my son. They won't have to hurt him."

"We'll tell them that, won't we?" Tighe said to Yarn.

Yarn grinned and nodded. "Maybe we can hang a sign around his neck. 'Handle with Care.' Something like that."

Gladys Citron leaned forward in her chair. When she spoke, her tone was surprisingly soft, but her stare was hard and un-wavering. "I must not be making myself clear."

Tighe finished his drink. "Sure you are, Gladys. You're play-ing Mommy—maybe forty years late, but you're playing it pretty well. You have to understand something, though. If it comes to choosing between your son and us, and I'm talking about *all* of us, then a hard choice will have to be made. I mean, if it comes to us or him, who do we choose?"

Gladys Citron leaned back in the chair and again closed her eyes. "I've got a migraine," she said. "Why don't you two run out and play somewhere."

"Who, Gladys?" Yarn said.

"It needn't come to that," she said, her eyes still closed.

"But if it does?"

She opened her eyes and stared up at the ceiling. "He was a very pretty baby. One of the prettiest I've ever seen. But then I was never really very much of a mother."

"He was never much of a son either, was he?" Yarn said.

It was several moments before Gladys Citron answered, her gaze still fixed on the ceiling. "No," she said, "not much."

They drove to the restaurant in Santa Monica in Velveeta Keats's dusty yellow Porsche, a 911 model that had been given to her on her thirtieth birthday.

"I just went out to get the mail that day," she told Morgan Citron, "and there the keys were with a little note in the mailbox that said, 'Happy Birthday, honey—Love, Mama,' but of course it was Papa that went out and bought it and all."

She was not a good driver. At the corner of the Pacific Coast Highway and Topanga Canyon she ran through a red light and just missed a pickup truck that had two large brown dogs in its bed. The dogs barked at her as she barely scraped by on the right. Citron closed his eyes automatically and opened them only when he was sure the danger had passed. "When was this?" he said.

"My birthday? Last August. August ninth. I turned thirty. How'd you feel when you turned thirty?"

"I'm not sure," he said. "I think it was just another day."

"How about forty?"

"Forty. Well, forty wasn't so hot."

"Where were you?"

"In jail. In Africa."

"What'd you do?"

"On my fortieth birthday?"

"Uh-huh."

"I think I cried," he said. "In fact, I'm pretty sure I did."

"Did you do that much? Cry, I mean."

"No," Citron said. "Only that once."

They drove in silence for nearly a minute until she broke it with a question. "Did he say anything about me?"

"Your father?"

Velveeta Keats nodded as she stared straight ahead, her jaw clenched, her hands wrapped tightly around the wheel. Her sudden tension was almost palpable, and Citron at first thought it might be because she feared the car, but then he realized she wasn't a good enough driver to be afraid of the car. His answer was really what she feared. He answered carefully.

"We talked about you quite a lot, your father and I."

"He tell you I made all that up about me and Cash, you know, going to bed together?"

"He said your brother died when you were seven and he was, I think, nine."

"My old man," she said slowly, choosing each word with care, "is a fucking liar."

"I see."

"Jimmy—I told you about him—he was my husband?"

"Right. Maneras, wasn't it? Jaime Maneras, the one whose family used to own all the milk in Cuba."

Nodding again, she said, "Well, it was just like I told you. Jimmy caught us in bed and shot Cash dead. With a pistol. Then Papa killed Jimmy, or had him killed, I reckon, and they shipped me off out here to be a widow woman."

"When was all this?" Citron said. "I don't think you said."

"Last spring. June. The first part of June."

"Did you ever know anyone else called Maneras whose first name started with an R?"

She gave her head a small hard shake. "The only other Maneras I ever knew was Jimmy's brother, Bobby."

"Roberto, maybe?"

She took her eyes off the road to look at him. "Yeah, that would be his real name, wouldn't it? But nobody I ever knew called him that. Everybody always calls him Bobby."

"What did Bobby do?"

"He did coke with Jimmy and Papa. I told you about all that, didn't I?"

"Not about Bobby."

"He's older'n Jimmy was. Five, maybe six years older."

"Where is he now?"

"In Miami, I reckon. At least, he was the last I heard. Why?"

"Somebody mentioned his name to me."

"Papa?"

"No, not him."

"Did he, Papa, I mean, did he, well, say anything else about me—anything at all?"

"He said for me to tell you hello," Citron paused only briefly before deciding to embellish the father's sketchy greeting to his exiled daughter. "And to give you his love."

Again, Velveeta turned to stare at him, disbelief on her face and in her tone. "He really say that?"

"Watch the road," Citron said, and added, "He really did."

They had dinner in the front parlor at Vickie's, which was the name of an expensive restaurant on the south edge of Santa Monica. The menu claimed, in a small italic note, that Vickie's was named for the Victorian mansion in which it was housed, a sixteen-room structure built in 1910 and painstakingly moved in 1977 from Boyle Heights in East Los Angeles to its present location, where it had been, according to the note, "lovingly restored."

Velveeta Keats read all this to Citron as they waited for the waiter to return and take their order.

"If it was built in 1910," she said, "then it really couldn't be Victorian, could it? She died before that, didn't she? Queen Victoria, I mean."

"1901, I think."

"Then it's Edwardian, isn't it? And instead of Vickie's they oughta be calling it Eddie's."

Velveeta Keats's small attempt at humor, the first that Citron could recall, transformed her. She smiled broadly and her eyes half closed into arcs through which something merry slyly peeped. She even laughed, although it was really no more than a chuckle that sounded seldom used, but not at all rusty. Gone was the somber poor-thing look, as Citron thought of it, and in its place appeared a look of near radiance that was not too far from beauty.

Still smiling, she looked at him and said, "You know what I used to do a lot? I used to giggle a lot."

He smiled back. "You should take it up again."

Her smile went away, but slowly, as she picked up the menu again and studied it. "Maybe I will," she said, looked up, smiled again, and asked, "Would it be okay if I had the sole?"

The sole proved to be excellent, as did Citron's steak, and between them they finished off a bottle and a half of wine. When the coffee came, she declined a brandy and, bare tanned elbows on the table, leaned toward Citron. The wine, or perhaps the evening, had given her face a higher color that was more glow than flush. Her eyes also shined with something, either pleasure or excitement or possibly anticipation. Citron felt it might even be all three.

"Can I talk to you about something?" she said. "Something I maybe should've talked to you about before?"

"Sure."

"It's about last night when you came with the flowers and those two men were there." She paused. "Can I talk to you about that?"

"I don't see why not—if you want to."

"Well, they came up over the balcony from the beach and in through the sliding doors. They had those wet suits on and their masks and they had the gun, of course. Well, they didn't say anything."

"Nothing?"

"Not to me—not a word. One of them just pointed the gun at me and the other one, he just kept looking at his watch like, well, you know, like he was waiting for somebody."

"Then I knocked."

She nodded. "Then you knocked and came in and threw the flowers at them. They could've shot you."

"I know."

"But they didn't. All they did was leave. Then I got real scared and you were so great and everything, and I just never said anything about them just—you know—waiting for you. I reckon I should've, shouldn't I I—said something?"

Citron smiled. "I don't know," he said. "Maybe. But then again, maybe not."

"Well, I've said something now. Does that make it all right?"

"That makes it perfect," Citron lied, trying to determine what it was that caused the cold prickling on the back of his neck. Apprehension? he wondered. Dread? And then he realized it was neither. It was something far simpler, far more elemental, and so familiar that Citron almost said hello. It was fear.

20

IT HAD TAKEN TWO MEN from Bekins Moving and Storage to carry the thing up the stairs and into Draper Haere's enormous room. The men, irritated because they had to work so late, were gone now, mollified by the twin $20 bills that had been thrust into their hands by the white-haired man in the $800 suit who watched, grinning broadly, as Draper Haere slowly circled the seven-foot-tall hatrack.

It was made from black cherry with two deep dishlike cast-iron weights at the bottom where the tips of wet umbrellas could be left to drain. Two beveled arms reached out and curved in on themselves. The curved arms were there to embrace the umbrellas. The main support, all scalloped and nicely carved, held an oval mirror. Surrounding the mirror were six protruding twisted steel pegs that ended in china knobs. On these, coats and hats could be hung. It was an imposing, even dominating piece of furniture, completely ugly, and Draper Haere found it magnificent.

Haere circled the hatrack two more times and then turned to the white-haired man. "Where'd you say you found it?" he asked.

"Out in Alexandria. I was just poking around one Saturday afternoon and there it was, all by itself, way at the back."

"Did you recognize it?"

"Draper, I can't say I did. But I swear it looked familiar. You know, I was out to his place a time or two back when I was just a kid, no more'n twenty-six, twenty-seven, so I asked about it and when they said it'd belonged to John L., well, I thought of you, dickered a bit, and bought it." The white-haired man reached out and touched one of the knobbed pegs. "On this peg hung the hat that sat on the head of John L. Lewis. Of course, old John L. wasn't exactly a politician in the sense that he ever ran for public office. But he was something."

"He'll do," Haere said softly, using his coat sleeve to give one of the curving arms a quick brush. "He'll do fine."

The white-haired man had arrived unannounced and unexpected at 7:45 while Haere was watching MacNeil-Lehrer, which he did religiously despite having privately nicknamed the pair, not unkindly, the dull boys. After the white-haired man rang the buzzer, Haere asked who it was over the intercom.

"It's me, Draper. Or more properly, it is I, Dave Slipper, and I've got a pair of fine lads down here with me who're going to tote something up the stairs, if you'll just ring the buzzer."

Haere rang the unlocking buzzer and then went out onto the small landing and watched with surprise as the two men from Bekins lugged the hatrack up the stairs and into the room, supervised by David Slipper.

The white-haired man was then seventy-one years old and had first arrived in Washington in 1935 after graduation from Swarthmore with an additional year of postgraduate study at the London School of Economics. He had been, at various times, a New Deal White House aide, or to hear him tell it, "Harry Hopkins's office boy"; a spy of sorts for the wartime Office of Strategic Services; a syndicated columnist (121 daily newspapers); a biographer of the iron-willed Speaker of the

House of Representatives, Thomas Brackett (Czar) Reed; an Assistant Secretary of Agriculture (six months); a deputy Undersecretary of the Interior (ninety days); ambassador to Chad (one year, "the longest year of my life," he later said); and for the past fifteen years a political fixer and consultant who charged outrageous fees for his sensible, hardheaded advice.

Many in Washington considered David Slipper to be the village wise man. He dwelt in a small mews house behind the Supreme Court, the same house he had lived in off and on since 1936. Joe McCarthy had once been a neighbor. A man of infinite grace and Southern charm, although some despised his elegance, Slipper still retained a trace of a Memphis accent that came and went depending on the grimness of the situation. For when they needed to send the bad news, they often sent it by David Slipper. And as one party wheelhorse in Boston had once told Haere, "When old Dave cuts your throat, Draper, you don't smell no fuckin' magnolias."

Haere took another admiring walk around the hatrack. "How the hell'd you ever get it out here?"

Slipper shrugged. "Oxy was deadheading one of its 727s back out, so I made a couple of calls and bummed a ride." Oxy, of course, was Occidental Petroleum.

"Just to see me?"

"Among other things. Have you dined?"

"Not yet."

"Got any eggs?"

"Sure."

"Then I'll just whomp us up an omelette."

The omelette was perfect, as was the salad that Slipper created out of a head of rather dubious iceberg lettuce, garlic, and some hot bacon grease. They ate at the scarred library table in the dining area and shared a bottle of wine. The table had once graced the study of Rep. Vito Marcantonio (D., N.Y.), or so it was claimed by the Brooklyn dealer who had sold it to Haere.

Slipper put down his fork, patted his lips with a paper napkin, and said, "So. How's the Candidate?"

"Veatch is fine."

"And the lovely Louise?"

"Great."

Slipper produced a thin silver cigarette case that was almost the size of a Number 10 envelope. He offered it to Haere, who shook his head. Slipper selected a pale-brown cigarette and lit it with a gold Ronson that Haere knew to be forty years old. Slipper inhaled, blew out the smoke, and smiled. "I didn't see you at Jack's funeral," he said, "but then you don't go to funerals, do you?"

"No," Haere said. "I don't."

"It was a nice do, a fine crowd. The Unitarian preacher mentioned God once—in passing, of course—and Maureen was awful, but then Maureen always is, isn't she?"

"I talked to her on the phone. She was a bit put out at having been turned into a widow."

"Stick to your rule, Draper, and keep away from funerals. They're simply a reminder of mortality, and, God knows, at my age, I don't need any reminders. But I go, I go, and the amazing thing is, they're all growing younger—the departed, I mean. What was Jack? Sixty or thereabouts."

"Around in there."

"When I was young, sixty was ancient. Now it's what—middling middle age? Roosevelt, for example. Only sixty-three when he died. Almost a young man by today's standards. But old then. Old and tired and used up." He shook his head sadly. "The war, I suppose." His moment of mourning over, Slipper looked at Haere again. "Jack was in the war, wasn't he?"

"Navy pilot."

Slipper nodded, as if remembering. "What was it, hit-and-run? You were with him, Draper. What d'you think—really?"

Haere sighed, produced his own cigarettes, and lit one. "Slippery, when you come on like that, my ribs get all tensed up waiting for the blade to slip between them. Now, I want to thank you for the John L. hatrack. It's a fine addition, and I really appreciate it. And you make just one hell of an omelette. But deliver it, will you? The message. Whatever it is."

Slipper smiled. "Do you have a drop of brandy by any chance?"

"Martel."

"Why don't we have a drop and some coffee? That be too much bother?"

As Haere poured coffee from the Bunn Pour-omatic and measured out two brandies, Slipper's eyes wandered over the room. "Remarkable place, Draper. It must be unique. Do you still have that wicked cat?"

"He's around," Haere said and set the coffee cups on the table.

"Hubert, right?"

"Hubert," Haere agreed, served the two small brandy snifters, and resumed his seat.

"How was New York?" Slipper said. "I'm curious."

"He couldn't make up his mind, so I saw his mother. She told me to forget it."

"Remarkable woman," Slipper said. "She and I had a small thing going once. My Lord, it must have been back in the late forties, around in there. We planned a tryst, an assignation, in Hershey, Pennsylvania, of all places. I showed, of course; she didn't." He sniffed deeply. "I can still remember the smell of all that chocolate." He sighed. "Well, that's one down, isn't it?"

"That's what I told Veatch."

"What d'you really think his chances are?"

"In 'eighty-four? Zero."

"I'm, well . . . I'm not so sure," Slipper said carefully. "His name keeps cropping up here and there in some rather interesting places. After all, California will have twenty percent of the delegate strength. That's a sound base. He's got time—two years. Money should be no problem, right? I mean, hell, Draper, you can take care of that. And, my stars, he is presentable, if a trifle glib for my taste, but they're all that way nowadays. Glib, I mean. They have to be. A mumbler, a hemmer and hawer, just won't do. Not on television. The only thing is . . ." Slipper let his sentence fade away.

Haere didn't ask him what the only thing was. Instead, he let the silence grow. Hubert wandered over, yowled, and jumped up on the table. Haere scratched his ears and said, "Who sent you, Slippery?"

Slipper sipped his brandy. "You know, for a fact, it's really difficult to say."

"Who?" Haere asked again.

"Wilde, Harrington and Litz," Slipper said, giving the names of the founders of the Washington–New York–Paris law firm, only one of them still alive, a mock-sonorous intonation. Among Wilde, Harrington and Litz's senior partners were six former U.S. Senators, three former cabinet members, and a failed Presidential nominee.

Slipper sighed. "It was actually old Gene Litz himself, eighty-seven if he's a day. He dropped by my place cold at eight A.M. No warning. I think it must have taken us thirty minutes to get him out of that fool Packard he's still driven around in and then into my place. Shuffle. Shuffle. Shuffle. That's the body. But the mind. Ah, that mind. He was born in 'ninety-five, Draper, and he hasn't forgotten one meal he ever ate, one crap he ever took, one person he ever met, or one word he ever read. And yet I must confess he remains the world's greatest bore. All fact and no charm. No charm at all. You ever meet him?"

"No."

"I'll try to give you the flavor. He comes into my house, looks around, nods, and says by way of greeting, 'Still live in the alley, I see.' Well, the chauffeur and I finally get him lowered into a chair. He looks up at the chauffeur and says one word:

'Out.' The chauffeur leaves. Old Gene looks at me and says, 'I'll have a toddy with one spoonful of sugar. I want the water just off the boil.'

"Well, I fix his toddy and he takes a sip. Then he says, 'There is a serious problem that must be solved. You are authorized to proceed to California. There you will confer with the governor-elect. Know him?' I said I did. 'Thought so,' he says. 'Knew so, in fact. You will inform young Veatch that if he entertains any hopes at all of securing the party's nomination in either 'eighty-four or 'eighty-eight, he will immediately abandon his research into the circumstances surrounding the death of John T. Replogle. Is that clear?' "

"What'd you say?" Haere asked.

"I asked him who his client was and he comes back with one of his Delphic answers. 'The nation,' he says. 'Mark you, not this administration. I care not a fig for this administration. Third-rate people. Madmen, knaves and actors. But we will not see this nation crippled.' So I ask, 'Who is we?' His answer is another question: 'You knew Replogle, of course?' I told him I'd just returned from his funeral. Well, he stares at me with those eyes of his that'll still freeze marrow and says, 'Those who destroyed him, we will destroy. Tell young Veatch that, and also that other young man out there, Haere, the one whose father was a radical. Tell them it will all be taken care of in time. If young Veatch refuses to accede to our request, inform him that he will never . . . never . . . never win the nomination.' Then he says, 'Call my man and help me up.' So I call the chauffeur in and we start shuffling him back out to the Packard. But just before we get to the door, he stops and says, 'Your fee for this particular service will be one hundred thousand dollars. The amount reflects my principals' deep concern.' Then we start for the door again, but again he stops and looks back. 'I didn't see your wife around,' he says.

" 'She's been dead for twenty years, Gene,' I said. 'That's

impossible,' he says, shuffles on out the door and into the Packard, and drives off."

David Slipper rose, moved to the sink, picked up the brandy
bottle, read its label, put it down, came back to the table, and
resumed his seat. "My advice, Draper? Call Veatch off. If he
won't listen to you, have Louise work on him."

"No," Haere said.

Slipper sighed. "Then I'll have to go see him and lay it all
out."

"Tell them this back in Washington, Slippery. If Veatch
backs out, I'll go it alone."

"Why?"

"Because I'm in too deep."

"Already?"

Haere nodded.

"Is Veatch?"

"No," Haere said. "Not yet."

"Then I'd better go bail him out."

"You'll have a problem with Louise."

"Will you help?"

"No."

Slipper again rose, turned to the sink, again picked up the
brandy bottle, and this time refilled the two glasses. "It's not
just the money, Draper," he said.

"Isn't it?"

Slipper shook his head as he sat back down. "I've got enough
money. More than enough. What it is, if you don't mind an old
man's embarrassed confession, is that I need to know if I can
still help change things."

"If you still matter."

"That's right. If I still matter."

"You matter, Slippery, you've just picked the wrong side."

David Slipper nodded, smiled, and rose. "Well, it won't be
the first time." He continued to smile down at the still-seated

Haere. "This one's going to be interesting, isn't it, Draper?"

"Very," Haere said as he rose. "I want to thank you again for the hatrack. That was a damn nice thing to do. Can I call you a cab?"

"I've got a limo waiting." He paused by the hatrack, which still stood in the middle of the room. "They'll send somebody after you, Draper. Somebody nasty. But you know that, don't you?"

"I know."

"Well, just so you do." David Slipper turned, smiled his most charming smile, and stuck out his hand. Haere accepted it without hesitation.

"Take care, Slippery," he said.

The white-haired man winked, turned, and was gone. Haere listened to his footsteps hurry down the stairs, taking them two at a time.

21

On their way back from the restaurant, Velveeta Keats drove and revealed in a low, hesitant voice a half-dozen of her more bizarre sexual fantasies. She wanted to know if Morgan Citron would be interested in helping her realize some of them. Citron said he found the first two interesting, but the third one, the one involving a generous use of Log Cabin syrup, sounded a little messy. And although the remaining three offered intriguing possibilities, he wasn't quite sure they could get around to all of them in a single evening. Velveeta Keats suggested that they limit themselves to the first two or three, and then see what happened. Citron said that seemed sensible to him.

"You don't think I'm weird, do you?" she asked.

"Not at all."

"They just come to me."

"Your ideas."

"Uh-huh. Do you think they're awful?"

"I think they're fine," he said. "All except the Log Cabin syrup thing. That doesn't do much for me."

She frowned and then brightened. "Maybe we could try it with Wesson oil instead."

Citron said he thought that might be an idea.

It was nearly midnight when Citron gently detached the sleeping Velveeta Keats's iron grip, sat up on the edge of her bed, and started pulling on his shorts.

She stirred, awoke, and smiled sleepily. "You leaving?"

"I've got a couple of things to do."

"I want to thank you for a real wonderful evening."

"It was different," he said as he zipped up his pants. Velveeta Keats giggled her agreement as Citron slipped on his shirt and started buttoning it up. "Do you have a passport?" he asked.

"Sure. Why?"

"I may have to take a trip. Maybe you'd like to come along."

"Where?"

"Central America."

"When?"

"Tomorrow or the next day."

"How long?"

"A week. Ten days at the most."

"You going to do one of those writing-traveler stories of yours?"

"Research mostly, I think."

She smiled. Citron saw that it was a happy, trusting smile, full of anticipation, but it disappeared almost immediately.

"Is this his idea—Papa's, I mean—or yours?"

That's better, Citron thought. Don't trust them, don't trust me; don't trust Papa behind that tree. "Mine," he said. "All mine."

"You sure?"

"Positive. It's just a junket actually—all expenses paid. We'll fly down, look around, and then come back."

"And you really want *me* along?"

"Very much." He waited for her to say no. Please say no, he

thought, and I'll just excuse myself ever so politely, go load up the Toyota, and head north. Maybe the Cadillac People have a chapter up in Oregon or Washington State. He made himself smile as he willed her to refuse.

"Well, sure, darlin'," she said. "I'd love to go."

Citron telephoned Draper Haere at nine minutes past midnight. The phone was answered halfway through its second ring.

"You're up," Citron said.

"I'm up."

"We need to talk."

"Here okay?"

"Give me twenty minutes."

"Fine. You can help me move the hatrack."

"What hatrack?"

"The John L. Lewis hatrack," Haere said and hung up.

Together, Haere and Citron moved the heavy hatrack to a point near the door where it would be the first thing any visitor saw. Haere gave it a few more tugs and pushes until he thought he had got it just right, stepped back with an admiring glance, and asked, "What d'you think?"

"It's . . . well, hideous," Citron said.

Haere smiled happily. "Yeah, isn't it?" The smile went away as he turned to Citron and said, "What've you got?"

"An answer or two, a few questions, some paranoia, and an idea."

"That's a start. You want a beer or something?"

"A beer would be fine."

Citron was sitting on the old leather couch when Haere handed him a can of beer and a glass. Haere took his usual seat in the Huey Long chair where Drew Meade had sat his last. "Where do you want to start?" Haere asked.

"With my landlady."

"Craigie Grey?"

Citron nodded, poured beer into his glass, tasted it, and said, "How well do you know her?"

"Not well. She's a cause type, a mild leftie, makes a good stump speech, works hard, and from what I understand is a pretty sharp businesswoman. I also think she's not a bad actress."

"She recommended me to you?"

Haere shook his head. "To Louise Veatch. Not to me. She and Louise are fairly close."

There was a lengthy silence as Citron seemed to study the beer in his glass. Haere grew impatient. "Let's have it."

Citron looked up. "When all this began I was dead broke, living out of my car. The rent on my post-office box was due, but I couldn't even afford that. So I decided to give the box one last check. In it was an invitation to an ACLU fund-raiser. It offered free food and something to drink, so I went. Out of the blue, Craigie Grey offered me a job as caretaker or super of her place in Malibu. The first person I met there, in Malibu, was Velveeta Keats."

Haere nodded.

"I took her to dinner tonight."

"You said you were going to. Where?"

"Vickie's."

"Nice place."

"Expensive," Citron said. "On our way there we talked about, among other things, her brother-in-law. He's called Bobby. Or Roberto. Or B. Maneras."

"Oh shit," Haere said and picked up the phone beside the Huey Long chair. He punched a number. When a woman's voice said hello after five rings, Haere said, "Louise."

"Christ," she said, "I was almost asleep."

"Where's Baldy?"

"Still at some meeting."

176

"Is Craigie Grey working?"

There was a brief silence. "I'm trying to remember. No. I don't think so. Why?"

"Take her to lunch tomorrow, will you?"

"I can try."

"Try isn't good enough."

"Well, I can see her sometime probably. Coffee or drinks or something. What do you want?"

"Talk to her about Citron. Find out everything you can. Why he was invited to an ACLU fund-raiser. Why she offered him the job. Who put her up to it—if anyone did. Everything."

"Has something happened to Citron?"

"No, he's fine. He's right here. A little paranoid maybe."

"What do you want me to be when I talk to Craigie—subtle, tough, direct, devious or what?"

"Whatever it takes."

"I'll call her first thing in the morning. Speaking of calls, did you know old Dave Slipper's in town?"

"I know."

"He called Baldy. In fact, that's where he is—with Slippery. What's it all about?"

"Baldy wouldn't tell you?"

"No. He just said it was important."

"They want Baldy to drop it."

"Huh," Louise Veatch said. "I reckon I'd better wait up for him then, hadn't I?"

"Maybe you'd better," Haere said, told her goodbye, and hung up. He turned to Citron. "Louise will get it out of her tomorrow."

Citron nodded. "Let me try something else on you."

"Okay. What?"

"Suppose I came up with something really god-awful—a top-grade political mess, say—what would you do with it?"

"Try to elect somebody President, somebody smart, like Veatch."

"Not brilliant?"

Haere shook his head. "I used to think we needed a brilliant President, but then I realized that if he was brilliant, and still wanted to be President, he'd probably have a few bolts loose."

"And that's all you want to do?"

"Jesus. Isn't that enough?"

Citron didn't bother to answer. Instead, he said, "Tomorrow, or the next day, I want to fly down to Tucamondo. I'll need to take two things with me."

"What?"

"Money. Quite a lot."

Haere nodded. "No problem."

"And some insurance."

"What kind of insurance?"

"Velveeta Keats."

Haere went into one of his long silences. His normally sad expression deepened into one of near despair, which by now Citron had learned to interpret as keen interest. "It's all linked together somehow, isn't it?" Haere said. "Everything."

Citron nodded. "I think so."

"Yeah," Haere said. "It's got to be."

22

THEY HAD AGREED to meet in the Polo Lounge for what Craigie Grey called brunch. Louise Veatch was driven to the Beverly Hills Hotel by Charlie, one of the two state policemen who had been assigned to the governor-elect and his wife. Charlie was a flirt. When he got out of the car and went around to open the door for Louise Veatch, she told him he could go play with his hoop in the park for the next hour.

"Hoops," said Charlie, who was three years younger than the governor-elect's wife. "I've seen pictures of hoops in books. Is that what they played with when you were a kid, Mrs. Veatch?"

"They went out just before skateboards came in, Charlie," she said.

"Olden times," Charlie said. "They must've been wonderful."

"They were," she said. "Be back in an hour."

"Yes, ma'am," Charlie said, deciding he would have just enough time to drop in on a Pan Am stew he knew who lived on Hillcrest a block down from Sunset.

A few people waved at Louise Veatch as she entered the Polo Lounge and slid into the corner banquette where Craigie Grey was waiting. The two women touched cheeks, ordered coffee, and then studied the menus. When the waiter returned with the coffee, Craigie Grey asked for grapefruit and a single slice of whole-wheat toast. Louise Veatch said she would have the cantaloupe, but no toast.

"How's the governor-elect?" Craigie Grey asked as she dug into her grapefruit.

"Trying to act gubernatorial."

Craigie Grey looked up slyly. "Not Presidential?"

"One thing at a time, Craigie."

"Folks are talking."

"Good."

"Is he really gonna go for it?"

"He keeps saying people probably feel they've had enough Presidents from California to last 'em awhile." Louise Veatch carved off a slice of cantaloupe with her spoon and chewed it thoughtfully. "Morgan Citron," she said. "Do you think he'd make us a good press secretary?"

"Good Lord, honey, I don't know. Is that what Baldy's thinking of?"

Louise Veatch shrugged. "Draper Haere brought it up the other night. You know Draper?"

Craigie Grey nodded.

"Well, Citron's been doing a little work for Draper, thanks to you, and we were all sitting around the other night, Baldy, Draper, and me, and Draper came up with Citron's name. For press secretary. After all, he did almost win a Pulitzer once, and you know how Baldy likes to do the unexpected. What d'you think? You hired him."

"I honestly don't know, Louise. I just met him that one time."

"Where was that?"

"At that big ACLU fund-raiser last week. The one you all couldn't make. I did my anti-national-ID-card speech, the one where I really get all steamed up."

"I know," Louise Veatch said. "I've heard it. What was he doing when you hired him?"

"Nothing I know of."

"Who invited him?"

"To the ACLU thing?"

Louise Veatch nodded.

"Well, I just hired him, sort of on impulse, you know, and then I got to thinking about it, so I checked around a little, not much, but some, and it seems his mama had sent us a check and a list of folks she thought might be possible members and contributors. So we sent them all an invitation and he was one of them."

"His mama?"

"Gladys Citron."

"No kidding? That's his mama? The ice lady?"

"Uh-huh."

"Jesus."

"I don't think they get along too well, him and his mama."

"Well, I don't know," Louise Veatch said.

"Know what?"

"I mean, hiring a press secretary whose mama's West Coast editor of *The American Investigator* is not the slickest PR move I can think of."

"It's not his fault."

"Craigie, let me tell you something. You can afford to collect strays. Baldy can't. What'd you do, anyway—just walk up to him and say, 'Hi, there, I'm Craigie Grey and I'd like you to be my new super'?"

"Well, no, I didn't do it exactly like that. But you know me, sugar. Somebody pointed him out at the reception, and there he was over by the food, just gobbling it down and looking like he hadn't had a square meal in nine days, so I went over and we got to talking and he seemed so nice and polite and, well, lonely, and then I got curious and asked him about Africa, because I'd read about that, and if that Emperor or President or whatever he was was really a cannibal, and then, well, why not?

181

I needed somebody so I asked him if he'd like to be my new super because that little fag who was there had just up and run off to San Francisco."

"And he said yes."

Craigie Grey nodded. "And then the next day, I think it was the next day, you called and asked me if I knew any investigative reporters around and I said, sure, how about Morgan Citron? Isn't that what I said?"

"That's what you said," Louise Veatch acknowledged, shaking her head regretfully.

"What's the matter?"

"I just wish his mama wasn't Gladys Citron."

"Well, sugar, all I can say is it's not his fault."

"No," Louise Veatch said. "But it's the reason he won't get the job."

They walked out of the hotel together. Louise Veatch turned, waved goodbye, and then climbed into the rear of the black Mercury sedan that Craigie Grey noticed was driven by a young blond man whose cool blue eyes swept the hotel drive and entrance before he closed the door and circled around to the driver's side. Craigie Grey remained standing on the top step until the Mercury rolled away. She turned then, went back into the hotel, and headed for a phone booth. She dropped a coin and dialed a number. When the telephone was answered, she said, "Gladys Citron, please. This is Craigie Grey."

Gladys Citron leaned back in her chair with the phone to her ear and listened patiently to Craigie Grey's rambling description of her brunch with Louise Veatch. Finally, Craigie Grey ran down and concluded her report with, "And that's all I said."

"What was she wearing?" Gladys Citron said.

"That real pretty green silk of hers she bought at Neiman-Marcus last fall. The one with the dolman sleeves."

"I've seen her on TV in that."

"She wears it a lot."

"And that's all you told her?" Gladys Citron asked.

"That's all. I swear."

"You did very well, then."

"Gladys?"

"Yes."

"That means you're not going to run that . . . stuff, doesn't it?"

"Of course it does," Gladys Citron said.

The call from Baldwin Veatch was more summons than invitation. After Draper Haere said he would be there in fifteen minutes or so, he hung up the phone and turned to the wife of the man he had just been talking to. Louise Veatch was slipping her green silk dress down over her head. Haere was wearing his Jockey shorts and an unbuttoned white shirt.

"He wants me there in fifteen minutes," Haere said.

"I heard," Louise Veatch said, smoothing the dress down over her breasts and hips.

"He wanted to know if I'd seen you. He thinks you ought to be there, too."

"That means he wants out."

Haere picked his pants off the back of a chair and started putting them on. "I thought you had him in line."

"That was at three this morning," she said, picking a few cat hairs off the sleeve of her dress. "I wish that goddam Hubert would stay the hell off my clothes."

"You could hang them up."

"Passion carries them straight to the floor." She turned to look at Haere. "At three this morning, I thought I had Baldy wavering, but that may have been just to shut me up. He wouldn't say much, but I reckon Dave Slipper took him way up the mountain and showed him the valley down below."

"Slippery's good at that," Haere said, picked up a paisley tie,

183

and examined it critically. "In fact, he's the best there is." Haere sawed the tie back and forth underneath his shirt collar, started to knot it, but said, "Well, hell," turned to the phone instead, picked it up, and punched a number from memory. When it was answered he said, "This is Draper Haere, Carlotta. What flights have you got going to Tucamondo tomorrow?" He listened and then said, "I'd rather change in Houston than Miami." To a question he replied, "Two. First-class. Put them on my American Express. The names are Morgan Citron and Velveeta Keats. Velveeta like in the cheese." He listened again as the details were repeated. "Right," he said, "and thanks. I'll have somebody pick them up."

Haere hung up the phone and went back to knotting his tie. Louise Veatch examined him with saddened eyes. Her mouth played with a small half-smile. "You reckon this is the fork in the road for us?"

Haere finished with his tie before answering. After slipping the knot firmly into place, he said, "You could leave him."

"Is that a proposition, an invitation, or what?"

"Both."

"Then I'd never live in the White House, would I?"

"You won't anyhow."

She looked around the enormous room as if seeing it for the first time. Haere couldn't tell if she thought what she saw was sad or only ridiculous.

"I could just move in here with you and dumb old Hubert, right?"

"Hubert's not so bad."

"But then I'd never meet the Queen or try out my Cajun French on Mitterrand or anything."

Haere smiled slightly. The possibility of Louise Veatch's meeting the Queen of England was one of their oldest private jokes. "We could get married," Haere said, adding quickly, "and if you're dying to meet Mitterrand, I could probably fix that up somehow."

Louise Veatch stared at him for long moments before whispering, "What about the Queen?"

"I don't think I can swing that."

"You're sweet."

"But?"

"You know what we'd be in five years?"

"What—dull?"

"Never dull, Draper. Just quaint."

"Well, what's wrong with that? I'm sort of quaint already."

She smiled. It was a melancholy smile of complicity and promise and love that almost convinced Haere he would never lose her. Then she was in his arms, and they were kissing frantically. When the kissing ended she said, "Aw, Jesus, Draper. Jesus. Jesus. Jesus."

"I had to ask."

She leaned back to look at him. Her smile was still there and tears were now rolling down toward the corners of her mouth where he knew she would lick them away. She always did.

"You know what?" she said.

"What?"

"After you asked, I almost—for a second there—I almost said yes."

Haere smiled, but only a little, and used his forefinger to mop up one of the tears. He tasted it. "Salty, like they say." He kissed her again, this time on the tip of her nose. "You'll like the Queen," he said.

23

THE HUGE LIVING ROOM in which Baldwin and Louise Veatch did most of their entertaining, if scarcely any of their living, was minimally furnished and almost devoid of color except for a few curious paintings by some long-dead Mexican artist. The paintings hung near the tiled concrete staircase that swept down in an S-curve from the second floor. A wall of glass looked out over the patio, the pool, the tennis court, and a fine old stand of pines and eucalyptus. The trees should have helped. Instead, they only barred the sunshine and made the room gloomy and tomblike and even menacing. It was a room that caused guests to drink too much and talk too little at the infrequent parties that were held in it. Louise Veatch hated the room. Her husband, when he thought about it at all, which was seldom, found it only drab, but not drab enough to spend any money on.

The Mexican maid's sandals slapped against the large square purplish tiles as she served drinks from a silver tray. There was only silence until the maid left. Then David Slipper raised his glass of bourbon and water and said, "Well, here's to all of us."

Slipper was seated in a cream-colored chair of boxy design. Draper Haere stared at him coldly and then shifted his gaze to the governor-elect, who was seated at one end of the long cream couch. At the other end was his wife. The governor-elect was fondling a glass of white wine. Louise Veatch had a glass of vodka on the rocks to her lips. She had the feeling she would need it.

"Okay, Baldy," Haere said. "Let's have it."

Veatch met Haere's cold gaze with a cool one of his own. His mouth, before he spoke, was drawn into a firm line. His big chin looked bold and resolute. It's his hail-to-the-chief look, Haere thought.

"I've decided we should drop our little investigation before it goes any further than it already has," Veatch said.

Haere nodded thoughtfully without shifting his gaze. "You've decided?"

"That's right."

Haere looked at David Slipper. "What'd you promise him, Slippery, besides the moon and the stars and the key to the vault?"

The white-haired man shrugged and smiled. "I never promise anything, Draper. You know that. I only mention . . . possibilities."

Haere smiled sadly and turned back to Veatch. "Baldy," he said, "let me ask you just one question. What the fuck makes you think you can call it off?"

Suspecting a trap, Veatch summoned his warmest, most lopsided grin. "I only meant, Draper, that my involvement, which you'll have to admit has been minimal, will end." He paused. The grin disappeared. "Forthwith," he snapped.

Haere was seated on a chair made out of chrome tubing and leather. He leaned forward, his arms resting on his knees, both hands clasping his glass of beer. It was an earnest position and the same that most assume when seated on a toilet. "Baldy,"

187

he said softly, "you're up to your neck in it. It was your idea to begin with. Jack Replogle came to you first, not to me. But what you've boarded is a runaway train. You certainly don't want to stay, but you sure as hell can't jump either."

"I say jump, governor," Slipper said.

"Shut up, Slippery," Haere said. To Veatch he said, "I've caught a glimpse of what this thing might be. Just a glimpse— somewhere out of the corner of my eye. I'm almost convinced it's big, awful, and absolutely devastating, and I'm guessing— just guessing—that in the books it could fall somewhere in between Teapot Dome and Watergate. If I'm right, then I wouldn't presume to tell you how to use it. You know. You could ride it right into the White House. Maybe even in 'eighty-four. But regardless of what you do, Baldy, I'm going after it—if necessary, all by myself. There're plenty of other would-be Presidents out there who'll know what to do with it—except I prefer you, God knows why. So what I'm offering you is your last best chance to go live in the White House. In or out?"

It was fifteen seconds before the obviously tempted Baldwin Veatch gave his one-word answer. "Out," he said.

"Well, shit," Louise Veatch said.

He turned to her, surprised, perhaps even hurt. "You don't agree at all, do you?"

"I just think you're dropping out too soon. You could wait, see what Draper comes up with, see if it's really worth it, and then make up your mind."

"That would be a bit too late, I'm afraid, Louise," Slipper said from around the cigar he was carefully lighting. "The—uh —possibilities I mentioned to Baldwin are contingent upon his immediate, let's say . . . disassociation." Slipper smiled a comfortable, confident smile that seemed to signal he had nearly completed what he had been sent to do. Or maybe, Haere thought, he's just found out that he can still matter after all.

Haere slowly got up from the chrome-and-leather chair and stood staring down at Veatch. "By next June, Baldy, they won't even know who you are. By next July, even Slippery here won't be taking your calls."

"I'm out," Veatch said.

Slipper came up quickly from the boxlike chair with a curious display of easy, fluid grace. He crossed over and stood searching Haere's face for something he apparently couldn't locate. "Draper, I'm fond of you. You know that." He paused and then continued in a soft, almost pleading tone. "And I admire you. By God, I do. Now I'm begging you not to go through with this thing. Begging you. If I thought it'd do any good, I'd get down on my knees and beg."

"You know what it is, Slippery?" Haere said. "What it really is?"

The white-haired man shook his head. "What doesn't matter, Draper. But it's big and it's bad, just as you said. I can judge its . . . its badness by the people who sent me and who're going to be mighty unhappy when I go back and tell 'em what you aim to do."

"How unhappy?" Louise Veatch said.

Slipper looked at her and shrugged. "They'll send somebody else out. And it won't be some old coot like me, either."

"Who?" Louise Veatch demanded, rising quickly, the concern sweeping over her face. "Who'll they send?"

"Louise," Slipper said, "I don't even like to think about it."

She quickly turned on Haere, her face suddenly pale, her hands clutching her empty glass as though to keep them from shaking. "You knew, didn't you?"

Haere nodded. "Slippery made it all pretty plain the first time he and I talked."

She turned to her husband. "Make him drop it." The governor-elect only looked away. Louise Veatch turned back to Haere. "Goddamn you, Draper, get out of it!"

Haere smiled slightly. "I either can't, or won't," he said. "I'm not sure which." He turned then and walked from the room. All three of them, two standing and one seated, watched him go. Nothing was said. No one tried to stop him.

Haere ran two errands on his way home. The first was at the travel agency near Seventh and Wilshire in Santa Monica, where he picked up the two first-class tickets to Tucamondo from Carlotta Preciado, the pretty twenty-six-year-old who examined him dubiously as she handed over the tickets along with his American Express card.

"Now what's wrong?" he said.

"You don't look so hot, Draper."

"I always look like this."

"No, usually you look like the world's going to end next month. But today you look like you just heard they moved it up a week."

He smiled. "That better?"

"Not much." She indicated the two tickets he held in his hand. "Nobody's going down there, you know. I haven't booked that flight in over two months. What the hell're they going down there for, anyway?"

"Honeymoon," Haere said.

"I can get them a real deal in Jamaica."

"They're looking for excitement."

"Excitement," she said. "Well, getting shot at or disappeared should be sort of exciting."

"That's just the kind of thing they're looking for."

Carlotta Preciado sniffed. "Velveeta. Who in the world would ever name their kid Velveeta?"

"Fondu freaks?"

"Tell your honeymooners something for me, will you, Draper? Tell them if they don't like Jamaica, I can get them a real sweet deal in Barbados. And if they want excitement, they can go to a cockfight and watch two chickens beat up on each other."

Haere grinned. "See you, Carlotta."

"Velveeta," she said. "Jesus."

Haere's next stop was the parking lot of the Crocker Bank. He opened the old Cadillac convertible's glove compartment, rummaged around, and finally found a small white paper sack that had once contained something he had bought at Brooks Brothers. He stuck the folded sack into his hip pocket, entered the bank, and was left alone in a small room with his safety deposit box. He tore a check from his checkbook, turned it over, and on the back wrote, "IOU $10,000," signed his name, and then wrote in the date. He opened the box and counted out $10,000 in fifties from the pig-fucker fund. He put the money into the Brooks Brothers sack and folded it so that it looked as if the sack might contain his lunch. He put the IOU in the safety deposit box, returned the box to its proper slot, agreed with the guard that it was indeed warm for November, went back out to his car, and locked the money away in its trunk.

When he found a parking place only a block from his building, Haere wrote the location down on a card in his wallet. He took the money from the trunk, walked home, up the stairs, and into his enormous room, where he found John D. Yarn and Richard Tighe waiting for him.

"Well," Haere said. "You're back." He turned, closed the door, and put the money sack down on a small oak table.

"We're back," Tighe agreed. He was sitting in the same chair he had sat in before, the Henry Wallace one. Yarn was back on the Wayne Morse couch. Hubert, the cat, was in Yarn's lap, almost asleep.

"We've been waiting quite a while," Yarn said. "We'd almost decided to go and leave you a message. We were going to break pussy here's neck. As an attention grabber, that'd be pretty good, wouldn't you say?"

"You don't have to break his neck," Haere said. "You've got my attention."

"This mess you've been poking around in ever since Mr. Replogle got himself killed up there in the mountains and we came around pretending to be with the FBI." Tighe stopped talking and raised his eyebrows in mock wonderment. "You do know we're not with the FBI?"

"It dawned on me."

"We thought it might," Tighe said. "Well, you'll have to agree that what you're poking around in is a real mess, right?"

Haere nodded. "A real mess."

"It's also more fluid than you might realize. Alliances are made, broken, remade, dissolved, and made again."

"You're not making sense," Haere said.

"He's not trying to," Yarn said. "What he's trying to do is give you a message."

"Which is what?"

"We're asking you to drop the whole thing," Tighe said. "We're asking you to forget all about it."

"All right," Haere said. "I will."

Yarn smiled. "I don't believe you, Mr. Haere."

Tighe picked the cat up underneath its front legs and stared into its sleepy blue eyes. "We might have to break your neck after all, pussy."

"Mr. Tighe doesn't believe you either," Yarn said.

"I'm no actor," Haere said.

"No, of course not," Tighe said as he put Hubert gently down on the floor. "But you do understand we're quite serious."

Haere nodded. "I can believe that."

"Good," Yarn said brightly and turned to Tighe. "Well, we've made our request, delivered our threat, so I guess we can go." He nodded toward the white Brooks Brothers paper sack. "What's in the sack?"

"Ten thousand in cash," Haere said and saw that they didn't believe him.

Both men rose and moved to the door, accompanied by Hubert. Haere followed closely. "Keep out of it, Mr. Haere," Yarn said, "for your own sake."

Haere nodded, but said nothing.

"So long, kitty," Yarn said and opened the door. Tighe went through it. Yarn started to follow him, but paused. "I almost forgot," he said, whirled quickly, and drove his left fist hard into Haere's stomach. Haere doubled over. Yarn stood watching him for a moment. "Just to make sure we really did get your attention," he said and left.

Haere straightened up slowly, clutching his stomach and gasping for breath. He moved slowly out onto the landing and watched the two men reach the bottom of the stairs and go through the door and out into the street. Haere turned and stumbled back into the enormous room. The pain came again, almost doubling him over. He straightened and moved, one slow step at a time, to the phone, picked it up, and punched a number. When it was answered he said, "Carlotta? This is Draper again. That honeymoon flight to Tucamondo tomorrow? Get me a seat on it, will you?"

24

AT THIRTY, Velveeta Keats still called her mother ma'am. They had been talking long-distance for nearly twenty minutes, Velveeta Keats staring out at the Pacific, her mother, Francine Keats, staring out at Biscayne Bay. In California the temperature was seventy-two degrees and dry; in Florida it was eighty-five with a humidity of around seventy-five percent.

There was a fifteen-second silence before Francine Keats spoke again. "And you're sure this Mr. Citron is a nice boy, Vee?"

"Yessum, except he's not really a boy. He's forty at least."

"Well, you know what I mean."

"Yessum, I know. But Papa's met him, Mama. Ask Papa about him."

"Well, I don't know, flying off down there to Central America with someone you just met, it could lead to—well, you know the kind of fixes you get in."

"Yessum."

"How's the weather out there?"

"It's real nice, Mama."

"It's warm here." There was another silence and then a long sigh from Florida. "When you all fixin' to leave?"

"Right away."

"And you'll be gone how long?"

"He said about ten days or so."

"And what'd you say this Mr. Citron does for a living?"

"He's a writer, Mama. He writes travel articles."

"Huh," Francine Keats said, her disapproval total. "Well . . ." She paused again. "Well, you all have a good time."

"Yessum, we will."

"And I'll tell your papa hello."

"Yessum. You do that."

"Well." There was another pause. "Send me a postcard, hear?"

"Yessum."

"Well, goodbye then."

"Goodbye, Mama."

After Francine Keats put down the phone, she continued to stare out into the bay where a white fifty-six-foot Chris Craft was putting out to sea. She knew the boat. It was the *Sea Savvy*, and it was owned by that New York couple down the road, that stuck-up Jewish lawyer and his wife, the one with all the red hair who claimed to be from Charleston. My Lord, the people who claim to be from Charleston nowadays. Francine Keats turned away from the window, sighed again, and examined herself in a mirror. She put two forefingers just in front of her earlobes and pushed up. The lines went away. So did ten years. At least ten, she thought. But they'd have to put you under to do it and B.S. won't stand for that because he knows you'd talk just like you do in your sleep and Lord knows what you'd say. But maybe if you could find a surgeon in Mexico City or Buenos Aires or someplace, one that didn't understand English, maybe you could have him do it. It sure was worth looking into.

She turned from the mirror and crossed the large room, which she called her sitting room because it sounded nice, went through the door and down the long hall to the door at the very end. There the man she always thought of as the skinny French nigger, the one they called Jacques, sat reading his American comic book, or probably just looking at the pictures. Jacques raised his eyes from the comic book and smiled.

"I . . . need . . . to see . . . him," Francine Keats said, raising her voice and spacing the words to make the English penetrate.

"*Oui, madame,*" Jacques said, rose, turned, knocked softly on the door, and waited for the "come in." He opened the door and Francine went into what she called her husband's den. The man was still there, the one B.S. called General, although he didn't look like a general to Francine Keats. He looked like Mr. Bilgere who had taught her Sunday-school class in the Calvary Baptist Church when she was eleven.

"Sorry to bother you, B.S., but—" She stopped and looked timidly at the general.

"But what?" Keats said.

The general was now on his feet. He even bowed slightly. Francine Keats liked that. She liked any display of nice manners.

"I just talked to Vee and—"

Keats interrupted his wife. "You sure it can't wait, honey? We're kinda busy here."

Francine Keats spoke in a rush. "I just thought you'd better know that Vee's flying down to Tucamondo with that Mr. Citron you met out there in California. You know, the boy you told me about."

Keats rose from behind his large teak desk and leaned across it toward his wife, his hands pressed flat against the desk's leather top. When he spoke his voice was quiet, so quiet and low and hard that Francine Keats began backing toward the door. "When?" Keats said. "When's Velveeta leaving?" He glanced at the general with a small apologetic smile. "Velveeta's my daughter."

The general nodded.

"Why, right away, she said."

"Right away could be a couple of hours, honey, maybe a day even."

"I got the impression they were on their way to the airport."

"I see," Keats said. "Well, thank you, Francine. Thank you for comin' in and tellin' me. I appreciate it."

"I thought maybe you oughta know," she said, turned, and hurried from the room.

When she was gone the mild-looking general sat back down and crossed his legs. He was wearing a double-breasted blue blazer and gray slacks of very fine light flannel. On his feet were the black laceless shoes that he still had made in London. His hazel Sunday-school teacher's eyes were covered by rimless bifocals. His face was round and unremarkable. His gray hair was thinning. Only his voice was distinctive. It was a deep clipped bass.

"She said Citron, I believe. Your wife."

Keats nodded and sat back down behind his desk.

"Gladys's son, I presume."

Again Keats nodded. "Yeah, he's Gladys's kid all right."

"Well," the general said. "That does present us with yet another problem, hmm?"

"You mean my daughter?"

"The problem—or question—as I see it, is why did young Citron ask your daughter to accompany him, hmm?" The general usually ended his questions with "hmm?" It was a habit he had picked up from an upperclassman at Virginia Military Institute, where he had been sent by his father, himself a general, after his eyes prevented him from being admitted to West Point. The general was actually a colonel-general and his name was Rafael Carrasco-Cortes. He was fifty-six years old and looking forward to an extremely comfortable retirement. However, his retirement now seemed to depend almost entirely on the man who sat behind the large desk in the book-lined room.

The general was sure the books were unread, probably un-opened. To the general, B.S. Keats was a social inferior, clever perhaps, but crude and ignorant and, of course, dangerous. B.S. Keats invariably thought of Carrasco-Cortes as the spic general. Their mutual contempt made for a curiously effective partner-ship.

"You wanta know why Citron took my daughter along?" Keats said. "Well, that's simple enough. He probably wants to fuck her some more, that's why." Keats smiled at the general's wince of dismay and then continued: "That's one, and two, I'd say, is he figures she might be useful as sort of a hostage. I don't reckon that sucker trusts me after all, despite all the time I spent butterin' him up."

"We are so close to complete success," the general said, his tone full of regret. "So extremely close."

"Hell, Ralphie, we're still gonna make it," Keats said. "But you and me might as well get one thing straight. Ain't nothing gonna happen down there to my daughter, understand?"

The general nodded his agreement. "But that still leaves us the problem of young Mr. Citron, doesn't it, hmm?"

"Yes, sir, that it does."

The general sighed. "Gladys, of course, won't like it. She won't like it at all."

"Now that's just too fuckin' bad about Gladys, isn't it?" B.S. Keats said, grinned his cold gray-toothed grin, and added, just for spite, "Hmm?"

They met for the first time outside the door of the grungy downstairs front apartment, the tall gray-haired woman in the dark-blue suit and the young blond woman with the sun-streaked hair and deep tan who was dressed in jeans and shirt and carrying in her right hand a small expensive Mark Cross suitcase made out of bleached pigskin.

Gladys Citron was about to knock on the door of Unit

198

A when Velveeta Keats said from behind her, "I'll bet you're his mama. You two sure look alike."

Gladys Citron turned. "I'm Mrs. Citron."

Velveeta Keats smiled, shifted the suitcase to her left hand, and stuck out her right. "I'm Velveeta Keats, and Morgan and I're just fixing to leave for the airport."

"Velveeta," Gladys Citron said, accepting the offered hand.

"Like the cheese," the younger woman said.

"Well," Gladys Citron said, smiling her most brittle smile and turning back toward the door. "Let's see if he's receiving."

She knocked. A moment later the door was opened by Morgan Citron, dressed in his new tan suit. He looked first at his mother and then at Velveeta Keats. "I take it you two have met."

"We introduced ourselves," Gladys Citron said.

"Come in." He moved away from the door.

Velveeta Keats backed up a tentative step or two. "I'll come back later if you two'd like—"

Citron interrupted. "Don't worry about it, Velveeta. Come on in. Please."

Gladys Citron was now inside the apartment and turning as she swept it with her eyes. "I was just in the neighborhood and thought I'd drop by to see where you were living."

"Would you like some wine?" he said as Velveeta Keats came in and put her suitcase down.

"Yes, please," his mother said. "I think I would."

"We usually sit around the table," Velveeta Keats said, drawing back one of the bent-iron chairs.

"How cozy," Gladys Citron said and settled herself into the chair the younger woman held for her. Gladys Citron smiled her thanks and said, "What do you do to keep busy, Miss Keats?"

"I sort of fool around."

"Velveeta's a remittance woman," Citron said as he put three

Kraft-cheese glasses of red wine on the table and sat down between the two women.

"Really," Gladys Citron said. "How fascinating. If you're a remittance woman, then you're not from California, are you?"

Velveeta Keats shook her head. "Miami."

Gladys Citron turned to her son. "You two are taking a trip, I understand."

"That's right."

"Might I ask where?"

"Tucamondo."

"Well," she said, "the current bang-bang capital of the world. I'm surprised."

"Why?"

"It's not your usual kind of peaceful backwater, Morgan, all quaint and curious. People keep getting shot down there, and decapitated, and kidnapped, and what-have-you Not your sort of country at all."

Citron sipped some wine, smiled indifferently at his mother, and turned to Velveeta Keats. "My mother is an authority on danger and violence. During the war she was with the Resistance in France."

"Was that World War Two?"

Citron nodded. "See this ribbon?" He touched it. "That's the Légion d'Honneur. It was given to her by de Gaulle himself because of all the Germans she killed. An even three dozen, wasn't it, Gladys?"

"Around in there."

"She's really quite proud of it."

"I don't blame her," Velveeta Keats said. "Lordy, that must've really been something."

Citron turned back to his mother. "Come on, Gladys, what's the real reason Velveeta and I shouldn't fly down to Tucamondo?"

They stared at each other for several seconds until Gladys

Citron shrugged and looked away. "None really—if neither of you minds getting shot at or beat up or made to disappear. In fact, I understand the climate is rather pleasant down there this time of year. Not too hot." She paused and then asked as casually as she could, "Just the two of you going?"

"Yes," Citron lied.

"Well, if you run across something unusual down there in the way of a story, Morgan, do remember your dear old mother. We pay awfully well, you know."

"All right."

"Where will you be staying?"

"I suppose at the Inter-Continental, if there is one."

"There is," Gladys Citron said as she rose. "There always seems to be an Inter-Continental in places where the people spend much of their time shooting at each other." She smiled at Velveeta Keats. "It was so nice meeting you, Miss Keats. I don't think I've ever met a real remittance woman before. I do hope we see more of each other."

Citron rose as his mother moved to the door, opened it, and then turned back. "Have a good trip, Morgan, and do be careful."

"Thanks. I will."

Gladys Citron said something very quickly in French, looked long and carefully at her son, and then left, closing the door behind her. Citron resumed his seat at the table. Velveeta Keats stared at him curiously. "What'd she say—in French, I mean?"

"Roughly translated, she said life is full of pitfalls for the unwary."

Velveeta Keats continued to stare at him. Finally, she said in a very soft sad voice, "Gosh, you two sure do hate each other, don't you?"

Citron thought about it. "Yes," he said, wondering why two utter strangers should hate each other. "I suppose we do."

25

Velveeta Keats met Draper Haere for the first time up in the enormous room, which she examined with wide-eyed delight and wonder. They packed Hubert into his carrying case, checked him into the Musette Hotel for Cats, and then drove in Citron's old Toyota to Los Angeles International Airport, put the car in a lot, and checked into American Airlines for flight 451 to Houston with its connection to Tucamondo.

There would be a thirty-minute wait before the flight was called, and Draper Haere suggested a drink. Velveeta Keats asked Citron to order her a Bloody Mary and then excused herself because she was just dying to go to the bathroom.

After the drinks came, Haere took a swallow of his and said, "My Candidate chickened out."

"Oh?" Citron said, thought about it, and then asked why.

"They sent an arm-twister out from Washington. An old pro who told my Candidate if he'd drop the Tucamondo thing, they'd hand him the nomination on a plate in 'eighty-eight, or maybe even 'eighty-four."

"Veatch believe them?"

"Not really. But there was an implied threat that if he didn't do what they asked—or demanded—he'd be a dead political duck after this term is over and maybe even have to go to work for a living—or something equally unspeakable."

Citron nodded, his expression thoughtful. "I don't think I need to ask who they are."

"No."

"You're one of them, actually, aren't you?"

"I'm a drawer of water, a hewer of wood. They're philosopher-kings."

"What about the Candidate's wife, the fair Louise?"

"Her."

"Yes."

Haere had another swallow of his beer. "Let's say she remained loyal to her husband's decision."

"I see." Citron had some of his own beer and said, "What else?"

"Those two fake FBI types you checked out. Well, they dropped by again."

"When?"

"Yesterday afternoon. Evening."

"And?"

"They told me to drop it."

"And if you don't?"

"They'll break my cat's neck, and then mine, and then maybe even yours."

Citron studied the beer in his glass. "I see."

"You can still cut out. I certainly wouldn't blame you."

"No," Citron said. "I don't think so."

"Why not? It can't be the money; it's not that much."

Citron drank some more of his beer before answering. "It's just that I've been away for more than two years now, and I've finally started back. I have a feeling that if I don't keep on going, I'll never get there. Back, I mean."

"Back from where?"

Citron shrugged. "Who knows? A mild madness?" He grinned at Haere. "You don't mind my being a little crazed, do you?"

"Not at all. What was it—Africa?"

"That—and maybe being the last American cannibal."

"No shit?" Haere said, trying to decide whether to look surprised or shocked, but managing to look only amused.

"One of the last, anyway," Citron said, remembering the young Mormon missionary from Provo.

"It still bother you?"

"It never did bother me—not really—because almost right away I came up with the answer—or the rationalization. It was the usual one."

"What?"

"Simple," Citron said. "I was hungry."

He smiled again, and in the smile there was no madness that Haere could detect, only the strange, utter calm that sometimes follows absolute despair.

There was no line at the Tucaereo Airlines check-in counter at Houston, but the clerk on duty still took forever to scrutinize the visas that Carlotta Preciado, the travel agent, had obtained from the Tucamondian consulate in Los Angeles.

The clerk, a Tucamondian himself, was no more than twenty-five and wore on his lip a fierce mustache so carefully waxed and tended it could only have been a hobby. "Are you going on business or pleasure?" he asked Haere.

"Pleasure."

"There is no pleasure there," the clerk said, slapping the tickets and passports down on the counter with absolute conviction.

"The flight on time?" Haere asked as he gathered them up.

"Yes, on time. And why not? There will be more crew than passengers. You three and two others will have an entire DC-8 to yourself. You wasted your money buying first-class tickets."

"He is an innocent in such matters," Citron told the clerk in a Spanish that had a slight, pleasant French accent.

"Of course," the clerk said. "You are all innocents. Who else would go to my country but fools, innocents, and missionaries?" He produced a small hand mirror from down behind the counter and examined his mustache. "The flight will be called in forty-five minutes," he said as he twisted one end of his mustache into needlelike sharpness. "If you miss it, I will understand."

As the three travelers turned from the counter, the tall man with the big ears and the nearly green eyes swept off his Stetson with a smile, a nod, and almost a wink. "Howdy, folks," he said and gave Velveeta Keats a small courtly bow. "Miss Keats, isn't it? And you're Mr. Haere, I bet, and you must be Mr. Citron. Welcome to Houston."

"Who the hell are you?" Haere said.

"MacAdoo. Bill MacAdoo, and I'm your hospitality committee of one who's hoping you'll join me up in Captains Country for liquid refreshment and, if you'd like, a bite to eat." He paused to deliver another smile and nod. "I sure hope you folks'll join me, because I need to pass on some information that you might find of deep interest and mutual benefit."

"MacAdoo," Haere said, looking the tall man up and down. "Any kin to the MacAdoo that Al Smith kept from being President?"

MacAdoo beamed. "Distant kin, Mr. Haere, very distant."

"And since the MacAdoo you're kin to married Woodrow Wilson's daughter, Elly," Haere continued, "that means you're even more distantly related to Wilson. So despite all that Texas bullshit, you must've gone to Princeton, and from Princeton where? It almost has to be Langley."

The broad MacAdoo smile vanished and with it went the chamber-of-commerce affability. The merry, nearly green eyes

205

narrowed themselves into suspicious slits. The big nose sniffed something bad. The booming voice lost its twang and turned cold and Eastern. "You make a nice intuitive leap, Mr. Haere," MacAdoo said. "Can we talk?"

Haere turned to Citron. "You want to talk to the CIA?"

"Not much."

"He'll buy us a drink."

Citron shrugged. "Okay, let's see what he's got to say."

They took the escalator up one flight to Captains Country, where all was dark paneling and deep leather chairs and shuffling old white waiters with impeccable manners and clawhammer tailcoats. It was Houston's version of a gentlemen's club as seen through a Hollywood prism.

After one of the old retainers took their orders, Velveeta Keats looked guardedly around, lowered her voice, and asked MacAdoo, "You really with the CIA, Mr. MacAdoo?"

"I work for my government, Miss Keats."

She took this for a yes and said, "Morgan's mama was sort of a spy with the French Resistance way back in World War Two, wasn't she, Morgan?" Before he could reply, she smiled at MacAdoo and continued. "I met her just today, Morgan's mama, and she told me all about it. Well, not really all, but some."

"Gladys Citron, right?" MacAdoo asked the son.

"Right."

"She's still something of a legend, your mother," MacAdoo said.

"Or a myth," Citron said.

The old waiter reappeared and served the drinks with identifying murmurs. Beers went to Citron and Haere, another Bloody Mary to Velveeta Keats, and to MacAdoo a Dewar's and water. MacAdoo had ordered by brand name.

After the waiter went away, Haere said, "Okay, let's hear it."

"It's really quite simple," MacAdoo said. "It would be better if you didn't continue your trip to Tucamondo."

"Better for who?"

"For everyone."

"Why?"

"What do you know about Tucamondo? I mean, what do you know for a fact?"

Haere looked at Citron. "You're the writing traveler."

"Well, it's larger than El Salvador, smaller than Belize, much poorer than both, and it's in a mess. But then it's always been in a mess ever since the Spanish first dropped anchor there in fifteen-something-or-other."

MacAdoo shook his head. "It's more than a mess. It's a virtual anarchy. I mean that. There is no government."

"There're the generals," Haere said.

MacAdoo began shaking his head again. "There are thirty-two generals who rule principalities, fiefdoms, some of them as large as fifty square miles, a few as small as twelve city blocks. There is no law. None. No accepted currency other than American dollars, gold, and drugs. The soldiers have become highwaymen, road agents, whatever you want to call them. The countryside is a deathtrap. Only the capital is relatively safe, and that's because it's ruled by a colonel-general called Carrasco-Cortes. He has the money to pay his soldiers."

"Where'd he get it?" Haere asked.

MacAdoo shrugged. "We estimate that Carrasco-Cortes has enough money to last another three weeks, perhaps only two."

"Then what?"

MacAdoo only shrugged again. "Chaos."

"You didn't answer Haere's question," Citron said, "so let me put it another way. Where did this colonel-general, this Carrasco-Cortes, lay his hands on enough money to pay his troops?"

"I have no idea," MacAdoo said. "None."

"You know," Citron said. "You have to know." He turned to Haere. "And now we know what they don't want us to know."

"We've got some questions is all, but no answers."

"Same thing," Citron said.

"Maybe," Haere said and turned back to MacAdoo. "What're you, anyway, the stopper?"

MacAdoo smiled his loose-lipped Texas grin again. He had very white teeth that seemed almost perfect. "I'm just a cautioner, Mr. Haere. I'm only here to suggest that you folks go on back home and forget all about that little bitty country down there that nobody gives two hoots in hell about."

"You could stop us easily enough," Citron said. "All you'd have to do is have State yank our passports."

"Well, sir, if we did that, then Mr. Haere might kick up all sorts of fuss in Washington—right, Mr. Haere?"

"I might."

"What I really don't understand," Citron said slowly, "is why you've said what you have. You must know what we want, and now you've as much as told us how to go about getting it."

MacAdoo produced his final smile. It's his goodbye smile, Haere thought, all thin and cold, all Princeton and Presbyterian. It was a smile of bleak predestination and sorry ends.

"We are fully content with having cautioned you," MacAdoo said, a bit of piety creeping into his tone from which all trace of Texas again had fled.

"Content," Haere said. "That's a funny word."

"Our contentment, Mr. Haere, stems from our utter certainty that should the three of you continue your journey to Tucamondo, then—well, we'll never be bothered with you again." MacAdoo glanced at his watch and rose. He frowned regretfully, as if late for some less enjoyable engagement, examined each of the seated trio in turn, seemed saddened by what he saw, and then said, "Goodbye, all." After that he turned and left the paneled room in long strides that were almost a lope.

Haere turned to Citron. "Well, what d'you think?"

"I think we should have another drink."

As Haere signaled for the old waiter, Velveeta Keats turned to Citron, gnawed on her lower lip, and said, "I don't know, Morgan, maybe I should've said something."

"About what?"

"That colonel-general he was talking about."

"Why?" Citron said. "I mean, why should you have said something?"

"I talked to my mama this morning down in Miami?" Velveeta Keats made it a question. Citron nodded. She looked at Haere, whose full attention she now had, and then back at Citron. "Well, I asked about Papa like I always do and she said he was in a meeting and—" She broke off to gnaw on her lower lip some more.

"And what?" Citron said.

"Well, Mama said Papa was in a meeting with a man and the man was a general and his name was Carrasco-Cortes."

"Jesus," Draper Haere said.

26

WHEN THE TELEPHONE RANG at 1:00 that same afternoon in Gladys Citron's living room, the blue-eyed man who sometimes called himself John D. Yarn rose from the wing-back chair in which Drew Meade had died, crossed to the telephone, picked it up, and said hello. The voice that screamed into his ear made him wince, lower the phone, and press it against his chest. He turned to Gladys Citron.

"It's him," Yarn said, "and he's not happy."

Gladys Citron glanced first at the brown-eyed man seated on the couch, the one who sometimes called himself Richard Tighe. He shrugged. She put down her drink, rose, crossed to the phone, and accepted it from Yarn. She removed a pearl earring, put the phone to her left ear, and said, "Well?"

"*Goddamnit, Gladys!*" The voice was loud enough to be considered a yell, and it belonged to B.S. Keats, who was yelling from Florida.

" 'Goddamnit, Gladys' isn't going to get us anywhere, B.S.," she said and motioned for Yarn to hand her the drink she had put down. Yarn gave her the glass and then lit a cigarette, which he also handed her.

"You claimed that kid of yours was gaga," Keats said, almost

screeching the words. "That he had scrambled eggs for brains."
The screech dropped back down to a yell. Tighe had risen from
the couch and moved over to stand by Yarn. Gladys Citron had
lifted the phone away from her ear. Both men had heard Keats's
voice quite clearly. It sounded like tin being torn.

"I told you he was disturbed, B.S. That's all. That he was
suffering from depression."

"Depression, huh? Well, your melancholy baby who wasn't
supposed to be able to find his ass with both hands sure as shit
seems to have snapped out of it. You know where he is right
now?"

"Probably on a plane."

"And you know who's with him?"

"Your daughter."

"My daughter, the nut case."

"I met her this morning," Gladys Citron said and paused to
take a swallow of her drink. "I found her rather sweet and
charming in a fey sort of way."

"You did, huh?"

"Yes."

"Well, guess who they took along as keeper, my fruitcake
daughter and your Sad Sam son?"

"Keeper?"

"That's right. Keeper."

"Who?"

"Draper Haere."

There was a long silence that was finally broken when
Gladys Citron said, "I see."

"You fucked up, Gladys." Keats was no longer shouting. His
voice had grown soft and almost tender. Gladys Citron inter-
preted the new tone as a threat, a quite serious threat.

"We warned Haere off," she said.

"We? You mean those two gigolos of yours? Shit, they
couldn't warn flies off a peach."

"You're wrong."

Keats sighed. "I hate to say this, Gladys, but it sure looks like you just went and fucked up everything."

"I don't fuck things up, B.S. I straighten things out. Let me remind you of a couple of items. More than a couple. When your daughter was playing Crazy Mary down in Miami, and about to go to the police, I lured her out here with an invitation from a movie-star landlady to come live on the beach in Malibu. And after Colorado, when we suspected Draper Haere would start looking for a professional snoop, I managed to lumber him with my own son, who, I felt then and still feel, is so emotionally damaged he's virtually useless. Then let's not forget old Drew Meade. I took care of that little problem, too. So now we have another one: Draper Haere. But he's really no big problem. My people can leave this afternoon and be in Tucamondo early tomorrow morning."

There was a silence from the Florida end and then Keats said, "Well, you did use your own kid, I gotta admit that."

"And one more thing, B.S. I brought you in on this deal, which is something else you might remember occasionally."

"I don't forget anything." There was another brief silence which lasted until Keats said, "I'll give you credit, Gladys, it's one sweet deal."

"How's the general?"

"He's all set and on his way back."

"Then there's no reason why we can't proceed."

"None except for this Haere fella."

"I'll take care of that."

"Gladys."

"What?"

"I don't want Velveeta hurt."

"No. Of course not."

"I mean, I don't want her touched."

"She won't be."

"Well, just to make sure, I'm gonna be sending my two French niggers down there tonight, and you might as well know if anything happens to Velveeta, well, my two niggers will have to take care of that boy of yours."

"I see." She looked up, studied the ceiling for several seconds, then sighed and said, "B.S., I'm going to say something very simply and I want you to listen most carefully."

"I'm listenin'."

"If your people touch my son, I'll kill you." She slammed down the phone and finished her drink in three long swallows.

Yarn grinned at her. "Think he believed you?"

"Hell, I believed her," Tighe said. "Why wouldn't he?"

She looked first at Yarn, then at Tighe. "There's a three-P.M. flight to Miami."

"We'll be on it," Tighe said.

Gladys Citron looked at her watch. It was 1:10. "Well," she said, "nap time." She reached up and ran her forefinger gently down Yarn's right jawline, turned, and went down the hall that led to her bedroom. Yarn started to follow, but paused at the entrance to the hall, turned back, and looked at Tighe. "Coming?"

"Yeah, sure," Tighe said. "In a second."

The only other passengers on Tucaereo flight 9 to the capital, Ciudad Tucamondo, were a thirty-four-year-old American and a young, drably dressed Venezuelan woman who tried to make herself invisible and who, Haere suspected, was a mule for some cocaine smuggler now homeward bound.

The American and the Venezuelan woman had thriftily bought tourist seats, but were promptly moved up into the first-class section once the plane was in the air. There, all five passengers were cosseted by the purser and the five flight attendants until they could eat and drink no more. Finally convinced they could do nothing else for their passengers, the crew gath-

213

ered in the front of the first-class section and either slept or gossiped among themselves for the rest of the four-hour flight.

After his opening conversational gambit was rebuffed by the young Venezuelan woman, the American went looking for someone else to talk to. His glance fell on the face of the melancholy saint who sat by himself across the aisle from the remaining two passengers, the man and the woman who slept leaning against each other. The American moved down the aisle and stopped at the seat of the saint, who was staring out the window into the dark.

The American cleared his throat. Draper Haere looked up at him.

"First trip down here?" the American said.

"Very first."

"Mine, too," the man said and slid into the seat next to Haere. He held out his hand. As Haere reached for it, the man said, "I'm Jim Blaine."

Haere brightened. "Any relation to James G. Blaine?"

"That's my full name, all right. Where's the James G. you know from?"

"From Maine," Haere said. "A long time ago. He wanted to be President but never quite made it."

"All my relatives are from Kansas. Not too many Blaines in Wichita, where I'm from, but there're a lot over in Kansas City, except most of that's in Missouri, you know."

Haere nodded his understanding and asked, "What takes you down to Tucamondo?"

"Well, it's sort of a funny story. I'm a doctor, an M.D., and I'm going down there for the Friends—you know, the Quakers?" Haere nodded again.

"The folks down there need doctors," Blaine said. "They need 'em real bad from what I hear." He shook his head regretfully. It was a largish head with a high forehead, made even higher by a rapidly retreating hairline. Blaine had grown a blond mustache beneath his snub nose, and under the mustache was a small, almost prim mouth that rested uneasily on a sledgehammer chin. Blaine's eyes went with the chin rather than the mouth. The eyes were sky-blue, almost unblinking, or perhaps just steady, and curiously skeptical. Haere wondered what Blaine specialized in and decided that whatever it was, he must be good at it.

"Are you going to work in a hospital?" he asked.

Blaine gave his big head a decisive shake. "A clinic out in the boonies. The Friends set it up a couple of years back. It did okay until about two months ago when somebody disappeared the guy who was running it." He shook his head almost angrily and the big chin seemed to take an apparently fearless swipe at the world. "He was a friend of mine," Blaine continued. "Joe Rice. We started out in the first grade and went through med school together. So when they disappeared him, I thought, well, the hell with it. I got in touch with the Friends, farmed out my patients to some other guys, kissed the wife and kids goodbye, and here I am." He smiled. "Damn fool thing to do, I guess."

"It sounds more dangerous than foolish," Haere said.

"I'm not a Quaker, you understand," Blaine said, then paused. "Hell, I don't guess I'm anything. Haven't seen the inside of a church in twenty years. Didn't even get married in one. But Joe Rice, he was a Quaker." Blaine smiled. "When we were kids, real little kids, I used to try and knock it out of him." He chuckled. "He'd beat the shit out of me. Some Quaker."

"There's no word about what happened to him?" Haere asked.

"Nothing. One day he started off for the clinic in his car, and zap. That was it. They never even found the car. There's no law down there, you know. I mean, they got soldiers and what they call federal police, but there's no *law*."

"So I hear."

"Well, maybe I can cure a few sick folks. Set a few broken

215

bones. Deliver a few babies. Old Jim wrote me once that he was getting to be a specialist in gunshot wounds. Maybe that's why they took him. He patched up the wrong people."

"Maybe."

Blaine cocked his head as he examined Haere. "You're not a missionary, are you?"

Haere shook his head.

"When I first saw you, I thought you might be. You sort of look like what I think a missionary would look like. What line're you in?"

"Direct mail," Haere said.

"Well, that must be pretty interesting," Blaine said and even managed to put some conviction into his tone. He yawned then, covered it with a hand, looked at his watch, and said, "I guess maybe I'd better try and get some sleep." He rose. "Been nice talking to you."

"And to you," Haere said.

The plane landed one hour and thirty-five minutes later at Tucamondo International Airport. The Venezuelan woman was first off the plane. Next down the ramp went Dr. James Blaine, followed by Velveeta Keats, Morgan Citron, and Draper Haere.

When Dr. Blaine reached the bottom of the ramp he was confronted by four men in civilian clothes, questioned briefly, and led away in handcuffs.

27

BECAUSE DRAPER HAERE'S Spanish was at best rudi-
mentary, consisting of two or three hundred disjointed words
that enabled him to rent a room, order food and drink, flatter a
woman, and get a car repaired, he let Morgan Citron take over
at the immigration and customs counter.

Citron collected the passports from Velveeta Keats and
Haere, glanced through them, walked over to a window as if to
examine them in a better light, and then moved up to the
counter, where a sullen, baldheaded man in a green uniform
eyed him with either boredom or contempt or both.

Citron tapped the three United States passports on the
counter and shook his head regretfully. "I'm afraid there is a
problem."

The baldheaded man brightened and nearly beamed. "A
problem, you say."

"Yes. With our visas." Citron turned to indicate Haere and
Velvecta Keats.

"You are traveling together?"

Citron nodded. "The three of us."

"What is the problem, may I ask?"

217

"As I said, it lies with our visas."

"I see. Continue, please."

"We obtained them, the visas, at your consulate in Los Angeles."

"I know their work."

"Is it sometimes inaccurate?"

The baldheaded man now stared at Citron with something akin to respect. "It happens," he said slowly, "although not often."

"My visa, for example," Citron said and slid his passport across the counter to the baldheaded man, who picked it up, looked left, then right, peeked inside, glimpsed the folded-up $100 bill, placed the passport back on the counter, and covered it with the palm of his hand.

"Are the other two passports the same?" he said.

"Exactly the same."

"Then there is, as you say, a problem," the baldheaded man agreed. "But it may be only minor. I will have to confer with my chief."

He picked up the three passports, turned, and disappeared through a door. Haere moved over to Citron. "See if you can find out about the guy who got arrested," he said. "The doctor."

"He's an M.D.?"

"Right."

Citron nodded. "Okay."

The baldheaded man came back through the door looking almost cheerful. He picked up a rubber stamp and opened the three passports. "It was a small problem," he said as he banged the stamp down on them. "A mere clerical error."

"I am relieved," Citron said, gathering up the passports. "The other man traveling with us, the American doctor, the one who was led away. Did he also encounter a problem?"

The cheerful look went away, replaced by a stony gaze. "He was of your party?"

"We merely met on the plane."

"You are not colleagues?"

"No."

"Do you plan to meet him later?"

"We have no such plans."

"Good. His papers were not in order. He is to be questioned."

"By the police?"

"Why do you ask?"

"I have an unseemly curiosity. It is a failing, I fear."

"Yes," the baldheaded man said. "It could be."

"I thank you for your courtesy."

"Welcome to Tucamondo," the baldheaded man said.

Citron led the way across the small room to the door that was marked as the exit. He opened the door and led them into a huge waiting room filled with fear. It was also filled with people who sat, stood, and leaned against walls, clutching suitcases and valises and shopping bags and cardboard boxes bound with rope or twine. Six men in black visored caps and ill-fitting dark-green uniforms moved among the people. Seemingly at random, an officer in a Sam Browne belt used his swagger stick to touch this person, then that, male and female, young and old, husband and wife, brother and sister, parents and grandparents. Those touched by the swagger stick were led away, leaving their possessions behind. No one watched them go. No one looked at the men in uniform. Instead, they gazed at the floor, the ceiling, the walls, and sometimes at each other, but never into each other's eyes. Many stared down at their own hands, and often seemed surprised to find that they were twisting themselves together.

Haere spotted the purser who had been on the flight from Houston. The purser was hurrying toward the street exit. He looked neither right nor left. As he went by, Haere touched him on the shoulder. The purser shuddered, stopped, and turned slowly. Relief spread across his face.

"What's going on?" Haere said, gesturing toward the packed-together people.

The purser didn't look where Haere gestured. Instead, he looked up at the ceiling.

"How many people do you see?" he asked.

"I don't know. Six or seven hundred, maybe."

"And how many will fit aboard a DC-8?" the purser asked, still staring at the ceiling.

"Two hundred and fifty?"

"Two hundred and thirty-two."

"What happens to the ones who don't make it?"

"They wait," the purser said. "Some have been waiting for four weeks."

"What about the ones the police are leading off—what happens to them?"

The purser decided to examine the floor. "Each passenger is given a number," he said. "Each number is called in precise order. A fair system, no?"

"Yes. Sure."

"Those who are led away are led away because they supposedly have problems—tax problems, exit-visa problems, almost any kind will do. These problems are quickly cleared up. Then the persons are invited to contribute to the police welfare fund. If they contribute adequately, they are returned to their former place in line."

"And if they don't?"

"They go to the bottom of the list, if they are lucky. The less fortunate, those without money, well, no one is really quite sure what happens to them." The purser looked at Haere for the first time. "I really must go, Mr. Haere."

"Yes, I understand."

"No, Mr. Haere. I'm afraid you don't." The purser turned and hurried toward the street doors. He looked neither right nor left, but only up at the green sign above the doors that read: *Salida*. Exit.

* * *

The airport was built on a narrow plateau that jutted out from the range of mountains that divided Tucamondo both geographically and economically. On the eastern slope, the mountains ran down into the broad marsh that fed into the Caribbean. The western slope descended more abruptly, finally spreading out into low hills that formed a natural harbor around which Ciudad Tucamondo had been founded by the Spanish in 1519.

They made the eleven-mile run from the airport to the edge of the city in an eight-year-old Chevrolet Impala taxi. The first thing the young driver had tried to sell them was dope, either cocaine or marijuana. He was a poor salesman and knew it, and his pitch was at best half-hearted. He became only a bit more eloquent during his second proposal, which was for a guided tour of the city's fleshpots where he promised sights that defied imagination.

"These are not old crones, señor," he said to Citron, who sat beside him in the front seat, "but young girls of no more than thirteen, some perhaps even twelve."

"Virgins, of course," Citron said.

"Only one, but her deflowerment by the large dog is the climax of the exhibition."

"Where do they find so many virgins?"

"In a poor country like ours," the driver said, "virgins are both cheap and plentiful."

"How's business otherwise?" Citron asked.

"It is better here in the west than the east. There they are starving. Here we only go hungry."

The road from the airport was a fairly new but already pot-holed four-lane highway, largely devoid of traffic, and lined with burned-out shells of trucks and buses and passenger cars.

"A fine road, true?" the driver said. "It was built with money from your country. Many of the President's relatives grew rich from it and now live in fine apartments in Miami. The President himself, of course, never lived to enjoy his share."

"They shot him."

"Yes. The generals. In front of the Presidential Palace against the wall. I will show you the exact spot when we go by. You may recall it was a public execution. People came from all over. It was like a feast day almost. They led him out and put him against the wall and the generals themselves, thirty-two of them, formed the firing squad. They were not expert marksmen, but eleven bullets managed to hit him. I myself was there. When it was done, there was only silence. And then there was a long sigh—like this." The driver sighed deeply. "It was almost like a gust of wind. Everyone was relieved."

"And now?"

The driver shrugged. He was a young man, still in his twenties, with eyes that were too large and wrists that were too thin. Like the clerk in Houston, he wore a mustache with carefully tended, sharply pointed ends. Citron wondered if the mustaches were a badge of some kind, perhaps a sign, or just something that helped pass the time and cost nothing. He decided not to ask.

"The generals," the driver said and again shrugged. "They cannot agree. So we have no government." He paused. "Only soldiers and bandits." Again he paused. "And much death." With a nod he indicated a burned-out bus. "These wrecks. They were full of people fleeing to the airport after the President was executed. The people in these wrecks were also executed. And robbed."

"By the bandits?" Citron said.

"Or the soldiers. There is really no difference."

The driver turned down the Avenue of the Fifth of September and pointed out the Presidential Palace and the wall where the luckless President had been executed. Next came the large square which boasted both the cathedral, open, and the baroque national theater, boarded-up, and farther on the offices of *La Prensa*, a once much-respected newspaper, also boarded-up.

"We get our news from television now," the driver said. "The television station still functions. There are many North American programs. There is the one about the attorney Perry Mason. It is a favorite. There is also the one called *Leave It to Beaver*. Did I pronounce it correctly?"

Citron replied that he did.

"That, too, is a great favorite." He paused. "No harm ever comes to anyone in that program. It is very popular."

The Inter-Continental Hotel was nine stories of steel and tinted glass built on a cliff above the sea. A drive curved up to it from the Avenue of the Nineteenth of January. The driver charged $15 for the trip in from the airport, and Citron gave him $20. The driver thanked him graciously and again mentioned the exhibition of the thirteen-year-old virgins, should the gentlemen change their minds. And the lady, too, of course. Citron said he would take it under advisement.

Their bags were carried into the lobby by a doorman who wore a chrome conquistador's helmet and a costume to match. Velveeta Keats and Citron decided to share a room. Haere was assigned one a few doors down. Both rooms were on the top floor with views of the ocean. The hotel seemed almost empty of guests. When Haere commented on this to the room clerk, the clerk replied that it was not yet the season. Haere asked when the season began. The clerk said next month—or the month after at the latest. When Haere was asked how he intended to pay, he said with his American Express credit card. The clerk said that would be acceptable. However, should the gentleman wish to pay cash in dollars, there would be a twenty percent discount. Haere said he would think about it.

Velveeta Keats was in the bathroom with the door closed when the telephone rang. Citron picked it up and said hello.

"Morgan Citron?" a man's voice said.

"Yes."

"I think we should talk." The man spoke in Spanish.

"What about?"

"A matter of mutual interest."

"Who are you?"

"I am Mr. X," the voice said, giving the X the Spanish pronunciation of either "equis" or "eckys."

"I suppose we could meet in my room."

"I prefer not to."

"Where then?"

"Tomorrow morning at ten."

"That's when. What about where?"

"I will let you know."

The phone went dead, and Citron put it down just as Velveeta Keats came into the room from the bath.

"Who was that?"

"Mr. Eckys."

"That's a funny name."

"Yes," Citron said. "Isn't it?"

28

THE THREE OF THEM entered the almost deserted restaurant in the Inter-Continental at nine that night. They were shown to a table by a bearded maître-d' who also provided them with menus. A busboy arrived and replaced the napkins, which did not seem to need replacing. Citron unfolded his on his lap and caught the folded piece of paper before it fell to the floor.

Citron looked around. The two other diners were a man and a woman who were seated across the room and interested only in what they were eating. Citron unfolded the piece of paper behind his menu, read it, and stuffed it into his pants pocket.

"Who's it from?" Haere asked, studying his menu.

"The guy who called."

"Mr. Eckys?" Velveeta Keats said.

"Mr. Eckys." Citron ran his eyes down the menu. "It's still set for ten tomorrow morning," he said, "but it's out in the country. I'll need a car."

"We'll rent one at the desk," Haere said. "What're you having?"

"Steak."

"Velveeta?"

"I think I'll have the fruit of the sea thing."

When the waiter came, Haere ordered steaks for himself and Citron and the seafood for Velveeta Keats. He and the waiter discussed wine, Haere in his broken Spanish, the waiter in his equally fractured English. They finally agreed it would probably be wise to skip the wine, which was of doubtful merit, and try the local beer instead. The beer was called Two Brothers and turned out to be exceptionally good.

Haere put his glass down and said, "While you're with Mr. Eckys tomorrow, I think I'll drop by the embassy and do my outraged-American-citizen turn."

"Over what?" Citron said. "The doctor?"

"If that's what he is."

"The embassy folks'll like that. They always do."

Velveeta Keats looked first at Citron, then at Haere, and again at Citron. She frowned. "Can I ask a question?"

"Sure," Citron said.

"What're you guys really up to?"

Citron leaned toward Velveeta Keats and smiled in what he felt might be a conspiratorial manner. "You want the truth, of course."

She nodded.

"Well, the truth is we don't really know."

"Right," she said, nodding wisely. "That's about what I figured."

Citron lay naked on the bed and watched as Velveeta Keats, also naked, sat crosslegged in a chair by a lamp and painstakingly applied the clear polish to her fingernails. They had acted out one of her sexual fantasies earlier, something to do with a mild form of bondage, and after it was over and Citron lay exhausted, she sat up in bed, popped up really, and announced the need to repair her nails. It seemed to be more than a need. It seemed to Citron almost a compulsion. He lay watching as she hummed softly, almost tunelessly, and carefully applied the small brush to each nail. He wondered if there really were such things as born liars and, if there were, whether Velveeta Keats could be classified as one. Was the trait inherited or acquired? Did she need to practice her skills as a liar, or was she a natural? And why were good liars usually better company than the truth-bearers who, he felt, were all too often stolid and dull and sanctimonious? Citron decided to request another performance.

"Tell me about him," he said.

"Who?"

"Your brother."

"The one I used to go to bed with?"

"Him."

"I just made that up," she said, still concentrating on her manicure. "I thought it might turn you on. Incest does that to a lot of people, did you know that?"

"So I've heard."

"He died when he was nine and I was seven."

"Of what?"

"Polio." She blew on her nails. "I still miss him."

"What happened to your husband, then? Jimmy. Wasn't that his name?"

"Jimmy. Jimmy Maneras. Jaime really."

"What happened to him?"

"He died."

"When?"

She held her hand out at arm's length to examine it. "Oh, I don't know. About six months ago, I reckon."

"What of?"

She waved her hand to dry the fingers. "Papa shot him."

Citron sighed. "Come on, Velveeta."

She looked at him, and her expression seemed hurt. "I'm telling you the truth. Papa shot him."

"Why?"

"You wouldn't believe me if I told you."

"I think I would."

"That's why they shipped me out to Malibu. I was going to the police. But then I got this call out of the blue from Craigie Grey inviting me to come out and stay in her beach place, and so, shoot, I didn't really want to get Papa in trouble with the police, so that's what I did. I went. He still won't speak to me, though, but you know that."

"Why'd your father shoot your husband?"

She was working on the other hand now, the left one, concentrating on each small brushstroke. "Self-defense," she said. "You know, I really shouldn't be telling you all this."

"Your husband was about to kill your father?"

"Uh-huh." Her concentration on the brushstrokes was now absolute.

"Why?"

"Why'd Jimmy want to kill him?"

"Right."

"Because he found me in bed with Papa."

She blew on her fingers, held her left hand out to admire her work, picked up the bottle of nail polish, recapped it, put it back on the table, and stared at Citron. He found her gaze cold, hostile, but not altogether mad. "Does that turn you on?" she asked in a flat tone.

"No."

"It does some guys. Women, too."

Citron sat up on the edge of the bed and looked at her carefully. She stared back, the hostility in her gaze slowly diminishing. He nodded slowly and said, "You're really telling the truth this time, aren't you?"

"The truth," she said. "Well, sugar, the real truth is that

we've been fuckin' each other ever since I was thirteen." She
looked away, and although her cold expression and flat tone
didn't change, the tears began to trickle down toward the corners of her mouth. "So maybe," she said, "just maybe that's
why I'm a little bit spacey sometimes. What d'you think?"

Citron lay back down on the bed, folded his arms behind
his head, and stared up at the ceiling, suspecting that he had
just been spooned a large dose of truth. As usual, lies were
more palatable. "I don't know," he said in a carefully neutral
reply to her question. "Maybe it is."

The United States embassy, located on a wide curving avenue that bore the name of Simón Bolívar, was a large sprawling
two-story building some twenty or twenty-five years old and
decorated with a series of pastel masonry screens that testified
to the influence of Edward Durell Stone.

Apparently as an afterthought, the embassy had surrounded
itself on all four sides by an eight-foot-high concrete brick wall
of such crude design that it spoke of hasty, perhaps even pan-
icky construction. As if to compensate, all the pieces of broken
glass imbedded in the wall's top were brightly colored. The wall
was also capped by concentric coils of very sharp-looking
barbed wire whose only conceivable function was to produce
deep painful cuts.

The American diplomats were flanked on the left by the
French and on the right by the British. The French had put up
an elegant fence of black iron bars that ended in rather sharp-
looking arrowlike points. Through the iron bars one could admire the three-story chateau that might have been transported
stone by stone from the Loire. The British had not bothered
to put up a fence at all, and apparently had spent their money
instead on magnificent landscaping, which almost compensated
for the uninspired architecture of their rather slapdash two-
story stucco structure.

Citron pulled up and stopped across the street from the U.S. embassy in the Ford Fiesta that Haere had rented through the hotel. Both men examined the embassy.

"Hell of a wall," Haere said.

Citron agreed with a nod. He looked at his gold Rolex. "It's nine-fifteen now. When do you think you'll be back at the hotel?"

"By noon anyway. One at the latest."

"Let's meet for lunch."

"What about Velveeta?" Haere said.

"She's going sight-seeing and shopping around ten or ten-thirty and won't be back until two."

"I'll either come by your room or call," Haere said, got out of the car, and watched Citron drive off. Wearing his light-weight dark-blue three-piece pinstripe suit, his white shirt and striped red-and-blue tie, Haere walked quickly across the broad avenue toward the marine guard who waited behind the obviously locked gates that were made out of thick steel bars. In his blue suit and gleaming black shoes, Haere knew what he must look like to the marine: like ancient history.

When he reached the gate, he stared through the bars at the embassy building. He ignored the marine, who was a twenty-two- or twenty-three-year-old corporal with one hashmark, a hand-carved Mexican Indian face, and surprisingly light gray eyes that were too old for the face.

The marine let a minute go by until he said, "Yes, sir. Can I help you?"

Still staring at the embassy building, Haere said, "Anybody in there up and about yet?"

"Yes, sir. Everybody."

"I'd like to see whoever's in charge of lost or strayed American citizens."

"Male or female, sir?"

"Why?"

"Well, sir, we usually let Miss Steadman handle misplaced wives. They get down here, the wives, and they meet some guy with real white teeth and his shirt open down to here and well, sir, they get, you know, like you said, lost or strayed."

"Miss Steadman handles them, huh?"

"Yes, sir."

"Who handles people who step off the plane and get led off by the cops?"

The marine unlocked the gate and swung it open. "That'd be Mr. Merry like in Merry Christmas."

"And what does Mr. Merry do?" Haere said once he was through the gate and the marine had relocked it.

"He's a counselor."

"Of what?"

The marine almost smiled. "Of people in trouble, sir."

After he talked to the marine sergeant at the reception desk and signed in, Haere waited a minute or two until a brown-haired woman in her thirties appeared, examined him briefly, introduced herself as Mrs. Crane, and asked him to please come this way. He followed her down the hall, up a flight of stairs, down another hall, and through a door into a reception room with a small desk that had her name on it. She knocked on a closed door, opened it, said, "Mr. Haere is here," and stood aside, indicating that Haere should go in.

The man who rose from behind the almost bare metal desk wore a seersucker jacket, a tie, and a smile. It was one of those wide white almost blinding smiles that immediately generate suspicion. Haere saw that the blue eyes above the smile seemed to be smiling, too, perhaps even grinning, although with all that crinkling it was hard to tell.

The man with the smile stuck out his hand as he leaned over the desk and said, "I'm Don Merry, Mr. Haere."

Haere shook Merry's hand. Merry waved him to a chair, sat

back down, kept on smiling, and said, "Well, now. How can I help you?"

"I arrived on the flight from Houston last night."

Merry nodded.

"I met a doctor on the flight, a medical doctor named Blaine. James G. Blaine."

Merry chuckled. "From Maine?"

"Kansas. He was coming down here to take over a clinic for the Friends, the Quakers."

Again, Merry nodded. "Joe Rice's clinic."

"He mentioned Rice. He said they were old friends, but that Rice had disappeared."

The smile went away and Merry looked grave, but said nothing.

"There were only five passengers on the flight," Haere continued. "Dr. Blaine was the second one off. He was arrested when he reached the bottom of the ramp and led away by four men who looked like cops to me." Haere paused. "I thought you should know. I might add that I find it extremely disturbing that an American medical missionary should be whisked away by the police the moment he steps off the plane. Extremely disturbing." Listening to himself, Haere was almost satisfied with the level of his indignation.

"Excuse me a minute," Merry said, picked up the phone, and dialed a single number. When it was answered with a faint yes, he said, "The name is James G. Blaine, supposedly a medical doctor from Kansas." Merry looked at Haere and raised an eyebrow.

"Wichita," Haere said.

"Wichita, Kansas," Merry said into the phone. "You've got the number of the Quaker clinic over on the eastern slope, don't you? Well, call them and see if they're expecting the arrival of Dr. Blaine, or if he has, in fact, already arrived safe and sound. If not, call Tucaereo and see if they had a J. Blaine on yesterday's manifest. If they did, then call our friend Suro and see if his people got their sticky mitts on the doctor and, if so, find out where they've stashed him. Then come tell Mr. Haere and me all about it."

Merry hung up the phone, put his smile back on, and looked at Haere, who decided that the carefully acquired tan made the smile seem whiter than it really was. The tan went well with the crinkly eyes and the lean jaw and the straight nose. It was all capped by a thatch of ginger hair that fell down over the high forehead in a careless wave. It all seemed calculated to produce an impression of warm, quick intelligence, and Haere was quite willing to buy it if only Merry wouldn't smile quite so often.

"Draper . . . Haere," Merry said slowly, spacing the name. He frowned as if trying to remember where he had heard it before. "Politics, isn't it?"

"Politics," Haere agreed.

"Whatever brings you down here?"

"Vacation?"

"Here?" Merry didn't try to hide his disbelief.

"Perhaps a little business?"

Merry shook his head as though business was simply awful. "Well, good luck is about all I can say. But if you want some advice—"

He was interrupted by the entrance of Mrs. Crane with note pad in hand. She looked at Merry, who nodded. Mrs. Crane turned to Haere.

"One," she said. "The Friends clinic. They never heard of any Dr. Blaine, so they couldn't be expecting him. Two, there was no J. Blaine on the Tucaereo flight from Houston yesterday —or the day before, for that matter. Three, I talked to Suro, who said he failed to arrest any gringos yesterday, although he might get around to it this afternoon after lunch."

"Commander Suro is something of a kidder," Merry explained.

"Yes," Haere said. "He seems to be. So does the mysterious

Dr. Blaine. What about this Dr. Rice? Has he turned up yet?"

"From where?" Mrs. Crane said.

"From wherever he disappeared to."

"Joe Rice hasn't disappeared anywhere," she said. "It was Joe Rice I just talked to at the clinic."

29

THE ROAD THAT CITRON FOLLOWED out of the capital
was a narrow blacktop, much potholed, and patched in long
stretches with gravel. It led through an exurbia of shantytowns
built out of scrap lumber and plastic sheeting and cardboard
and flattened tin cans. The road then curved up into the mountains, where no one at all seemed to live other than a few farm-
ers who grew straggly plots of corn and raised small herds of
goats and the occasional chicken.

The sub-subsistence farms gave way to what seemed to be
neglected or abandoned coffee plantations. Citron checked his
odometer. At precisely 3.6 kilometers after the coffee plantations
began he started looking for the side road that was marked on
the rough map slipped to him by the busboy in the Inter-
Continental restaurant. He almost missed the side road because
it was virtually hidden by some tall broad-leafed plants. They
looked like poinsettia to Citron, although they were actually
higuerilla or palma Christi or, more commonly, castor-bean
plants. Citron did notice they had been carefully planted to
obscure the dirt side road that turned out to be not much more
than a rutted path.

Citron backed up and eased the Ford slowly through the

screen of broad-leafed plants, which noisily scraped against the car's sides. After bouncing slowly along the dirt path for 1.3 kilometers, Citron stopped the car and turned off the engine.

He watched as the one-armed man stepped out from behind a clump of bushes which, for all Citron knew, were coffee plants. The man was fairly tall, at least six feet, and thin. His right arm was missing. The stump poked out from the sleeve of a clean blue T-shirt. In the man's left hand was a pistol of some kind. Citron noted that it was a revolver. Over his eyes the man wore a pair of dark, gold-framed aviator glasses. He was a narrow-faced, grim-mouthed man, and Citron judged him to be in his middle thirties. Beneath the clean blue T-shirt was a pair of white duck pants that were soiled with smears of either dirt or oil.

The man moved slowly over to the Fiesta. The pistol was not aimed at Citron, but rather at the Fiesta itself, as if the man were prepared to kill the car should it make any sudden move. When he reached the right-hand door the man shoved the pistol down behind his belt and used his left hand to open the door. He took the pistol back out, climbed into the car, and looked at Citron.

"You are Citron?" the man said in Spanish.

"Yes."

"I am Mr. X." This time he said "Mr. X" in accented English.

"Right."

"We wait."

"For what?"

"To see if you were followed."

"I see."

They waited five minutes in silence. Citron found it to be a comfortable wait without strain or tension. It was, he thought, something like waiting with an old and troubled friend. Citron had often waited like this with other Mr. Eckyses in other countries until they decided to speak of their hopes and fears. Finally, the one-armed man broke the silence with an observation. "You speak very good Spanish."

"Thank you."

"Your friend, Mr. Haere," he said, pronouncing Haere "Haair-ray," "his Spanish is not quite so good."

"No, I suppose not."

There was another silence, which lasted a full minute. "That is why I telephoned you."

"Because of my Spanish."

"Yes. My English is poor."

"For what other reason did you telephone?"

"You do not know?"

"Not exactly."

Mr. Eckys smiled without displaying any teeth. It was a slight smile, almost wan. "Suppose I said I was a bandit and that we intend to hold you for ransom."

"Good luck."

"You mean there is no one who would pay for your safe return."

"No one."

"You are a poor man yourself?"

"Very poor."

"Yet you wear a fine watch."

"A gift."

"From a rich friend perhaps?"

"My mother."

"Then your mother is surely rich and would pay well for the return of her son."

"I fear that you do not know my mother."

Mr. Eckys twisted slightly in his seat and raised the pistol so that it now was aimed at Citron. "I will take the watch."

Citron shrugged. "It is yours," he said and started to slip it from his wrist.

"Keep it," Mr. Eckys said. "It was a test. A rich man would hesitate. A poor man would not."

"Why wouldn't he?"

Mr. Eckys frowned as he considered the question. "I am not sure," he said finally, "but it is true. Perhaps it is because the poor have nothing to lose but their lives."

"I can see you are a deep thinker," Citron said.

"I think from here," Mr. Eckys said, tapping himself on the heart with the muzzle of the pistol. "You may start the engine."

Citron nodded and turned the key. "Where do we go?"

"Another two kilometers."

"And then?"

"I will show you where it took place."

"What?"

Mr. Eckys smiled, this time displaying a set of large white teeth. "The betrayal. That is why you are here, isn't it? To learn the details of the betrayal."

"Yes," Citron said, putting the Fiesta into drive. "That is exactly why I'm here."

They drove the two kilometers in silence until Mr. Eckys said, "Stop here."

Citron stopped. Mr. Eckys used the pistol to point to a low mound, no more than a foot high, which was covered by weeds. The mound was perhaps seven feet wide and nine feet long. "We buried them there, all of them," Mr. Eckys said.

"Who?"

"Myself and my comrades. We watched from over there." He pointed to a stand of trees.

"I mean, who was buried?"

"The gringos. All nine of them. They killed each other. Later they were dug up and taken away."

"When?"

Mr. Eckys thought about it. "It was six months ago—in

June." He opened the car door. "I will show you where it took place."

Citron didn't move. "I must ask a question."

Mr. Eckys, almost half out of the car, turned to look back. "I will try to answer it."

"How did you learn about me and Mr. Haere?" He paused. "That is my question."

"Ah. I see. You are puzzled."

"Yes."

"The answer is simple. We learned of you from your embassy."

"My embassy?"

"The embassy of the United States. You are a citizen of that country."

"Yes."

"That is where we learned of you."

"They told you?"

"Told us?" Mr. Eckys looked surprised. "*Us?* We are the Committee of a Thousand Years."

"I must apologize. I am not familiar with it."

A gleam flared in Mr. Eckys's eyes. A patriot's gleam. A look of fervor crossed his face. "If it takes a thousand years, we will win back our land and free our people."

Citron, finding himself in familiar territory, relaxed even more. He often had heard such talk in other hot countries. It was not only familiar, but also reassuring, even soothing. It somehow made him feel at home. "You are of the insurgents then," he said.

"Of course."

"And the struggle goes well?"

Mr. Eckys's face darkened. "Not well enough."

"But yet you were able to learn my name and that of Mr. Haere."

"We have our people in the embassy. Pot scrubbers, floor

sweepers, and such. A file was left untended. The Xerox machine was handy. It took only a minute. The woman who accomplished this pushes the coffee cart through the embassy. She pretends ignorance, but has a degree in economics from the University of Mexico."

"And what did the file on Mr. Haere and myself say?"

"That Haere will use the information we have to topple the repressive government in Washington."

"It said *that*?"

Mr. Eckys shrugged. "Words to that effect. I read only the translation, of course." A thought came to him that caused his hand to stray back to the pistol. "Is it not true?"

Citron answered carefully. "It is true enough. Mr. Haere has had wide experience in toppling governments. An expert. I am merely the . . . propagandist."

Mr. Eckys nodded his approval. "A vital role." He turned again to leave the car. "Come, I will show you where the betrayal took place."

Citron got out of the car and followed the one-armed man to the thick stand of trees. "What do you see?"

"Only trees," Citron said.

"Come."

Mr. Eckys led the way through the trees. There were stunted pines and a type of laurel and others that Citron didn't recognize. They formed a thick, almost impenetrable screen that Mr. Eckys twisted through, Citron behind him. Then the trees ended.

"Look," Mr. Eckys said. "They brought in a bulldozer to create it."

It looked something like a meadow that the trees were now trying to reclaim. It was at least fifteen hundred feet long and perhaps seventy-five feet wide. Citron nodded. "A landing strip," he said.

"Exactly." Mr. Eckys indicated the trees. "My people were

concealed here. The gringos' truck was over there." He pointed to the far end of the landing strip.

"The truck?"

"The cocaine truck."

"I see."

"The plane came in like this." Mr. Eckys used his one hand to show how the plane landed. "It was an old plane with two engines. Of the Douglas company manufacture."

"A DC-3."

"Yes. I believe so. It taxied to the cocaine truck. A dozen gringos, all armed, emerged from the plane carrying suitcases. The suitcases contained the money. The cocaine was packed in drums."

"Drums?"

"Oil drums."

"How much was there?"

"Of the cocaine? A ton, I believe. At least a ton. Perhaps two."

"Go on."

"While the drums were being loaded onto the old plane, the money was being counted. There was so much money that they weighed it on a special scale. Then the gringos who flew in with the plane and the money tried to arrest the gringos with the cocaine."

"Arrest?"

"Yes."

"What happened?"

"The gringos who had supplied the cocaine refused to be arrested. So the shooting began. Four of the drug buyers were slain, as were five of the drug sellers. It was glorious. The pilot of the old plane panicked. He started the engines. The gringo drug buyers who still lived ran for the plane and scrambled aboard. The drug sellers continued to fire at the plane as it rose into the air. It was a splendid sight. Dead gringos everywhere."

"What happened to the money?"

"Ah. That. It was loaded into the truck. The gringos left, leaving the dead behind. Some of my people followed the truck, of course. It went directly to the Presidential Palace, which was even then occupied not by a President, but by the repressor Carrasco-Cortes. Meanwhile, we buried the dead gringos, but first we photographed them, and then turned to our Cuban comrades."

"To identify the dead men?" Citron said.

"Yes."

"Who were they?"

"Nine were killed in the battle. Five were of the CIA."

"And the other four?"

Mr. Eckys smiled. "They were of the FBI."

30

CITRON AND MR. ECKYS WALKED BACK through the trees to the rutted trail in silence. When they reached it, Citron turned to the one-armed man. "You say the Cubans identified them—the dead men?"

"Yes. We contacted them and they dispatched an agent."

"From Havana?"

Mr. Eckys looked at Citron with pity. "Havana? Certainly not. From Miami."

"Yes," Citron said. "Of course."

"A strange man for a secret agent."

"How so?"

"He drank. He made advances to our women. He boasted of how rich his family was before Fidel came down from the mountains."

"Did he have a name?"

Mr. Eckys shrugged. "He had many names and several passports. Venezuelan. Chilean. U.S.A. At first, we suspected him. He was not of a serious disposition. But he was shrewd. Even when we got him drunk and supplied him with one of our cleverest women, he gave nothing away. All he wanted to talk with our woman about were the old days in Havana when his family owned all the milk in Cuba. Or so he claimed. Nevertheless, we decided to entrust him with the photos of the nine dead gringos. A week later he sent us their names and particulars by a Tucaereo purser who is one of our sympathizers." Mr. Eckys frowned at Citron. "Why do you smile?"

"I'm sorry," Citron said. "I did not know that I was."

"It was not a pleasant smile."

"I'm sorry."

"I suppose you desire the list."

"Very much."

"With the list can Mr. Haere topple the fascist government in Washington?"

"He can only try, but I assure you his desire to do so is a burning one."

"And the new government—would it be less supportive of our generals?"

"Who could promise that? But I fail to see how it would not be an improvement. A great improvement."

Mr. Eckys thought about it. "Yes," he said finally. "What you say is true. I will give you the list." He reached into his left hip pocket and brought out an 8½-by-11-inch sheet of ordinary typewriter paper that had been folded into quarters. "Perhaps in your propaganda you could mention us."

"The Committee of a Thousand Years."

"Yes."

"I will mention you."

"Thank you." Mr. Eckys handed over the sheet of paper.

Citron unfolded it. There were two headings. One was CIA and the other was FBI. Under the CIA heading were the names of five men along with their ages and their home addresses. Most of them lived in either Maryland or Virginia. Citron wondered if the Cuban secret agent had obtained their home addresses from telephone books.

The first two names of the four presumably dead FBI agents jumped up at Citron's eyes. He felt himself start. The first name was John D. Yarn. The second man was Richard Tighe, no middle initial. They really can leap out at you, he thought. They can actually jump right off the page.

"You are smiling again," Mr. Eckys said.

"What?"

"I said you are smiling again. That same smile. I have seen men of wide experience smile just like that. Their experience has been both good and bad, but mostly bad."

"This list," Citron said, waving it a little.

"Yes?"

"It will be extremely useful. Extremely."

"Good. It is what we hoped."

They turned and headed down the rough trail toward Citron's car. They walked in silence. When they reached the car, Mr. Eckys said, "I will leave you here." He offered his left hand. Citron shook it with his own left hand.

"Who knows?" Mr. Eckys said. "Perhaps some good will come of all this." He didn't sound too hopeful.

Mr. Eckys turned. He turned just in time to see the man who called himself Dr. James C. Blaine step out from behind a thick clump of bushes that Citron still thought of as coffee plants. Dr. Blaine was wearing a light windbreaker, a blue shirt, and chino pants. On his feet were striped blue running shoes. In his right hand was a .38 caliber Smith & Wesson revolver. He pointed the pistol at Mr. Eckys. He pointed it casually, with one hand, his right, much as he would point a finger, and fired three times as Mr. Eckys tried to tug his own pistol from his belt. Two of the rounds struck Mr. Eckys in the chest, the other one just above his belt buckle. Mr. Eckys fell forward. He tried to break his fall with his one hand, but failed and landed on his face in the red dirt, where he called on his mother once, on God twice, shuddered, and died.

"Well, now," Blaine said and turned to Citron. "You're Citron, right?"

Citron nodded, his fear making him either unwilling or unable to speak. Probably both, he thought, as he felt the fear grab at his lungs and trickle down from his armpits.

"Just wanted to make sure," Blaine said.

"Hey, Hallmark!" a man's voice called.

Blaine spun around in a crouch, both hands now on the pistol, searching for something to shoot at, someone to kill.

"Behind you, dummy," another man's voice called. Blaine whirled again and fired into the foliage. From behind Blaine, John D. Yarn stepped out from behind a clump of either dwarfed or stunted pines. Yarn shot Blaine in the back four times, aiming his shots carefully, squeezing them off, taking his time. Blaine stumbled forward two steps, then twisted around, struggling to look behind him, to discover who his killer was. The last expression that crossed his face was something like recognition. "Well, fuck you, turkey," he said and crumpled into the red dirt not more than a foot from the dead body of Mr. Eckys.

Across the road from Yarn, Richard Tighe stepped out from behind some of Citron's coffee plants. He moved over to Blaine, nudged him with a toe, reholstered a short-barreled revolver, and looked at Yarn. "What'd he say? I didn't quite get it."

"He said, 'Fuck you, turkey,'" Yarn said.

"That'll go down on my list of famous last words." Tighe looked at Citron, who stood near the Fiesta, his knees trembling. His hands were also trembling, but he had jammed them down into his pants pockets. There was apparently nothing to be done about his knees.

"I don't suppose you remember us?" Tighe said.

"I remember your voices," Citron said, thinking that his own voice sounded high and scratchy and probably frightened. "I'm good at voices."

"You mean when you threw us the bouquet in the Keats girl's apartment?"

Citron nodded.

Tighe looked at Yarn. "Hell, I don't think we said more than five or six words, did we?"

Yarn shrugged. "Like he says, he's good at voices."

"But you don't know who we really are, do you?"

"One of you claims he's Yarn and the other claims he's Tighe, but you're not really because Tighe and Yarn were buried back over there about three hundred yards."

"I don't mean who we pretend to be," Yarn said. "I mean who we really are. You don't know that, do you?"

Citron wordlessly shook his head.

"We're your baby-sitters, friend," said Tighe with a chuckle.

Yarn nodded happily at the description. "That's right, your baby-sitters."

"Then Mommy must have sent you."

"She gets worried about you, Morgan."

"What about him?" Citron said, nodding toward the dead Blaine. "Who sent him?"

"You've made a lot of enemies, you and Haere," Yarn said. "Any one of them could've sent him."

"Who was he?"

"Him?" Yarn said, moved over a few steps, and stared down at the body of the man who had killed Mr. Eckys. "Well, that's the Hallmark." He looked up. "What name was he using?"

"Blaine," Citron said. "James G. Blaine."

"His real name was Livingstone Creek, although everyone always called him either Stony or the Hallmark." Tighe paused. "He was pretty good."

"That still doesn't tell me who he was."

"Well," Yarn said, "the Hallmark here was the one they always sent when they wanted to send their very best."

* * *

They walked Citron away from his Fiesta and down the rutted trail and around a curve to where a green BMW 320i was parked. They went past the BMW and the only comment they gave it was when Tighe said, "The Hallmark always did like a nice machine."

Around another curve in the trail was parked a dusty four-door white Volkswagen. Tighe opened the rear door and indicated that Citron should get in. "Ours," he said. "He followed you and we followed him."

"I thought he was supposed to be the best," Citron said as he got into the rear seat.

"We're the best," Tighe said, getting in beside him.

Yarn slipped in behind the wheel of the VW and backed it down the trail until he came to a spot where it was wide enough to make the turnaround. They drove in silence along the bumpy dirt road until Citron said, "You can drop me off at my hotel. The Inter-Continental."

"Afraid not," Tighe said.

"I thought you were supposed to be my baby-sitters."

"Oh, we are, we are. But we don't want to wind up doing life in Leavenworth—or Atlanta either, for that matter, and neither does Gladys."

"Especially Gladys," Yarn said.

"So what happens to me?"

"Well, we just might have to tuck you away for a while," Tighe said.

"Where?"

"That's what we're gonna talk to the general about," Tighe said. "They've got a pretty nice jail right here in the capital, and then there's another one over on the east coast that's not so nice. Sort of hot over there. On the east coast."

"No jail," Citron said.

"That's right, I almost forgot," Yarn said. "You just got out, didn't you, about a year ago? In Africa."

"Yes," Citron said. "Africa."

"Tell me something," Tighe said. "Was that chief spear-chucker over there really a cannibal like they all claimed?"

"Yes."

"No kidding? Well, I don't know what kind of jail he ran, but I imagine it's going to seem like the Ritz compared to the one over on the east coast here."

"No jail," Citron said.

"You hear that?" Tighe asked. "Morgan here doesn't like the idea of spending two, three, maybe four years in some beaner jail."

"Can't say I blame him," Yarn said.

"Of course," Tighe continued, "you may not have to go. It all depends."

"On what?"

"On how much you know."

"I don't know anything."

Tighe sighed heavily. "Morgan, let me tell you something. For your own good. All Gladys said was that we've got to keep you alive. That's all. I mean, Gladys is probably just one hell of a mother, but for some reason I don't think she's the type who'd spend the rest of her life in the slammer for her baby boy, although, like I said, she really must be some mom."

"But it's not up to us, you've got to understand," Yarn said.

"Who's it up to?"

"The general."

"You see, Morgan," Tighe said, "the general's going to want to know what you know."

"Very little," Citron said. "Almost nothing."

"Well, I believe you, and Yarn up there, he believes you, but the general, well, he's going to want to take you down in the cellar and beat the shit out of you and stick hot wires up your dong just to make sure."

"A very cautious guy, the general," Yarn said.

"And mean. About the only thing meaner is a Cuban."

"Or a Uruguayan. They're pretty mean, too."

"So what do you want?" Citron said.

"Tell us what you know," Tighe said. "Tell us what you know, and what you think you know, and what you've guessed, and even what you think you've guessed. Then we'll tell the general that all you've done is to make some pretty wild guesses and we don't see any reason to keep you in the pokey for more than a month at the most, and no reason at all to take you down in the cellar and shove hot wires up your dong."

"A month," Citron said. "I'm not sure I can take a month."

"What about the hot wires?"

"No, I couldn't take that either."

"Then let's hear it," Yarn said from the front seat. "Your version." He pulled the car to a stop, turned off the engine, and twisted around in the seat.

Citron took a deep breath and let it out slowly. "You suckered them, didn't you?" he said. "Langley, I mean."

There was a long silence until Yarn said, "That's right. We suckered them."

31

DRAPER HAERE WALKED BACK to the Inter-Continental from the American embassy. It was a four-mile walk that led him past the Presidential Palace. He paused to examine the bullet holes in the wall where the President had been executed and wondered if the generals might someday commemorate the spot with a plaque.

Haere walked slowly, because it was hot and because the leisurely pace enabled him to gawk at whatever caught his interest: a three-hundred-year-old Spanish colonial house, a pair of eleven-year-old prostitutes, a forty-one-year-old Buick Roadmaster taxi, and a man in his late twenties who played the guitar while his five-year-old son sang a sad song about how desperately poor they were and held out an International Harvester cap into which no one but Haere dropped any money.

Across the square from the cathedral in a large crowded outdoor café, Haere found a vacant table and ordered a cup of coffee. He was halfway through the cup when a man sat down beside him. The man was young, somewhere around twenty-three or twenty-four, and wore a white short-sleeved shirt and dark pants. Haere thought he looked vaguely familiar.

"Naturally, you do not remember me," the man said in English which had almost no accent.

"You look familiar."

"Really? I'm surprised."

"Why?"

"Busboys are rarely remembered."

It came to Haere then. "At the hotel last night. You replaced the napkins that didn't need replacing."

The man smiled politely as though Haere had remarked upon the weather. "We are being watched. In a moment a taxi will arrive. I will get into it. You will remain here. They will follow me. Agreed?"

Haere nodded. "What's the problem?"

"Please listen carefully," the man said and looked up at the sky as if to check on the chance of rain. "The man your Mr. Citron met with this morning has been murdered. Smile, please."

Haere made himself smile. "And Citron?"

The man smiled back. "He was taken to the Presidential Palace by two North Americans. In their early thirties. They shot and killed the man who murdered our leader. Please laugh a little."

Haere chuckled and nodded.

"Very good," the busboy said. "The man who killed our leader arrived with you on the flight yesterday."

"He called himself Dr. Blaine."

"We have reason to believe he was a hired killer, one without politics, who was sent to kill both you and Mr. Citron. Another small laugh, if you can."

Haere chuckled appreciatively. "The two North Americans who took Citron to the Presidential Palace?" he asked, still chuckling.

The busboy grinned broadly and wagged his head. "One had blue eyes, one had brown. That's all I know." He looked at his watch. "Please remain here until I've gone."

Haere tried, but failed, to keep smiling as the busboy rose with a grin and made his way through the tables to the sidewalk. A taxi pulled up. Haere noted that it was the same 1941 Buick Roadmaster he had seen earlier. The busboy reached for the rear door handle. He had his hand on it when two men in open-necked shirts, sport coats, and blue jeans moved up to him from behind and jammed short-barreled revolvers into his back. The busboy tried to wrench the Buick's door open, but the old taxi was already pulling away when the two men with the revolvers began firing.

One man shot the busboy three times; the other man shot him twice. The old Buick sped away and a woman screamed. Some café patrons rose and began to race toward the cathedral, either to hide or to pray. Others ducked beneath the café tables. There were more screams and shouts. One man cursed steadily in a low, calm voice. Haere watched as one of the two gunmen knelt by the fallen busboy and shot him through the neck. Haere wondered why, since the busboy already seemed quite dead.

The kneeling man rose and said something to the other gunman. Both turned to look at Haere. Still staring at him, they slowly put their short-barreled revolvers away in small belt holsters. They entered the café, made their way through the tables, and stopped at Haere's. He saw that they were younger than he had thought, neither of them much more than twenty-five. Their black eyes seemed bottomless. Neither wore any identifiable expression, although one of them, Haere noticed, was a mouth breather. The mouth breather was the one who had knelt and shot the busboy through the neck.

"Do you understand Spanish?" the mouth breather asked.

Haere nodded. "A little."

"Good. Leave our country. Today."

"Do you understand that?" the other one asked.

"Yes," Haere said. "I understand."

"Good," the mouth breather said. They stared at Haere for a

moment longer, then turned and walked back through the tables to the sidewalk and over to where the busboy still lay. A new green Volvo sedan pulled up. The driver popped the trunk latch. The two gunmen bent down, picked up the dead busboy, and folded him away into the Volvo's trunk. They slammed the lid down, turned, gave Haere another thoughtful look, and then climbed into the rear seat. The Volvo sped away.

Haere rose. His knees felt as if they were going to give way, so he leaned on the table, his head down, gulping great gasping breaths. When the trembling finally subsided, he looked up. People were staring at him. They had all edged away until none was closer than twenty feet. Haere moved slowly through the café tables and onto the sidewalk. He looked down at the spot where the dead busboy had fallen. There was a large thick smear of blood. Haere stared down at it for several seconds, then slowly turned and started walking west toward the Inter-Continental.

In the Presidential Palace, Morgan Citron had been kept waiting for almost an hour in an anteroom just outside a pair of sixteen-foot-high doors through which Tighe and Yarn had gone. Citron did not wait alone. Seated across the room from him were a young uniformed captain and an even younger lieutenant, both armed with M-16 rifles. The rifles were pointed at Citron, one at his head, the other at his stomach. The fingers of the two young officers were on the triggers. The safeties were off. Citron sat virtually motionless, remembering that the last time he had gone through such a pair of doors, he had been given a diamond. This time he expected no gift.

One of the sixteen-foot-high doors opened and Tighe appeared. "Okay, Morgan."

Citron rose and followed Tighe through the immense door and into a room that was too large for any conceivable purpose other than a state ball. It was a dark room, made even darker by the heavy curtains that covered a long row of windows. Citron suspected the windows looked out over the grounds that led to the street. The entire room was paneled in a wood so dark it seemed almost black. The paneling only added to the gloom.

Citron followed Tighe across several large, old, and very expensive-looking oriental rugs and past a long library table that held the current issues of *The Economist, Business Week, Time, National Geographic,* and *People.* Citron read the magazine's names as he moved past the table and toward the desk at the room's far end. The desk was the size of a dining table that would seat twelve comfortably and seemed to have been carved out of the same dark wood used to panel the room.

On the front right corner of the desk, his legs crossed, his hands clasping one knee, perched Colonel-General Rafael Carrasco-Cortes. Three leather armchairs were pulled up in front of the desk. Yarn was seated in one of them. Carrasco-Cortes smiled at Citron and gestured toward the center chair. "Please," he said. Citron took the center chair and Tighe sat down next to him.

"So," the General said. "You are Gladys's son, hmm?"

Citron nodded. The general sighed. "Whatever are we to do with you, hmm?"

"Why not put me on the next plane out?"

The general smiled and eased himself off the edge of the desk. He was not wearing a uniform. Instead, he wore a dark-blue pinstripe suit with a vest and a white shirt and a blue-and-gray-striped tie. As he moved around behind the desk, Citron wondered if the general and Draper Haere bought their suits at the same store.

The general sat down, opened a drawer, took out a piece of Kleenex, removed his rimless bifocals, and began to polish them. Without the glasses, his eyes looked almost bewildered. Citron knew that they weren't.

Still polishing away, the general said, "I'm going to ask you to do something, Morgan." He looked up. "I hope you don't mind if I call you Morgan, but I've known your remarkable mother for so many, many years that calling you Mr. Citron makes me feel—well, old." He smiled and slipped the glasses back on.

"What're you going to ask me to do?" Citron said.

"I'm going to ask you to tell me exactly what you told our two friends here earlier."

Citron looked at Yarn. "This isn't quite the way it was supposed to go."

Yarn shrugged. "All bets are off."

"You see, Morgan," the general said, "what I'm trying to decide is whether to have you shot. I must confess that at the moment I'm leaning in that direction. This little session here will be, in effect, your trial—although I suppose court-martial would be more accurate."

Tighe turned to Citron with a grin. "I'm your defense attorney."

Citron nodded, turned to Yarn, and said, "What're you—the prosecutor?"

"Right," Yarn said.

"What's the charge?"

"We're going for espionage and see what happens."

The general took a large gold watch from his vest pocket, snapped its cover open, and placed it on the desk. "Could we begin with your statement, Morgan, hmm? I do have a rather busy schedule today."

"I don't have much choice, do I?"

"None," Tighe said.

"You put up a great defense."

Tighe shrugged. Citron looked at the general, who was now leaning back in his chair, his hands steepled in front of him. "All right," Citron said, "I'll tell you what I know, what I think I know, and what I suspect. A lot of it's conjecture."

"Of course," the general said and nodded encouragingly.

"After you lined the President up in front of the wall out there and shot him, you found that the coffers were bare. The country was bankrupt and you needed money. As I recall, before your coup the country was divided, mostly for administrative purposes, I guess, into two states or regions—the Eastern Region and the Western Region. You carved it up into thirty-two regions and parceled them out to the other generals according to seniority. You kept the largest region—the capital—for yourself."

"All this is common knowledge," the general said.

"A lot of what I know is only that—common knowledge."

The general nodded. "Continue."

"You needed money," Citron said. "You needed it for yourself and to pay your troops and to keep a semblance of order. But because of your human-rights record, which I think is usually called 'appalling,' Washington was out. They couldn't lend or give you a dime. Congress wouldn't let them. So you turned to your friends in the CIA. You do have friends in the CIA, don't you, general?"

The general smiled. "A few."

"Well, even the CIA couldn't slip you that kind of money under the table, but they came up with something just as good, although God knows where they got it. They came up with a ton or two of cocaine." Citron looked at Yarn. "What was it, one or two? I'm not sure."

"Two tons," Yarn said. "And they got it by calling in some past favors."

"Two tons of cocaine will fetch how much now?" Citron asked.

Tighe thought about it. "Seven hundred and fifty million a ton on the street," he said. "But wholesale, about thirty-five to fifty million a ton."

"Which wasn't quite enough, right?" Citron said. No one answered, so he asked again. "Right?"

"Continue," the general said.

"So you decided to buy the two tons of coke from the CIA with government money, steal it from yourselves, and then wholesale it in the States. And that's what you did. All of you."

Citron stopped talking. After seconds passed, Yarn turned to him. "I think the general would like a few more details."

"I have to ask a question first," Citron said.

The general nodded.

"How long have you known my mother?"

"Years. Twenty-five at least. We met in Barcelona."

"Then you knew her when she was still with Langley."

The general smiled his acknowledgment. "We were dear friends."

"I can imagine," Citron said. "So you went to her, described what you had in mind, and—I suppose—offered to cut her in. She put you in touch with an ex-big-time coke dealer called B.S. Keats. And Keats lined you up with just the people you were really looking for—the Maneras brothers, Jimmy and Bobby. Or Roberto and Jaime."

"Bobby was just in on the edge of things," Tighe said.

"Right. So let's talk about Jimmy, who was B.S. Keats's son-in-law. He was also a double agent of sorts working for both Cuba and the FBI, and Jimmy must've been the one who brought you two in." Citron looked first at Tighe and then at Yarn. Both men nodded slightly.

"You three worked out the details, am I right?" Citron said.

"The three of us—plus the general, of course."

"I'll bet you even had a name for it."

"We thought we'd call it the Spookscam," Yarn said, "but it never came to that."

"It was cute, though," Citron said. "The idea. The FBI supposedly would catch the CIA red-handed selling cocaine to finance the operation of a repressive Central American dictatorship. Imagine the flap." He looked at Tighe. "What was in it for the Bureau—South America?"

"Sure," Tighe said. "It was the Bureau's peapatch originally, and they'd very much like it back. Central America, too."

"So that's how you sold it to them: catching Langley with its hands dirty. Very dirty. And that's how you got that ton of money you needed to make the buy."

Yarn smiled. "We just borrowed that from the narcs at DEA. It was confiscated money. We took about all they had." The memory made Yarn smile some more.

Citron looked at the general. "I have one more question," he said. "What's my mother's connection with B.S. Keats?"

"You don't know?" Tighe asked.

Citron shook his head.

"She works for him," Tighe said. "When B.S. got out of the coke trade a few years back, he had all these millions sloshing around, so he set up this dummy corporation and bought himself a going business, or controlling interest in it anyway. He bought *The American Investigator*." Tighe paused. "He also bought himself a chain of shoestores, but they're not doing so hot."

"Please continue, Morgan," the general said.

"Well, it's pretty simple from here on. These two and maybe a half-dozen or so other special agents flew down with the money to make the buy. The CIA, of course, believed they were legitimate drug dealers. These two here stayed on the plane, I'd say, and loaded the coke on while the other FBI innocents paid over the money and then tried to arrest the CIA people. Well, from what I understand, the CIA wasn't having any. The shooting started. Nine people died: four FBI agents and five CIA people. But the CIA still got what it was after: the money. So the ones who weren't dead loaded the money up and delivered it here. You did get your money, didn't you, general?"

The general only smiled.

Citron looked at Yarn. "And you two flew back with the coke, dumped it off with B.S. Keats to peddle, and then went on to Washington with your sad story of how you'd lost not only the coke and the money, but also four men in a shootout with the CIA. And then the cover-up started." Citron shook his head dubiously. "Did they really believe you in Washington?"

"They didn't have any choice," Yarn said. "They couldn't press charges or the whole story would've come out. So they made us swear a blood oath of silence and then fired us. Can you imagine that?"

"What about the other FBI agents—the ones who survived?"

"We took care of them financially—and the pilot," Yarn said. "If you've got enough money you can take care of damn near anything."

"Except one thing," Citron said. "Jimmy Maneras. Something had to be done about him before he slipped what he knew to Cuba."

"B.S. took care of that for us," Tighe said. "He finally let Jimmy catch him in the sack with what's-her-name, that daughter of his."

"Velveeta," Yarn said.

"Old Jimmy went wild, pulled a gun, and B.S. shot him dead."

"In self-defense, of course," Yarn said piously.

Citron nodded. "So that left only brother Bobby—a very scared brother Bobby who skipped to Singapore, where he sold what he knew to a washed-up old hack called Drew Meade who immediately peddled some of it to a political type called Jack Replogle. Replogle knew exactly what he wanted to do with it, only he got killed up in the mountains of Colorado before he could tell what he knew to Draper Haere." Citron looked first at Yarn, then at Tighe. "Who killed Replogle—you two?"

Tighe nodded, almost imperceptibly.

"So, Morgan," the general said, "what now, hmm?"

"Now?"

"Yes. Your predicition of events to come."

"Well, now, I suppose, you take your millions and run. I don't think you can hold this country together much longer. No one could. Another month or so and they'll drag you out of here and put you up against that same wall out there."

"I shall be long gone before that happens. I've almost decided on La Jolla—at least, for part of the year."

"La Jolla's nice," Tighe said. "We're kind of thinking of Buenos Aires."

"Of course," Yarn said, "the Bureau, and especially Langley, still aren't too happy with us, but as long as we help keep it all under wraps, well, they're not going to be too difficult. They've scratched the kitty litter up over worse than this."

No one had anything else to say for almost a minute. Finally, the general sighed heavily and said, "You know, Morgan, sitting here listening to you just now, one phrase kept popping into my mind: loose cannon."

Citron said nothing.

Again, the general sighed, even more heavily than before. "Gladys will never forgive me, but I'm afraid I'm going to have you shot."

Citron only nodded and looked away. As usual, he thought, the prisoner showed no emotion. He merely shriveled up inside. Death in a very hot country. It was not an altogether unexpected end. Ever since Africa, he realized, he had been anticipating it somehow or, perhaps more accurately, dreading it.

"Well, at least you won't rot in jail," Yarn said.

Citron looked at him, still wearing no expression except for a certain deadness in the eyes. "Yes," Citron said. "There's that."

32

THE CALL DRAPER HAERE PLACED to Los Angeles had just gone through when the shooting started. He was in his room on the top floor of the Inter-Continental and the shooting sounded like small-arms fire. It also sounded faint and sporadic and very far away.

"Would you hold a moment, please," Haere said, put the phone down, went to the window, and looked out. All he could see was his splendid view of the Pacific Ocean. He went back to the phone, picked it up, and said, "Gladys Citron, please. This is Draper Haere calling. It's about her son."

"One moment," the woman's voice said.

Gladys Citron came on the line with a question. "What's this about Morgan?"

"How are you, Gladys?"

"I'm fine. What's wrong with Morgan?"

"He's in some trouble and I'm trying to get him out of it. He was involved in a shootout this morning and—"

Gladys Citron interrupted. "Is he hurt?"

"I don't think so, but I'm not absolutely sure. He was taken to the Presidential Palace by a couple of Americans who sometimes call themselves Tighe and Yarn. Ever hear of them?"

There was a silence of several seconds before Gladys Citron said, "Go on."

"That's all I know except that in about one hour from now I have an appointment with the chargé d'affaires at our embassy. His name's Rink. Neal Rink."

"You say they took Morgan to the Presidential Palace?"

"That's right."

"Have you tried to talk to Carrasco-Cortes?"

"That's the first thing I tried to do," Haere said, "but all I got was the usual *no habla inglés* runaround." He paused. "I've also got calls in to Washington to a couple of Senators I know. I thought if you knew anyone at State who—" Haere stopped talking because the line went dead. There was no click or buzz. Only silence. Haere recradled the phone, waited ten seconds, and picked it up again. It was still dead. He hung it back up and listened to the small-arms fire, which seemed louder and closer and not quite so sporadic.

Gladys Citron waited behind her desk until her Chinese secretary came in with the report. "All the circuits to down there are kaput," she said. "Nothing going in or out."

Gladys Citron turned her chair around so she could look out the window. When she turned back, her expression was resigned. She looked up at her secretary.

"I want you to get me a seat on the next flight to Miami. The very next."

The secretary nodded. "You want me to call Mr. Keats and ask him to have someone meet you?"

"No. Don't. What I do want you to do is take all my calls and tell them you don't know where I am or how long I'll be gone. And that means everyone."

"Even Mr. Keats?"

"Even him," Gladys Citron said.

*   *   *

Draper Haere walked down the hotel corridor until he came to the room occupied by Morgan Citron and Velveeta Keats. He knocked at the door. It was opened by a short, chunky black man.

"Who the hell are you?" Haere said.

"I?" the man said. "I am Cecilio. And you?"

Before Haere could reply, Velveeta Keats was at the door. "It's all right, Cecilio. This is Mr. Haere." To Haere she said, "Morgan's not back yet, but come on in."

Haere entered the room to find that it was occupied by yet another black man, a tall thin one. "This is Jacques," she said. "He and Cecilio work for my papa and he sent 'em down to, I don't know, baby-sit, I reckon." She paused. "They're Haitian and they speak French a whole lot better'n they do English. You speak French?"

"A few words is all," Haere said.

"Our English grows," Cecilio said.

"I can see that," Haere said and turned to Velveeta Keats. "We've got a problem."

"A problem!" Jacques said. "It is why we are present. Let us make the repairs."

Haere's forehead wrinkled with doubt. Cecilio looked hurt. "I can see by your visage you have much doubt. Is it because our skin is black and our English poor but growing?"

"You haven't heard the problem yet, friend."

Jacques nodded thoughtfully. "That is true. Tell us."

Again, Haere looked skeptically at Velveeta Keats, who said, "Papa swears by 'em both, Draper."

"Okay," Haere said. "Well, the problem is this: Citron got into a shooting scrape this morning. He was taken to the Presidential Palace. He may still be there. Or he may be in jail. I want to find out where he is and get him out."

"Was he hurt?" Velveeta Keats asked.

"No. At least I don't think so."

"Shooting scrape?" Cecilio said, his tone asking for a translation.

"Bang-bang," Haere said.

"Aaah. Please. Listen." Cecilio pointed toward the window. The small-arms fire could be heard quite clearly. It sounded even closer. Cecilio smiled. "Much bang-bang."

"You know what it's all about?" Haere asked.

Cecilio nodded. So did Jacques, who said, *"La contre-révolution."*

"Is this indeed the same Monsieur Citron who speaks the fine French?" Cecilio asked.

"He speaks French, Spanish, and I don't know what else," Haere said.

"English, clearly," Jacques said and turned to Cecilio. They conferred in their rapid soft Creole-accented French for almost a minute. Their conference over, they turned back to Haere with supremely confident expressions.

"We have experience considerable in such matters, Cecilio and I," Jacques said. Cecilio nodded. Jacques continued: "Money is essential."

"Bribes?"

"But of course."

Haere looked again at Velveeta Keats. She shrugged. "All I know is Papa swears by 'em."

Haere looked first at the fireplug Cecilio and then at the beanpole Jacques. "And you know Citron?"

"He is our dear friend," Cecilio said.

Haere started unbuttoning his vest and shirt. When open, they revealed a tan nylon money belt. Haere twisted the belt around until he could untie its ends. He took it off, placed it on the writing table, zipped it open, and counted out $1,000 dollars in $50 bills, which he folded and placed in his pants pocket. He handed the money belt to Jacques. "There's nine thousand in there," Haere said. "See what you can do."

"We are wise spenders," Jacques said as he caressed the money belt.

Both men started for the door, but stopped when Haere said, "By the way."

"Yes?"

"How's your Spanish?"

"Excellent," Jacques said. "Almost as good as our growing English."

"Except for a small Cuban accent," Cecilio said.

"Which we work to correct."

They went through the door, closing it behind them. Haere turned to Velveeta Keats and noticed the tears running down her cheeks.

"That won't do any good," he said, unable to think of anything else to say.

"I can't help it."

Haere found a handkerchief and handed it to her. "Here. Blow on that or something."

She wiped her tears away and blew her nose loudly. "What do we do now?"

"You and me?"

She nodded.

"We go raise hell at the embassy."

"Will it help Morgan?"

"Probably not."

She blew her nose again. "Draper?"

"Yes?"

"They wouldn't shoot Morgan or anything like that, would they?"

"I really don't know," he said.

The prison that the young captain and the even younger lieutenant took Morgan Citron to had been built 206 years before on a cliff facing the sea. It was high-walled and damp and smelled of rotting fish and human waste.

Citron stood in the chief warder's office, his wrists locked behind him in handcuffs. The warder studied the papers on his desk that contained the instructions for the disposition of the prisoner. The warder was an army major called Torres. He was fat and overage in grade. A trace of saliva leaked from the left corner of his mouth. He wiped it away with a green silk handkerchief as he studied the papers. After finishing the papers he glanced up at Citron and then leaned back in his chair, his eyes shifting to the young seated captain. Citron thought the warder's eyes spoke of corruption. He hoped he was right.

"The telephones are out," Major Torres said, keeping his tone casual, almost indifferent.

"When are they not?" the captain said.

"And the firing? It seems to be coming from nearer the city center."

The captain shrugged. "A small band of drunkards with old M1s and eight rounds each."

Major Torres nodded. "And the television?"

"I have not watched the television," the captain said.

"Nothing but *Gunsmoke* episodes. On the radio there is no news either. Nothing but martial music. Each time I turn it on they are playing 'The Washington Post March.' "

"It both soothes and inspires," the captain said.

"And what of the general?"

"He is well and fully in command of the situation. Already he has taken corrective measures."

Major Torres nodded doubtfully, wiped his mouth again, and pointed at Citron with his chin. "And this one. He is to be shot tomorrow morning. Why not do it now and get it over with?"

"Tomorrow morning," the captain said firmly. "Everything must be done exactly according to your orders. It is a matter of some delicacy."

Major Torres grunted. "Executions are never delicate." He studied Citron. "Is he rich?"

"No," the captain said.

"Important?"

"He is a convicted spy. That's all you need to know."

Again, Major Torres grunted. "If he is neither rich nor important, we should shoot him now."

"You have your orders, major," the captain said.

Torres ignored the captain and examined Citron carefully. "Well, spy, what have you got to say?"

"I have no wish to be shot."

"You speak very good Spanish."

"Thank you."

"Do you have money?"

"None."

"If you had money, you could buy a fine last meal."

"I have no money."

"Then you will eat what the rest eat." Major Torres pressed a button on his desk. A guard entered. The young lieutenant rose and unlocked Citron's handcuffs. The guard looked questioningly at Major Torres.

"He is to be shot in the morning," Torres said. "Find him a nice cell."

The guard nodded, took Citron by the left arm, and led him away.

The cell was on the ocean side of the prison. There was a barred window high up. The cell was small, no more than five by seven. It was lit by a single bulb and contained a plastic bucket, a clay jug of water, and a low stone bed. A folded blanket was on the bed.

"I can sell you cigarettes and food and even liquor, if you have money, " the guard said.

"I have no money," Citron said. "It was taken from me."

The guard shrugged as he closed and locked the cell door. The door was made of iron bars. Citron looked around the cell and sat down on the stone bed. He sat there for nearly an hour, staring down at the floor, his head bowed, his arms on his knees, thinking of past mistakes, old loves, untaken paths, and the final indignity he would have to brook, which was death. After that, no more surprises ever. He absolved himself of all sins, if sins there were; almost but not quite forgave his enemies; rose, and urinated into the plastic bucket. When he was through urinating, he sat back down on the stone bed and took off his right shoe. He then rolled down his sock and slipped the gold Rolex from his ankle. He put the watch in the plastic bucket. It would be safe there, he knew, at least for a while.

He folded his jacket into a pillow. He lay down on the stone bed, his hands locked behind his head. He stared up at the high stone ceiling. After a while he closed his eyes. After a while he even slept—and dreamed of Africa.

The office was large enough to pace in. It belonged to the chargé d'affaires of the United States embassy, who sat behind his teak desk and watched the man in the three-piece blue pin-stripe pace up and down as he cajoled, implored, and even threatened.

The chargé d'affaires was Neal Rink. He was fifty-nine years old and had risen as high as he would ever rise in the Foreign Service of the United States. Threats, even threats from such smooth articles as Draper Haere, no longer bothered him. Ten years ago, he thought, you might've hopped; fifteen years ago you would've leaped. Now he smiled, leaned back in his chair, and said, "So it's come to this, has it?"

Haere stopped pacing and looked at Rink. "To what?"

"To threats."

"I'm not threatening you, Mr. Rink. All I'm—"

Rink, still smiling, interrupted. "You *are* threatening me, Mr. Haere. You're threatening me with assorted members of the Senate Foreign Relations Committee, with a gaggle of Congressmen you seem to have in your hip pocket, with crucifixion in both the *New York Times* and the *Washington Post*, and with disgrace, dishonor, and possible bankruptcy."

Rink reached down into his bottom drawer and came up with a bottle of J&B Scotch whisky. "I suppose I should tell you that I've got a rich wife and that I'm retiring from the fudge factory in exactly two months and nine days. With that in mind, maybe you'd be willing to drop the act and join me in a glass of whisky. I'm sure Miss Keats would also like one."

Velveeta Keats nodded. "Yes, sir, I would." She looked up at Haere from her chair in front of Rink's desk. "You sounded awful mad there, Draper."

Haere grinned. "I was selling. I always sound mad when I'm selling."

"You're really quite good," Rink said as he poured the Scotch and added water from his desk carafe. "I assume it's quite effective when dealing with candidates for public office."

"It's one of the first things I learned," Haere said as he accepted his drink. "If you sound angry, you also sound convinced. People like conviction. Especially in politics, where it's a reasonably rare commodity." Haere took a long swallow of his drink, sat down in the chair next to Velveeta Keats, and looked at Rink. "Okay. Let's hear it. What can you do about Citron?"

Rink had some of his Scotch. He seemed to like its taste. Then he sighed and said, "Nothing."

"Nothing at all?"

"Nothing until Merry finds out what they've done with him. We need to know where the body is." He smiled at Velveeta Keats. "I didn't mean that literally, of course."

"No, sir. I didn't think you did."

"There's also another problem." Rink tilted his head toward the window. "Hear it?"

Both Haere and Velveeta Keats nodded. The gunfire, although still distant, seemed to be increasing in intensity. "That's the sound of counterrevolution," Rink said. "One that has at least a six-to-five chance of succeeding. For Mr. Citron's sake, you'd best hope that it does."

Before they could ask why, there was a knock at Rink's door. Rink told the knocker to come in. The door opened and Don Merry entered. His hair was mussed, his tie loosened; he looked haggard. There was no smile.

"Well?" Rink said.

"I've just come from the palace."

"Were you able to see the general?"

"No, sir. It was impossible. There's suddenly a siege mentality over there. But I did see Colonel Velasco."

Rink looked at Haere. "Velasco is the general's chief aide." He turned back to Merry. "Well, come on, Don, let's have it."

"They tried Citron this morning. They tried him, convicted him, and sentenced him."

"How long did he get?" Rink asked.

"Until tomorrow morning. He's to be shot at six tomorrow morning."

"Dear God," Rink said.

33

THE FIRST THING the two Haitians did with Draper
Haere's $9,000 was to suborn the assistant manager of an Avis
franchise. The Haitians wished to rent a Dodge van. The assistant manager was reluctant. He was convinced the counterrevolution would succeed and that the Avis cars and vans
would be expropriated by the new regime. Clearly, he would be
without work, because his politics, unfortunately, were not of
the left. He must now think of his future. Cecilio asked the
assistant manager if $500 would enhance his prospects. The
assistant manager said that, by strange coincidence, it was the
precise amount he had in mind. He could now rent them the
van with a clear conscience.

In the rear storeroom of a small shop that usually sold
leather sandals, the two Haitians bought two cases of blackmarket Ballantine Scotch whisky and ten cartons of Marlboros.
The whisky cost them $75 a bottle; the cigarettes went for $100
a carton: With the whisky and cigarettes in the rear of the van,
their next stop was the Presidential Palace.

At least three companies of infantry in full battle gear now
surrounded the palace. The van was stopped a block away from
the palace gates by a young private soldier armed with an M-16.

"Do you smoke, brave young soldier?" Jacques asked. The brave young soldier replied that he did indeed. Jacques handed him a carton of Marlboros and inquired as to the whereabouts of his commanding officer. The soldier said that Captain Vadillo at the moment was taking his ease in the park on a bench.

Jacques and Cecilio parked and locked the van. They entered the park and, after a few inquiries, were directed to Captain Vadillo, who sat dozing in the sun, conserving his strength for the battles yet to come.

Jacques addressed the captain by name and said, "We have a strange request."

The captain eyed them with absolute suspicion. "And it is what?"

"We come from the Inter-Continental Hotel, where a crazed North American paid us a small fortune to deliver a case of Scotch whisky and three cartons of Marlboro cigarettes to a friend of his. The friend is another North American with a rare name."

"What is the friend's rare name?"

"Morgan Citron."

"And where is he supposed to be?"

"In the Presidential Palace," Cecilio said. "Detained for some minor irregularity."

"Are you Cuban?" the Captain said. "You speak like a Cuban."

"Do we look like Cubans?" Cecilio said.

"There are many black Cubans."

"We are Haitian."

"I would not help you if you were Cuban."

"We would not expect you to." Cecilio smiled at the captain. "Shall we say two bottles of Scotch whisky and two cartons of Marlboro cigarettes?"

"Three," the captain said. "Three each."

273

"Done."

"Wait for me here," the captain said.

He returned from the Presidential Palace in fifteen minutes and told them, "The North American is no longer in the palace."

"Ah," Jacques said.

"He is in the federal prison."

"Well."

"He is to be shot tomorrow morning."

"A pity," Cecilio said. He looked at Jacques, who nodded sadly at the news. "Then we must surely get his whisky and cigarettes to him today," Jacques said.

The two Haitians turned and started in the direction of the rented van. Jacques turned back with a smile. "Coming, captain?" he asked.

The captain hurried after them and the promised whisky and cigarettes.

Morgan Citron stood with his back to the high stone wall and watched the squad of soldiers fumble with their rifles. Something was wrong with their barrels, which were bent like candles left in the sun. A woman's voice said, "You are still far too thin." He turned and looked up at the top of the wall. Miss Cecily Tettah of Amnesty International sat astride the wall as she lowered a rope ladder with glass rungs. Citron was worrying about whether the glass rungs would bear his weight when he awoke in the cell of the federal prison.

He sat up on the edge of the stone bed. He was not surprised that he had slept. Almost half the time he had spent in the Emperor-President's prison had been spent in sleep—in fast time, as prisoners everywhere called it. He reached into the plastic bucket and brought out the gold Rolex. He wiped it off on the trousers of the suit he had bought at Henshey's in Santa Monica. According to the watch, he had slept an hour.

It took Citron only two minutes to remove the gold expansion band from the Rolex. He put the watch itself back into the waste bucket, rose, moved to the barred door, and started calling for the guard.

After five minutes the guard shuffled down the corridor and stopped in front of the cell door. He was a round-shouldered, bleak-eyed man who had the beginnings of a potbelly. His uniform no longer fitted him. Citron estimated the guard's age to be a few years past forty, which was good. Ambition had gone, or was going. A younger guard might still have hope.

"You do not have to scream," the guard said. "My post is only a few meters away."

"How was I to know?" Citron said.

The guard thought about it and then nodded. "True." He paused. "What do you want?"

"I want food and beer and coffee."

The guard almost smiled. "Perhaps a nice steak?"

"I will pay."

"With what?"

Citron held up the watch band. "With gold."

The sight of gold produced its usual response. The guard smiled and squinted and licked his upper lip. He looked quickly to his right and left, and then back at the gold band that swung in a small arc from Citron's fingers. "Real gold?" the guard whispered.

"Eighteen-carat."

"Perhaps some beans and rice with your steak?"

"And beer and coffee," Citron said.

"Yes, of course. Beer and coffee. I will be back in thirty minutes." He turned to leave but stopped at the sound of Citron's voice.

"Wait."

"What?"

"Do you have any relatives?"

"Yes. Many."

"And some of them perhaps plan to emigrate soon to the States?"

"My youngest sister and her cousin."

"Bring me a notebook and a pen and I will write in it. When your sister and her cousin get to the States they can take the notebook to a man in California who will pay them for it. He will pay them at least two thousand dollars." Citron paused. "Perhaps more. The man is generous."

The guard hesitated. "What will you write? In the notebook?"

Citron smiled. "A story," he said.

After the guard returned with the food and the drink and the notebook and the ballpoint pen, and after he bit into the gold band to test its quality, and after the food was eaten and the beer and the coffee drunk, Citron settled down on the stone bed with the notebook. He opened it and on the first page wrote Draper Haere's name and address in Venice and then: "Draper: Please pay the bearer (or bearers) $2,000 for this—or more, if you like their looks. Regards, Morgan Citron."

After that, Citron wrote steadily for four hours. And because it was a strange tale that demanded a cold and logical style, he wrote in French.

When Gladys Citron arrived at Miami International Airport, she went to a phone booth and used her telephone credit card to call a man at his home in Middleburg, Virginia. The man was retired now from government service and had been for nearly four years. Gladys Citron had known him for nearly forty years. She had once saved his life in 1944 near Cannes. When the man seemed reluctant to do what she asked him to do, she reminded him of 1944 and Cannes.

"Gladys," the man said, "looking back on it all, you didn't really do me any favor."

"Come on, Harley."

"You really want to do me a favor, you'd come up here and we'd have a few drinks, and then I'd hand you my shotgun, that Purdey I bought in 'forty-five in London, remember? And then you could do me a real favor."

"Call them, Harley."

The man sighed. "Call me back in thirty minutes," he said and hung up.

Gladys Citron entered an airport cocktail lounge and ordered a martini, the first martini she had tasted in five years. A forty-year-old Cuban with eyes the color of hot fudge tried to pick her up and it helped pass the time. She ended it by paying for both her and the Cuban's drink, went back to the pay phone, and again called the man in Middleburg. He answered the phone on the first ring.

"I've got bad news," he said. "You ready?"

"I'm ready."

"According to a cable they got from the chargé down there, a guy called Rink, not a bad guy, by the way, well, the good general court-martialed your son today and they're going to shoot him tomorrow morning at six A.M., which would be seven A.M. Eastern Standard Time."

"I see," Gladys Citron said.

"That's my Gladys," the man said. "Tell her the fuckin' world's coming to an end at noon and she says, 'I see.'"

"It's solid, this information?" she said.

"They read me the fuckin' cable, Gladys. This guy Rink says he thinks the general himself may be due for the drop. They got a counterrevolution going on down there and Rink thinks it just might work."

"I see," she said. "Well, thank you, Harley."

"For what?"

After she hung up, Gladys Citron sat in the phone booth for at least two minutes until she dropped another coin in and

277

dialed B.S. Keats's number from memory. When Keats answered she told him she had just arrived at the airport and suggested they meet in one hour at the place where they usually met when they didn't want anyone to know they were meeting. Keats asked if she had heard anything. Gladys Citron said she had and that was what she wanted to talk about.

She drove in her rented Chevrolet past the Bob's Big Boy restaurant and parked a block away. She walked back to the restaurant, went in, ordered a cup of coffee, and took it over to the booth where B.S. Keats sat with a Coca-Cola in front of him.

Gladys Citron put the coffee on the table and sat down in the booth across from Keats. She held her large Coach purse in her lap.

"Well?" Keats said.

"They're going to shoot him in the morning. My son."

"That ain't so, Gladys."

"He's going to have him shot. Our friend, the general."

"Never happen. Never."

"Did you set him up—my son?"

"Me? Christ, I got my little girl down there. I even sent my two French niggers down just to make sure nothing happened to her or him. It's gotta be some kind of fuckup, Gladys. That's what it's gotta be."

"I know you set him up, B.S." she said, took the .32 caliber Colt automatic from her purse, and shot him under the table three times. Keats clutched his stomach, said something she couldn't understand, slumped forward over the table, and knocked over his Coca-Cola. Gladys Citron rose and shot him through the head, then turned and walked out of the restaurant. There were three other customers in the Bob's Big Boy restaurant, plus the staff. None of them tried to stop her.

She turned in the rented car at the airport and checked on the earliest flight out. It was American's flight 138 nonstop to

Kansas City. She paid cash for a first-class one-way ticket and gave her name as Mrs. Gordon Percy.

Seated in the first-class section of the DC-9, drinking the second martini she had had in five years, Gladys Citron came to the sensible conclusion that she might have gone quite mad. Her mind turned then to the comforting thought of suicide. When she arrived in Kansas City, she would check into a nice hotel, perhaps the Muehlbach, if it was still functioning, order dinner and a good wine up to her room, take a long bath, and think about suicide some more. It just might get her through the night. The thought did, in fact, get her all the way to Kansas City, where she was arrested by two homicide detectives as she came off the plane.

34

DRAPER HAERE AND VELVEETA KEATS WALKED BACK
to the Inter-Continental from the U.S. embassy. They walked
because all taxis seemed to have disappeared and because
Haere said he wanted to. The streets were almost deserted except for Jeeps and army trucks filled with soldiers, most of
whom seemed to be sixteen years old. Sometimes Velveeta
Keats would take flash pictures of them with her Polaroid
camera. None of the pictures turned out very well. Velveeta
Keats didn't seem to mind. After she examined each picture
and showed it to Haere, she threw it away.

"Why take them?" he said.

"I like to see if what I see is what other people see."

"And is it?"

"I don't think so. I think other people see more than I do.
When I look at the pictures I see a lot of things I missed. That's
why I use a Polaroid. I don't like to wait. Not for anything."
She stopped, turned, and aimed the camera at Haere. He looked
into its lens, unsmiling. She pushed the red button. The camera
whirred and the picture rolled out. They continued walking as
Velveeta Keats watched the picture develop.

She stopped and looked from the picture to Haere and back again. "You really are sad, aren't you? I mean, way down deep inside."

Haere smiled, took the picture from her, and looked at it. "Is that what you see?"

She nodded. "I thought it was just the way your face grew, you know, sort of accidental. But you really are sad. Not depressed. Just sad."

Haere could think of nothing to say, so he gave the picture back to her. She said, "I think I'll keep this one," and put it away in her purse. They walked on in silence, listening to the distant gunfire.

"How far away are they?" she asked.

"A mile maybe. It could be less."

"I wonder what Morgan's doing."

"I don't know."

She stopped again and stared at Haere. "We're not going to let them shoot him, are we? I mean, we're going to get him out. Somehow."

"Sure we are," Haere lied. "Somehow."

The lobby of the Inter-Continental was jammed with print and television reporters and their crews. Most of them were Americans, but there was also a sprinkling of Europeans. They were all bunched around the reception desk, shouting their demands, elbowing each other out of the way, cursing the hotel management, and declaring their individual and corporate importance.

"Jesus," Velveeta Keats said. "Where'd they all come from?"

"I guess they want in on the kill," Haere said. He looked around the lobby and spotted a tall, mournful, almost middle-aged man who stood leaning against the wall as he sipped reflectively from a pint of Smirnoff vodka. Haere turned to

Velveeta Keats. "Why don't you go on up to your room and I'll try to find out if these guys know anything."

Velveeta Keats headed for the elevator. Haere went over to the tall man and said, "You're a long way from St. Louis, Nessie."

The tall man turned and from his six-foot-five height stared down at Haere. Surprise replaced his mournful look. He even smiled. The man was Nestor Leed, and for almost as long as Haere could remember Leed had covered Midwestern politics for the *St. Louis Post-Dispatch*.

"Draper," he said. "My God. So you've sunk to this—fomenting revolutions in banana republics."

"Not me," Haere said. "I'm a tourist. What the hell do you know about Central America?"

"Nothing. Absolutely nothing. It's a learning experience. I'm joining management next month and they thought I could use a little foreign seasoning. I suggested London, but when this flared up they shipped me off down here—on the cheap."

"You fly in with the rest of them?"

"Just barely. We all chartered a plane out of Miami. At first, they wouldn't let us land. Then the rebels took the airport and so here we are."

"When'd they take it—the airport?"

Leed looked at his watch. "About two hours ago. After we landed they held a press conference—the Committee of a Thousand Years. They claim they'll have the whole city by morning. Noon at the latest. For such a ragtag bunch, they seemed awfully confident." He offered Haere the pint of vodka. Haere had a sip, handed it back, and said, "It should be a hell of a story."

Leed shook his head and the gloom returned to his face. "You know what the awful thing is, Draper? I don't even care who wins. I don't give a rat's ass. That's really awful, isn't it?"

"Maybe London would've been better," Haere said.

Leed nodded. "Yeah. Maybe it would've."

Haere knocked at Velveeta Keats's door, and it was opened by Jacques, who put a finger to his lips. "Shh," he said. "There is sadness. A death."

"Whose?" Haere said as he came into the room.

Velveeta Keats turned from the window. In her hand was a sheet of paper. Cecilio stood near her. Velveeta Keats gestured with the sheet of paper. "The embassy just sent this over by messenger."

"Who died?" Haere said.

"Papa. He died. Somebody shot him in a Bob's Big Boy. Mama's lawyer called the State Department and they cabled Mr. Rink at the embassy and since the phones are still out, he sent this over by messenger."

"I'm sorry," Haere said.

"Don't be," she said. "In a Bob's Big Boy. Wouldn't you just know it?"

Jacques cleared his throat. "This changes things."

"How?" Haere said.

"With the death of Monsieur Keats, we must withdraw."

"Your English gets better and better," Haere said. "Withdraw from what?"

"From tomorrow's affair," Cecilio said.

"What affair?"

Jacques looked surprised. "The rescue of our good friend Monsieur Citron, of course. It is all arranged. Did we not say we would arrange it?"

"Maybe, friend," Haere said carefully, "maybe you'd better tell me about it."

"You must understand that we committed the entire nine thousand dollars," Cecilio said.

Haere smiled. "Tell me about it."

"Yes, of course," Jacques said. "We will even draw you a map."

Morgan Citron finished reading what he had written in the spiral notebook at eleven that night. He rose from the stone bed, went to the door, and called for the guard. When the guard appeared, Citron poked the notebook through the bars.

"Here," he said. "Give this to your sister and her cousin and they will be two thousand dollars richer when they deliver it to the man in Los Angeles."

The guard thumbed through the notebook. "This is not Spanish," he said.

"No."

"It is not English either. I can read a few words of English."

"It is French," Citron said.

"I do not read French."

"It's a pretty language."

"So I have heard." The guard put the notebook away in a pocket. "Do you want a priest?"

"I am not of the faith."

"He would be someone to talk to."

"Thank you, but I would rather not."

The guard nodded. "Well, he's usually drunk by this time anyway, but if you change your mind, I can have him here in the morning."

"When does it happen?"

"At six. I will wake you at five, if that is all right."

"I will probably be awake by then."

"Yes. That is true. Well, if you change your mind about the priest . . ."

"I think not."

The guard tried to think of something else to say, but couldn't, and finally settled for goodnight. After he was gone, Citron sat back down on the stone bed. He thought about death and dying for a while, but found he could think of it only in abstract terms. Somehow it seemed extremely impersonal. He wondered when the fear would come. Probably about 3:00 in the morning, he told himself, when you start praying and calling for the priest. He suddenly realized they were actually going to kill him. A sense of near well-being swept over him as he also realized there was absolutely nothing he could do about it.

He bent over and reached into the plastic waste bucket, took out the Rolex watch, wiped it off on his pants leg, and slipped it into his shirt pocket. If they aim for the heart, he thought, they'll hit the watch. At least they won't get that. He chuckled as he lay down on the stone bed, his head now cushioned by the folded jacket. The thought of the watch made him smile as he stared up at the high stone ceiling. He was still smiling slightly when he fell asleep.

The three of them were eating dinner from trays in the immense room in the Presidential Palace when the young captain came in. Colonel-General Carrasco-Cortes looked up from his tray and said, "Well?"

The young captain looked uncomfortable. "A report by radio from Colonel Velasco. There will be a slight delay. A mechanical problem. With the rotor, the colonel said."

"How slight?" Carrasco-Cortes said.

The young captain looked even more uncomfortable. "An hour. Perhaps less."

"That's cutting it awfully fine," Tighe said.

The general glared at him. "Any suggestions?"

"Boat?" Tighe said.

"That yacht of yours?" Yarn asked.

The young captain cleared his throat. The general raised his fork, put a piece of meat into his mouth, looked up at the young captain, chewed, and nodded for the captain to speak. "The yacht was surrendered an hour ago by Admiral Beccio," the captain said.

"Beccio," the general said. "That pansy pig."

"We wait for the chopper then," Yarn said.

"How long do we have, my boy, hmm?" the general asked.

"Three hours at the most, sir."

"You will be going with me, you understand."

"I understand, sir."

"Keep us informed."

"Yes, sir."

The young captain turned and walked the long length of the huge room to the double doors. He turned, looked back at the three men, then opened one of the doors and went through into the anteroom, where six men stood, staring at him. Three of the men wore army uniforms. Two were majors; the other was the young lieutenant. All of the officers were armed with M-16s. The other three men, the civilians, were dressed in dark T-shirts and khaki pants. Around their necks were bright-green scarves. The civilians were armed with pistols: two .45 caliber automatics and one long-barreled .38 Colt revolver. The pistols were stuck into their belts. The civilians were all in their late thirties. None of the army officers was more than twenty-nine.

"Well?" the oldest civilian asked.

"They think the helicopter is still coming," the captain said. "I told them it would arrive within the hour."

"And they believed you?" the older of the two majors asked.

The captain nodded. "They continued to eat."

"They believed him," the other major said.

"Are they armed?" the oldest civilian asked.

"The two gringos have sidearms," the captain said.

"And the general?"

"A pistol in his desk drawer."

The oldest civilian nodded and turned to the older of the two majors. "We want them unharmed," he said.

286

The major nodded. "I understand."

The oldest civilian nodded at the young captain. He turned, grasped the knobs of the huge doors, and flung them open. The two majors and the young lieutenant raced through the doors and into the room, their M-16s aimed at the seated men at the room's far end. Carrasco-Cortes had just forked another piece of meat into his mouth. He looked up, obviously surprised, even shocked. He chewed once on the meat, then bent forward and spat it out onto his plate.

The oldest civilian moved past the long library table. "You are under arrest, all of you," he said. He had the .45 automatic in his hand now. The hand trembled noticeably.

"Under arrest?" the general said.

"By order of the Committee of a Thousand Years," the civilian said, rolling the name out a bit self-consciously.

Yarn was twisted around in his chair, staring up at the officers and the civilians. He looked at Tighe. "Well, shit, partner," Tighe said.

35

At just before dawn, the fat chief warder of the federal prison, Major Torres, strolled down the stone corridor toward the sleeping guard. In his right hand was a toothpick, which he was using to divest a molar of a bit of bacon. In the crook of his left arm was a sawed-off doubled-barreled shotgun.

When he reached the guard, Major Torres nudged him with the shotgun. The guard awoke and looked up sleepily. He started to rise, but Major Torres used the shotgun to pat him back down. The major put the toothpick away for later, reached into another pocket, and brought out a $100 bill. He handed it to the guard.

"You will sleep, my friend," he said. "You will sleep for the next hour with your eyes squeezed shut. Do you understand?"

"Yes," the guard said. "I understand. Perfectly." To show that he did, he put his head back down on the small wooden desk, cradled it in his arms, and closed his eyes so tightly that he frowned.

Major Torres moved down the corridor until he came to Citron's cell. Through the bars, he could see Citron sitting on the edge of the stone bed. Citron looked up at him.

"Well, spy," Torres said. "It is time."

"Is it?"

"Yes."

"The guard said six. It is not six yet."

"The guard was wrong," Torres said as he unlocked and opened the cell door. "He's a simple fellow and often wrong. Otherwise he would not be a guard. Come. Hold out your hands."

Citron rose, moved slowly to the open cell door, and held out his hands. Torres, the shotgun pressed against his side by an arm, clicked a pair of handcuffs around Citron's wrists.

"Just you and I?" Citron said.

Torres smiled. "What did you expect?"

"I don't know. More people, I suppose."

"A doctor. A priest. Guards. A firing squad. A slow walk down a badly lit corridor. Like in the cinema, true?"

"Something like that," Citron admitted.

"Sorry," Torres said. "Just you and I. And Carmelita here, of course." Torres patted the shotgun.

"A sawed-off," Citron said.

"Painless, I assure you. Let's go."

They went down the stone corridor, Citron in the lead. They passed the guard, whose head was still down on the desk, his eyes squeezed shut. When they were ten feet past the guard, he opened his eyes and sat up. He looked at the disappearing backs of Torres and Citron. Then he looked at his left hand, which was clutched into a fist. He opened it slowly. The $100 bill was still there. The guard crossed himself slowly.

It was just growing light when Citron and Major Torres came out of the building that held the cells and entered the exercise yard, which was not much larger than two basketball courts. The yard was surrounded on three sides by the prison buildings, and on the fourth by a stone wall that was at least twenty feet high.

Citron looked back over his shoulder at Major Torres. "Where to?" he said.

"The wall," Torres said and indicated the spot he wanted with a gesture of the shotgun.

They walked slowly across the exercise yard until they reached the wall.

"I will take the watch now," Torres said.

"What watch?"

"The gold watch that goes with the gold band that you gave the guard for food and drink. I can take it now or later."

Citron reached into his shirt pocket with his manacled hands, removed the watch, and handed it to Torres, who smiled. "A gold Rolex."

"A gift from my mother."

"Poor woman. She has my sympathy."

"She would only reject it."

"Turn, please, and kneel, facing the wall."

Citron turned and knelt. He closed his eyes. He could hear the hammers of the shotgun being cocked, one at a time. And then he heard a familiar voice. "Hey, Morgan," the voice said.

Citron looked up. It had to be a dream, of course. For he knew that only in a dream would a sad-faced forty-two-year-old man in an immaculate three-piece blue pinstripe suit, white button-down shirt, and neatly knotted tie be straddling a prison wall with a coil of green plastic garden hose in his hands.

"Catch the fucking hose," Draper Haere said and tossed one end of it down.

Citron rose slowly. He turned and looked at Major Torres, who had twisted away to light an after-breakfast cigar. Citron turned back and grasped the garden hose with his manacled hands. Slowly, laboriously, with much puffing and cursing, Haere pulled Citron up to the top of the wall. Once astride it, Citron looked down at Major Torres, who was now leisurely strolling back toward the door that led into the exercise yard.

As he strolled, Torres waggled the shotgun without looking around. It was his goodbye wave.

Citron looked at Haere. "You sure you're not a dream?"

"No dream," Haere said. "A nightmare maybe. Let's go." He indicated the aluminum ladder whose top was propped against the wall and whose legs rested on the roof of a tan Dodge van.

Citron was first down the ladder. Haere followed him and tossed the ladder down between the wall and the van, where it landed with a clatter. Both men jumped from the van to the ground and hurried around to the van's right-hand door. Velveeta Keats was behind the wheel. The engine was running.

"Hi, Morgan," she said.

"Well," Citron said. "Velveeta."

"Get in," Haere told Citron and opened the door. Velveeta Keats's Polaroid camera fell to the ground. Haere picked it up. Citron climbed into the van. Haere slammed the door shut.

"See you, Morgan," Haere said as the van moved away.

Velveeta Keats drove no better than she ever did, but Citron said only, "Haere's not coming?"

"No," she said. "He's got something else to do."

"Where're we going?"

"The nearest border," she said and glanced at him with a happy smile. "Surprised to see me?"

"Yes," Citron said. "Very." And to his surprise he found he really was.

Draper Haere walked back to the main gate of the prison. It was nearly a two-block walk. When he arrived at the gate, a guard asked him what he wanted.

"Major Torres," Haere said, adding, "I am Draper Haere."

The guard made two telephone calls. Shortly after the second one was completed, another guard appeared and motioned for Haere to follow him. They went through three doors and down two corridors and finally into Major Torres's office.

"Please," Torres said in English, indicating a chair.

Haere declined with a shake of his head, reached into his inside breast pocket, brought out a fat envelope, and handed it to Torres. The Major removed the packets of $50 bills from the envelope and counted them swiftly but carefully onto his desk.

"All there," he said after he finished the counting. "The Haitians said it would be." He scooped the money up, put it back in the envelope, and brought out a ring of keys. "I hear the fighting has reached the television station," he said as he selected a small key, unlocked a drawer, and put the money away.

"Who do you think will win?" Haere said.

"The rebels."

"Where does that leave you?"

Major Torres rose, smiling. "I'm sure the rebels will provide me with many, many customers, provided, of course, they don't shoot everyone. Well, I think it all went smoothly enough, don't you?"

"Yes," Haere said. "It did."

"And the two Haitians?"

"They decided to return to Miami."

"Charming fellows," the major said. "Can I offer you a ride back to your hotel?"

"No thanks," Haere said. "I'll walk."

The major patted his huge stomach. "I should do that, walk more." He took out his newly acquired gold Rolex and looked at the time. "You must let your walk take you by the Presidential Palace."

"Why?"

"Do you like historic occasions?"

"Very much."

"Then let your walk take you by the palace."

* * *

A crowd of some five to six thousand persons had already formed outside the Presidential Palace by the time Haere reached it. It was a strangely silent crowd whose members spoke to each other, if at all, in whispers. Civilians armed with M-16s and wearing green scarves around their necks had cleared a space in front of the palace gates. The space was in the shape of a squashed horseshoe.

As one of life's great gawkers, Haere worked his way to the front of the crowd with practiced ease. Something bumped against his thigh. He looked down and with surprise found that he was still carrying Velveeta Keats's Polaroid.

"You will have something to take a picture of in a minute," the man next to him murmured.

"What?" Haere said.

"Wait and see."

The gates swung open and the crowd sighed. The three older civilians, wearing their green neck scarves, came through the gates first. They were followed by Colonel-General Carrasco-Cortes in full dress uniform, his hands bound behind him. Next came the two men who sometimes called themselves John D. Yarn and Richard Tighe. They walked side by side. Their hands were also bound behind them. After Tighe and Yarn came the four young officers: the two majors, the young captain, and the very young lieutenant.

The army officers took over and led the general and the two Americans to the wall. The three prisoners were turned around so that they faced the crowd. The older of the two majors looked back at the oldest civilian, as if for confirmation. The civilian frowned and shook his head. He went over to the three prisoners and moved them down the wall to the exact spot where the late President had been executed. The crowd murmured its appreciation.

There were no speeches. The civilians and the four young officers lined up in a row in front of the general and the two

Americans. No more than twenty feet separated the prisoners from their captors. The eyes of the two Americans swept frantically over the crowd, seeking rescue. Yarn's eyes found Draper Haere.

"For God's sake, Haere!" It came out of Yarn's throat half-scream, half-yell.

Haere stared back at him. The four officers and the three civilians raised their weapons.

"Goddamn it, Haere, please!" This time it was indeed a scream.

Haere raised the Polaroid camera, aimed it, and pushed the red button just after the civilians and the officers fired. The camera whirred. The film rolled out. Yarn fell first, and then Tighe. The general, with three bullets in him, continued to stand. He cried, "Long live—" but was unable to complete his last command. He fell back against the wall instead, slid down it into an awkward sitting position, and sat there until he died a few seconds later.

Draper Haere took the film from the camera. He turned and walked away through the still-silent crowd. The film slowly developed. It turned out to be an excellent picture.

36

NINE DAYS AFTER THANKSGIVING, a Saturday, Draper Haere awoke in his enormous room at his usual time of 6:30 A.M. Hubert, the cat, was perched on Haere's chest, staring at him balefully. The cat was often there when Haere awoke. "Morning," Haere said. Hubert purred loudly.

Haere pushed Hubert aside, got out of bed, moved to the kitchen, plugged in the Bunn coffeemaker, and headed for the large bathroom. When he came out nine minutes later he was showered, shaved, and dressed in gray slacks, tweed jacket, and blue oxford-cloth shirt, but no tie. It was his Saturday costume and, in Haere's opinion, almost daringly informal.

After two cups of coffee and three cigarettes, Haere donned a denim apron and cracked two eggs into a pan in which the butter was already sizzling. Just as the eggs were beginning to fry, the downstairs buzzer sounded. Haere went to the intercom, pushed the button, and asked, "Who is it?"

A woman's voice replied in Spanish, but Haere couldn't quite understand what she said. He pushed the unlocking button and went back to his eggs. A few seconds later there was a soft knock at the door. Haere went to the door and opened it. There were two of them, neither more than seventeen years old. They were also a little plump and fairly pretty and completely terrified.

"Señor Haere?" one of them said.

Haere nodded. The one who spoke thrust a brown paper sack at him.

"One moment," Haere said in Spanish, hurried back to his eggs, and flipped them over with a spatula. He returned to the two young women and said, "Please," indicating that they should come in. They came into the enormous room warily and stared at everything with wonder.

Haere opened the paper sack and took out the spiral notebook. He flipped it open to the first page and read: "Draper: Please pay the bearer (or bearers) $2,000 for this—or more, if you like their looks. Regards, Morgan Citron."

Haere turned another page and saw that it was written in French. He flipped a few more pages. It was all French. Because of his almost nonexistent French, Haere said, "Shit," smiled at the two young women, said, "One moment," in Spanish again, turned, went back into the bathroom, and removed $2,000 from the false bottom in the medicine cabinet. He started out of the bathroom, but stopped, turned back, added another $500, and went to his desk, where he slipped the sheaf of bills into an envelope.

He went over to the two still-terrified young women, bowed slightly, said thank you very much in Spanish, and presented the envelope to the plainer of the pair. She looked inside the envelope and giggled. She showed it to her friend. The friend also giggled. Draper Haere smiled, went to the door, and opened it. The two young women started through it, but the prettier of the two grasped Haere's hand, raised it to her lips, and kissed it. Haere told them to go with God. They went quickly down the stairs, giggling all the way. Haere closed the door and smelled his eggs burning.

He hurried over to them, dumped them down the garbage disposal, lit another cigarette, picked up the kitchen wall phone, and dialed a number. On the fifth ring, Governor-elect Baldwin Veatch himself answered with a sleepy, muttered hello.

"This is Draper, Baldy. Let me talk to Louise. I've got something of an emergency."

"Aw, Christ, Draper. Hold on."

A moment later Louise Veatch came on the line. "Well?"

"Citron came through," Haere said.

There was a brief silence and then Louise Veatch said very softly, "No shit."

"I need you," Haere said.

"Give me an hour," she said. "It might take two."

"All right," Haere said, hung up, turned, and put some more butter into the pan.

The downstairs buzzer rang again as Haere was washing the last of his breakfast dishes. Again, he went to the intercom, pressed the button, and said, "Yes?"

A man's voice said over the speaker, "This is MacAdoo, Mr. Haere. We met down in Houston. At the airport."

"Woodrow Wilson's kin?"

"Yes, sir."

"What d'you want?"

"Five minutes of your time. That's all."

"That's all you'll get," Haere said and pressed the unlocking buzzer.

When MacAdoo came into the enormous room he looked around with frank appreciation. "Now, by God, this is something, isn't it?"

"Coffee?" Haere said.

"Appreciate it."

"Sit down."

MacAdoo moved into the living-room section and took his

seat in the Huey Long chair. His eyes roamed over the room and its eclectic furnishings as Haere poured coffee into two mugs.

"How do you take it?" Haere said.

"Black."

Haere handed MacAdoo a mug of coffee. MacAdoo took it with his right hand and patted the arm of the chair with his left.

"Nice old chair," he said.

"Belonged to Huey Long."

"No kidding. The Kingfish." MacAdoo sipped his coffee and smiled. "Now that's good coffee."

Haere said nothing.

"It's been sort of your life's study, hasn't it, Mr. Haere? Politics, I mean."

Haere only nodded.

"Your friend, Mr. Citron?"

Again, Haere nodded.

"In case you haven't heard, he's in Sri Lanka. With the Keats girl. Woman, I mean. Velveeta. Velveeta Keats. That is sort of pretty, isn't it, if you forget about the cheese and all?"

"Very," Haere said.

"You heard about Gladys Citron, I expect."

"I heard she died in her cell in Kansas City."

"Heart failure," MacAdoo said in an almost sorrowful tone.

"Heart seizure," Haere said automatically.

"What's the difference?"

"Everyone dies of heart failure."

MacAdoo thought about it. "You're right." He drank some more of his coffee. "I imagine you've pretty much got the whole picture by now, haven't you?"

Haere nodded. The nod was a lie, but he saw no reason to tell MacAdoo the truth.

"You going to run with it?"

"I don't know yet."

"We'd like to dissuade you."

"We?"

"Yes, sir. We."

"Langley, you mean."

MacAdoo smiled slightly.

"How do you intend to do that—dissuade me?"

MacAdoo frowned. "We don't really know, Mr. Haere. That's why I'm here. To find out what you want."

"I don't want much of anything," Haere said, "except a new President in 'eighty-four. Can you guys handle that?"

MacAdoo sighed, put his coffee mug down, and rose. "I was afraid you'd say something like that. No way I can change your mind?"

Haere shook his head, rose, and walked MacAdoo to the door. The tall man opened it, turned, and examined Haere somberly. "Mr. Haere, I'm sorry, but I just don't see how we're going to be able to leave you alone."

"Try," Haere said.

MacAdoo nodded, turned, and went down the steps. Haere watched him go. When MacAdoo reached the street door, he opened it, and then held it for someone. Haere could hear Mac-Adoo's polite, faint "Ma'am."

Louise Veatch came through the street door carrying a small suitcase. She started slowly up the steps. When she arrived at the landing, she brushed past Haere and into the enormous room. He closed the door. Louise Veatch looked around the room.

"Which one of those closets can I have?" she said.

Haere stepped over and took her bag. "You left him?"

"I left him."

"For good?"

"For better or for worse, anyway."

"What'd he say?"

"About what you'd expect. He was still yelling when I went

299

out the door." She smiled. It was a sad smile. "Well, are you glad? You haven't said."

Draper Haere put his arms around her, drew her to him, and kissed her. It was a long, tender kiss, full of promise. When it was over, Haere made her the one promise he felt he could keep. "It won't be dull."

Louise Veatch smiled. "I know," she said. "That's probably the real reason I'm here."

It took Louise Veatch more than an hour to translate aloud for Haere what Morgan Citron had written in the spiral notebook. When she was finished she looked at Haere and said, "Good God! Did you know all this?"

"A lot of it. Not all."

"Are you going to use it?"

"What do you think?"

Louise Veatch thought about it for more than a minute before she answered. "Use it, Draper."

He nodded, rose, and went over to the kitchen wall phone. "Get on the extension," he said.

Louise Veatch waited until Haere dialed eleven numbers. She then picked up the other phone. It rang three times before it was answered by a woman's voice with a hello.

"It's Draper Haere, Jean. Is he in?"

"Yes, of course, Draper. Just a moment."

The Senator came on the phone. "Hello, Draper." He had a deep, almost harsh voice.

"I need to ask you a question, Senator."

"Shoot."

"How would you like to be President?"

Almost ten seconds went by before the Senator softly said, "Very much."

"Then I think we'd better talk," said Draper Haere.

For a complete list of books available from Penguin in the United States, write to Dept. DG, Penguin Books, 299 Murray Hill Parkway, East Rutherford, New Jersey 07073.

For a complete list of books available from Penguin in Canada, write to Penguin Books Canada Limited, 2801 John Street, Markham, Ontario L3R 1B4.